THE
BLAMED

Emily Hourican is a journalist and author. She grew up in Brussels, where she went to the European School and learned how to fake it as a Eurobrat, and now lives in Dublin with her family. She has written for the *Sunday Independent* for fifteen years, as well as for *Image* magazine, *The Gloss*, *Time Out*, *Condé Nast Traveler* and *Woman and Home*. She was also editor of *The Dubliner* magazine.

www.emilyhourican.com
@EmilyH71

Also by Emily Hourican

Fiction
The Privileged
White Villa

Non-Fiction
How To (Really) Be a Mother

THE
BLAMED

EMILY
HOURICAN

HACHETTE
BOOKS
IRELAND

First published in Ireland in 2018 by
HACHETTE BOOKS IRELAND

1

Cataloguing in Publication Data is available from the British Library

ISBN 978 1 4736 8109 5

Typeset in Garamond by redrattledesign.com

Printed and bound in Great Britain by Clays Ltd, St Ives plc

Hachette Books Ireland policy is to use papers that are natural, renewable and
recyclable products and made from wood grown in sustainable forests. The logging and
manufacturing processes are expected to conform to the environmental regulations of
the country of origin.

Hachette Books Ireland
8 Castlecourt Centre
Castleknock
Dublin 15, Ireland

A division of Hachette UK Ltd
Carmelite House, 50 Victoria Embankment, EC4Y 0DZ

www.hachettebooksireland.ie

For my mother

CHAPTER 1

Now

'What's wrong with him?'

She said it in French, disapproving more than curious, certainly not helpful, in a voice cracked with age and self-righteousness.

'Glass,' Anna muttered. 'Stuck in his foot.'

Rudi continued yelling, so loudly that a crowd began to gather, drawn by the promise of drama. He sat heavy on the warm sand, foot drawn up onto his other knee, as Anna knelt in front of him, brushing away the dust. She swiped at the thick paste of blood and sand that smeared the sole of his chubby foot to get a better look at the cut. It was deep. The blood told her that much. Would it need stitches? If so, where would she go? Who, among these casual watchers, would help her?

Around them, outside the circle made by Rudi's cries and Anna's frantic repetitions of 'It's okay, lovie, it's okay' – charms already broken by the disaster she should have prevented – questions and suggestions flowed.

'What happened?'

'What did he do?'

'Qu'est-ce qu'il y a?'

The crowd – all women – addressed themselves to the first who had spoken, their queries laconic rather than urgent. This wasn't their emergency, so they settled in to enjoy it. They were censorious too, staring accusingly at Anna, as if she had stabbed the child. Or, at least, had failed to protect him. *If you were French, this would not have happened*, they seemed to say. In the heat of their gaze, Anna felt herself to be careless, lazy, without standards. Her chaotic foreignness had allowed this disaster, so, although they were prepared to stand and watch, the women did not offer to help.

The glass, green and Gothic, was stuck deep into Rudi's pudgy foot. The soft sand must have offered some hidden thing, Anna thought, a rock, perhaps, against which the glass had leveraged. Rudi, running unsteadily with a full bucket of water, had done the rest.

Trying not to think of severed tendons or tiny slivers working their way into Rudi's bloodstream, Anna plucked out the glass, then washed off the blood, slopping seawater from Rudi's bucket onto his sticky foot.

'Weren't you clever to bring this?' she said, forcing calm into her voice, trying to distract him from the pain.

A man from the crêperie at the far end of the little beach came over with a white plastic first-aid kit. He was small and dark, sympathetic, where the women, still murmuring to one another, were not.

'*Merci. Vous êtes très gentil.*' Anna knew that once she had got rid of the blood, and put a plaster over the wound, the drama would dissipate. The crowd would disperse and Rudi's sobs would quieten. By the time Maurice came back, there would be no trace of trauma, nothing to stop him tousling Rudi's hair and saying, 'I'm sure you were a brave boy,' with the same useless bonhomie he would have adopted had Anna told him Rudi had made a magnificent sandcastle.

Trying not to think about sand or glass embedded and festering, she promised herself she would soak the foot later in antiseptic, stuck the largest plaster in the first-aid box over the cut, and made Rudi lie on his back with his foot against her shoulder. Sure enough, the women were moving away now, in little knots and pairs, ready to continue their discussion of Anna's failings over *un thé*, perhaps.

She looked at Jessie, wanting to say something about the French Revolution and the *tricoteuses* because she thought it might draw her in. She had known not to ask her daughter for help at the moment of crisis, but now she hoped for a smile at least. But Jessie, with all the superiority and indifference of fourteen, ignored her. Her little brother's yells had seemed to cause her nothing but annoyance. As Anna watched, she turned on her front and closed her eyes.

'Shall I make you a sandcastle?' Anna asked Rudi, because she knew he would say yes. She pulled him onto her knee, ignoring the rough grind of sand between them, because she wanted to feel the warmth of his body curled into hers. He snuggled close and relaxed, rather than tensed, as Jessie did now whenever Anna came near her.

She looks at me as if I make her feel sick, Anna thought. It was the way Jessie looked at so much now. As if the world were made up of ugly, rotting things that could only be viewed through narrowed eyes, jaw tightened with disgust.

After a while, Rudi went to get more water, the empty bucket bouncing against his leg. He was limping, but only a little, and seemed not to notice it in his excitement at the building project.

Anna watched him at the water's edge, trailing his bucket in the surf, determined to fill it to the brim, unaware that each time he laid it on its side, as much water poured out as in. He, at least, still did the things he wanted to do, without calculating their effect on others. Beyond him, the sea stacks at the mouth of the little cove shimmered in a light that was almost silvery, which made Anna unhappy for reasons she didn't understand. Maybe it was just the lack of heat in the day – it so clearly wasn't summer. The morning mist hadn't fully cleared and there was a chill in the ragged sheets drifting in and out, like scraps of gauze trailed by an invisible hand.

It wasn't holiday season, was distinctly off-peak, and the small Breton town seemed ready to retreat into itself. Why did we come? Anna wondered. Because we felt we deserved it? That we had earned it, in doctors' visits and painful introspection? Or because we wanted to avoid reality for a while, do the things normal families do? Like holidays, where they take time off together and relax. *Unwind.* The word made her stab angrily at the sand with Rudi's little blue trowel.

'I got the papers.' Maurice sounded pleased with himself.

'Rudi cut his foot.' Shading her eyes against the sun, Anna began to tell her husband about the glass, the blood, the women judging. She tried the line about the *tricoteuses*, because she liked it, but Maurice ignored it, as she had known he would.

'He's alright, though?' he asked briskly.

'Yes, he's fine.'

'Good.' That was as much as he wanted to know. Everything else belonged to the realm of the imaginary, which was also the realm of the unnecessary – the many things with which Maurice did not concern himself. And maybe he was right, Anna thought, although that didn't stop her from moving away from him, closer to Jessie, who had blanked the exchange. Maybe it is self-indulgent to contemplate the might-have-beens and almost-weres. Maybe it's neurotic of me to do it, she thought, reassuring myself in the retelling that nothing bad had happened? That I managed the situation so that disaster did not, after all, befall us.

Neurotic. She thought about the word. Was it hers, or had she picked it up from Alison, in one of the family sessions?

She looked at Jessie again. Lying down, the knobs of her spine were less obvious, but as soon as she moved – to get water, her book, adjust the towel – they reared up out of her back like the coils of a sea serpent.

'You must feel like you're walking on eggshells', her mother had said when Anna tried to describe the cold fury Jessie turned on her.

'I feel like I'm crawling over them,' Anna had replied. 'Like a slug.'

Her mother had stayed silent at that.

The beach was emptying now, while the terraces of cafés and restaurants filled. Again Anna wondered at the clockwork-like precision of this country: failure to eat lunch at twelve thirty or one o'clock was inconceivable. Their own late arrival on the beach, a haphazard trail that began with Maurice and Rudi, then Anna, carrying bags and rugs, and finally Jessie, meant they were rarely ready for lunch when lunch was ready.

Jessie was wearing an ancient Mickey Mouse T-shirt, cut off and tied so that it ended just below her ribs, and a pair of black bikini bottoms. Where had she found the T-shirt? Anna was certain she had thrown it away years ago. Mickey, faded, leered jauntily at her. Jessie's choice of something so childish, worn provocatively, made perfect sense.

All morning, Jessie had been the object of sly glances from men and women. The women stared openly, the men obliquely. Did they see what Anna saw, or what Jessie saw, or something else entirely?

Did they realise that it was Anna who had put what flesh there was onto those bones, just as surely as if she had taken Plasticine and stuck it on hard, even as Jessie sought to shrug it off?

Aware of the gaze of those around her, Jessie had stretched out, elongating her gangly limbs and pointing her toes. Anna, watching her, as she always did now, had felt sickened that they would stare so nakedly, and that Jessie had all but smirked back. She took each sideways glance as a compliment, each expression of curiosity or shock as jealousy. A girl who had been happy and invisible to the world, now tense in the glare of its searchlight. She looks like the problem, Anna realised

– buttery brown hair, thin, toned from too much running, tanned, the childish T-shirt tied high to reveal her ambiguous body. She looked like the girl other girls might want to be, Anna knew, but she was like that because she couldn't bear to be herself.

She had made herself an object of envy, but also of pity, a plea for protection. And yet, although she invited these things, she rejected them too.

It was, Anna thought, with the part of herself that could still appraise and observe, like staging a car crash, then claiming to be disgusted with those who craned their necks to gawp.

In making herself small, Jessie made herself vulnerable, but also superior: 'I'm small and weak and feeble but I'm better than you.' In the same way she demanded her mother's attention, yet refused it. She made it impossible for Anna to come close, or to step away.

Jessie tossed her hair over her shoulder, lifting it up from the nape of her neck as if it were too heavy. The honey-coloured streaks were fake, just as the tan was fake and the eyelashes. Only the effort was real.

'Lunch, Jessie?' Anna said.

'I've just had breakfast.' Jessie paused between each word, the better to convey her irritation at having to say them.

'Hardly "just",' Anna said. 'Hours ago.'

'Not hours. About an hour and a half.' She spoke precisely, just as she did everything precisely now. 'And I'm not hungry.'

'Okay. Fine.'

Anna stopped herself asking what Jessie had eaten. She had seen the bowl and spoon going into the dishwasher at their tiny rental house, but had missed the bit where Jessie ate whatever had been in the bowl. 'Don't make it all about food,' the psychologist had said. 'You don't want every conversation with her to be a trigger.' *Trigger. Association. Stress factor.* All these words with new and urgent meanings.

'What about you?' Anna said, half-turning towards Maurice. As always, she found herself confronted with the problem of what to call him. Never marry a man whose name you hate, she thought. Maurice. She had always hated it, and its abbreviations even more: Maur, Mo, Ricky. At first, she had got round the problem by calling him 'darling' or 'love', but that no longer came naturally. When Jessie was small, she had called him Moss, which was probably the best option. She should have made it stick, Anna thought now, but she had so badly wanted Jessie to call him 'Dad'. Now Jessie, too, avoided calling Maurice anything. He was 'him' and 'you' to both of them. Perhaps that's where the rot starts, Anna thought. The Man Without A Name. Except to Rudi.

'Dadda, we're making a sandcastle,' the little boy said firmly, arriving back with his bucket and the delight that only he, now, could bring to them.

Jessie didn't have a name either, Anna realised. At least not one of her own. Calling her Jessie, after a dead girl, had seemed a good idea at the time because Anna had wanted to keep her best friend alive. But, of course, she couldn't. Instead, she worried more and more that she had infected Jessie with something of death, which was consuming her from the inside. As if her beginning had been tied in with another's end.

She had tried calling her 'Jess', to differentiate, but had soon found herself slipping into the familiarity of 'Jessie'. It had seemed a good way to remember the friend who had meant so much. And when it was too late to change, Anna had come to realise how much of her daughter's life was a hand-me-down.

A name that wasn't her own. A mother she had to share. A father who wasn't hers. Poor Jessie, she thought. No wonder she wanted to make such a statement with the things that did belong to her: first her hair and clothes, then her body.

'Dig.' Rudi put the trowel into Anna's hand and lay on his stomach in the sand, flipping at it with his spade, sending a shower of grit into the air.

As well dig as brood, Anna decided, bending to join him.

CHAPTER 2

Jessie

Alison told me to write and keep writing, express everything I feel, the things that happen, what people say and how *that* makes me feel. I knew she was going to say it because that's what people say in these situations, but also because I did two sessions of sitting and not talking to her, and she faked being really cool with that. I could see it was making her tense, though, and she felt we had come to an *impasse* – that's what she called it, stupid cow, as if saying it in French was cool – and she needed to move it on and this was her way of doing that.

Also, she hopes I'll make a mistake and tell her what's 'wrong' with me, and then she can tell me back, like she's just discovered it all by her stupid self.

So I'm writing everything down, but only because I'm not doing any of the other things she wants me to do. Anyway, it's not for her. It's for me. I've got a different place where I write the things I show her, and the two are nothing like each other.

Hers is for her and anyone she decides should see it: her boss, to prove what a great job she's doing; my parents, whoever. Mine is just for me.

And it doesn't matter what I write for her. Everything I give her she looks at and says: *How did that make you feel? What would that look like?* Always in a voice without expression, which I hate. It's as if she's afraid that any expression will 'trigger' me – I might get carried away and start doing what her tone tells me to do: get excited or angry. Like I'm a puppet. So she keeps her voice to a dull drone and I follow it, staying low and level.

The place where I write the real things? The password is husk. I like that word. Husk. Husky. Husky voice. Husky dog. I looked it up. It means the dry outer covering of fruit or seeds. It's lovely, like something secret where the inside and the outside don't match.

I hate Alison, but only because she's stupid, and because I'd hate anyone who had to do what she does – sit in a room with me for an hour every few days and talk about me. About *why* I do or don't do things. About *what* I feel and how feeling that *makes me feel,* as if my whole life is little tunnels that meet up and twist around each other when it's separate bits that don't touch. But I don't really hate her, not the way I hate some of the others.

I hate this holiday for three reasons.

The house is tiny. It's called a *gîte.* We're all crammed in together. I can hear them breathing and Rudi talking in his sleep. His bed is so close to mine, I could roll onto it. Maurice crackling his newspaper and using the folded edges to clean his nails. That's gross. Sometimes he sticks his little finger into his ear and waggles it around really hard. Whatever comes out he wipes on the corner of the paper. Then he carefully tears it off, folds it and leaves it on the table.

I hate it being so easy for them to watch me and see what I do. I hate the watching. Anna says I make them do it but I think she enjoys it. She always used to watch and stare anyway. Now she has an excuse.

I hate hearing Anna speak French. She's good at it. She's like someone else when she speaks it. She moves her hands a lot and is animated. Flirtatious. It makes me hate her even more because she shouldn't be playful. And because I hate watching her try to pretend everything is normal with us. I see her doing it with Alison too. She makes her voice all low and reasonable to show everyone what a great, reasonable person she is, so they're both talking in low, flat tones, like a humbling, fuzzy ball they pass back and forth to each other.

I bet she does the same in meetings. It's totally fake. She can scream and shout at me just as much as I can scream and shout at her. Neither of us gets the prize for being calm and sensible. I've watched her face go dark red when she's angry with me, and listened while she screamed so loudly her voice has gone scratchy and broken. That's when she stops.

Then she gets a look on her face like she's seen something terrible. She looks at me like I frighten her.

She doesn't do it so much – lose it like that – any more. Not since I got older. She does a different thing now: she stops whatever she's doing and just breathes, with a hand on her chest, to calm herself. I hate that almost more than I hated her screaming at me.

Back then, after the screaming, she would go all weak and hardly be able to stand up. Her legs would wobble, like she'd had a shock. She'd be so, so sorry, and cry, and say could I forgive her, and I always said of course, and then she'd make something specially nice to eat – pancakes with bananas she fried in butter and sugar, or hot chocolate with loads of cream. It was nice, after it was terrible.

She's never lost it like that with Rudi. I guess he doesn't scare her the way I did. But I've seen Maurice looking at her sometimes, when she gets really annoyed, and I know he's wondering if she's going to. He kind of hovers when she gets angry, like he's going to grab Rudi and run if she starts shouting, though I don't know where he'd go. He never hovered like that with me. Or grabbed me and ran. But I did see him try to say things to her sometimes to calm her when she was screaming at me. It didn't work much.

He didn't protect me from her, but I protected her from him, even though she doesn't know that.

Like, once, he asked me did I 'mind' when she got angry like that. He looked all worried, his face bunched up, like a squeezed fist, and he asked me sideways, so he didn't have to look right at me. I knew he didn't want to, in case I said something that would force him to do things. Actually, I think he was sorry as soon as he asked.

I said I didn't *mind*. 'Mind'? Seriously? What a jerk he turned into. And to think how much I liked him at first, when he was new and fun and Anna listened to him and he made her laugh.

We've only got another few days here and then we can go home. I can't wait. I want to get back to the places I'm used to, where I can work out what I'm doing and need to do. Here, I just have to go along with what they want. There's no point doing anything else. Other girls have told me to 'ride it out'. They mean just put my head down, keep quiet and go along with them.

Anna calls it 'picking your battles' and she's a great one for that. Always going on about how good she is at letting people at work get away with little things so she can go in hard on bigger things.

I guess I know what she means now. I pick my battles too. And because I have a bigger battle, I don't care so much about all the little ones that used to get to me. The battles with Harriet. With Jenna. With Zach.

I didn't tell them I was coming here on holidays. I thought they didn't need to know. That's a battle I pick now too: how much to tell anyone. Before, I would tell them all everything, Anna first. It's what we always did, her and me. I'd tell her about school and teachers and hockey and gymnastics and friends, and she'd tell me about work, and try to teach me things about life and people through what she'd done. I used to listen to what she wanted me to learn, so I could use it in my life.

'Never act in anger'; 'Think first'; 'Think backwards from what you want the outcome to be, then decide how to get it.' So pleased with herself, like she'd discovered the secret of life or something. So calm, so certain. Mostly.

She's like a never-ending fountain of life lessons. One of those YouTube motivation tutorials. A free one.

Maurice hates being here too. I can see he does. But that

doesn't make him and me any closer. My enemy's enemy isn't always my friend. Sometimes he's just another, smaller, enemy.

I think that's why everyone said how 'grown-up' I was when I was a kid: I was like a little carbon copy of Anna. All careful and reasonable and with the same expressions and words – her friends used to laugh. Sometimes I said things to make them laugh. Other times I wouldn't notice until something came out by accident, and then they laughed.

They loved it. Gran didn't. Her face would twitch and she would peer at me. The same way she didn't love me calling Anna by her name, instead of 'Mummy'. 'It sounds wrong,' she would say, face wrinkled like a raisin. 'Rude.'

'It's not rude,' Anna would say. 'It makes sense. I like it. We're not some kind of archetypal mother and daughter. We're friends, aren't we, Jessie?'

And I would smile at her and say, '*Best* friends,' because she loved that.

It hasn't been true for the last few years. I had other best friends. I don't now, but that doesn't mean she's back in the game.

Doing things her way didn't work for me. Alison tries telling me that just because something doesn't work it doesn't mean it was wrong from the start, or that the person who told me was malicious; just that it didn't work. She thinks too much about it.

I'm learning so much from this: what's important, what's not. How to get what I want without showing what it is. It's like I have an inner flame that they're all trying to blow out. Knowing I have it makes me feel I really am special, like Anna used to tell me I was. She would tell me again and again, and I'd pretend to believe it but I never knew what she was talking about because I was just ordinary, and then I realised that she meant *she's* special – or she wanted to be – and that therefore I had to be, too. Because if I wasn't special, then she, as my mother, couldn't be.

Her. Always her.

And then the point, oh, the point: that she is so great, so hot, that she made it happen – got the job, the husband, even with a slow start and a child. Damaged goods, broke, without enough money for shampoo, yet she won out. Anyone would want to hide from that. And I do.

There's a line I keep thinking of from a film about Muhammad Ali that she made me watch. She loves Muhammad Ali. I used to too. But in the film he's dancing around the ring and he's crowing, 'How is that man going to hit me if he can't find me?' And he's right there, dancing in plain sight, but he says George Foreman won't be able to find him.

That's me. If I don't show myself, they can't find me.

CHAPTER 3

Now

'Where will we have dinner?'

'Must we think about that now?' Anna turned her head towards Maurice. The sun had come out fully at last, late in the afternoon, and she was drowsy. She could see he was impatient, bored by the beach, but the crash of waves against the quieter bluster of the wind hypnotised her. Beside her, Rudi played with a heap of shells, chatting quietly to himself, while Jessie was fully asleep on the towel. She was so fragile, thought Anna, looking at the arms and legs, like bits of string, against the bright stripes of the towel.

'She needs to sleep,' she said, lowering her voice.

'Sleep is hardly her problem,' Maurice said, not lowering his. 'More often, getting out of bed is.'

'True, but that doesn't mean she's sleeping; just that she won't get up. Remember what Alison told us? That sleep and food are the priorities.'

'Fine.' He was clearly irritated by the new ordering of their lives, by any mention of therapy. 'But food is exactly what I'm suggesting. Or we'll end up leaving it too late again and not finding anywhere decent.' Finding somewhere decent was a big part of what Maurice liked to do on holiday. And by 'decent' he meant somewhere he could tell his friends was a 'great place. Only tiny, but the freshest seafood you ever tasted. Literally from the boat, into the kitchen . . .' Anna used to enjoy doing it too – 'lobster straight out of the sea, fifteen minutes from pot to plate, carrots from their own garden' – at the start, when being loved by him was something new and exciting, something she could return. But she had long since lost interest. Just another of the things they no longer did together.

'So why don't you book the one at the end of the beach that we thought looked nice?'

'For seven o'clock?' He was already standing, ready to go.

'Yes. Take Rudi with you. Maybe find a chemist and get some disinfectant for his foot.'

They left, Rudi bobbing along beside Maurice, the unevenness of his gait making him seem even younger than his five years, still chattering about the superheroes and villains who peopled his world. At that age, Jessie had been practical as a town planner, Anna remembered. Interested only in people – real people, people they knew – what they did and said and thought. Anna remembered the child's bafflement when she had described a neighbour as 'a dog person'.

'What's a dog person?' Jessie had asked. 'Is it like a werewolf? Half-dog, half-person?'

'No!' Anna had laughed. 'It's someone who likes dogs more than cats, sometimes more than they like people.'

'Why would anyone like anything more than people?' Jessie had asked, aged maybe six.

Anna tried to recall when last Jessie had shown interest in the doings of anyone they knew. Recently, her focus had been so narrow. How long was it since she had asked after any of their friends, Jayne, Marissa, Susie, the women who had almost brought her up, with Anna, before Maurice came along? They had babysat, sang to her, given her presents on her birthday. Now, if Anna tried to tell her even the simplest thing about her own life or what she thought, Jessie curled into a C, as if physically shielding herself from her mother's words. She supposed a year must have passed since Jessie had really shown any interest, but it was hard to tell. Like everything else, it had happened so gradually. A disengagement that at first Anna had told herself was normal until she began to understand that it wasn't.

She turned towards her daughter, trying to conjure up the image of a year before: Jessie smaller, plump, with straight dark hair, usually tied back in a low ponytail, and a round face in which only the eyes were remarkable. She had never been vain, not much interested in clothes or sparkly princess stuff. She hadn't been sporty either, not one of the hearty hockey girls. She had been, Anna had always thought, reassuringly normal, a sweet girl who wanted to be good and do well, content to stay close to her mother.

At first Jessie's lack of femininity – as Anna understood that word – had charmed her. She was so devoid of subterfuge, so unaware of the effect she produced on others. For Anna, who had always understood the light in which she appeared, who had always tried to manipulate that effect, and who knew just what those instincts could lead to, Jessie's indifference was magnificent. But as her daughter grew, Anna worried that she carried too few of the magnets she felt within herself, the silent lures that drew people to her. When eventually Jessie had seemed to wake up to the world's gaze, showing that, after all, she wanted to be noticed, Anna had been pleased.

The hair had gone first, layered so that it waved rather than hung straight, then streaked with blonde. Jessie's excitable friend Harriet had come up with the idea, animated by the thought of a makeover, by a desire to help. By then, she had looked at least a year older than Jessie. 'Doesn't she look amazing?' she had asked, lifting a section of Jessie's new hair and letting it fall through her fingers. 'So pretty. All the boys are going to fancy her now.' She had said it approvingly, but with the confidence of one who felt herself unassailable, whom all the boys fancied already.

'You have a good eye,' Anna had said, smiling at Harriet, even though she wondered, faintly uneasy, what might come of Harriet's confident predictions. Indeed, of Harriet's confidence. She had been right to be uneasy. There were many ways for a makeover to go wrong, and being too successful was one of them; Jessie's new prettiness had shifted the dynamic between the girls, in a way that Harriet must have grown to resent.

Soon afterwards, Jessie had begun to lose weight. The natural slimming down of a chubby kid, Anna had told herself. Suddenly she looked taller for being thinner, or maybe was actually taller, newly lanky with that lack of grace that is so completely graceful in itself.

Now, remembering how she had admired the emerging lines and shadows on Jessie's body, Anna felt ashamed. It had taken her so long to see past thin to sick.

Bit by bit Jessie withdrew, but so gradually that Anna noticed only once she had gone, shut behind her partition like Snow White in her coffin: perfect and untouchable.

Maybe if Jessie and Rudi had been closer in age, I would have noticed, Anna thought. Maybe if I'd had my children together, with the same father, doing the same things at the same time. Instead, preoccupation with one had led her to neglect of the other.

'Do you feel guilty? Responsible?' Alison had asked in one of Anna's private sessions.

No.

Alison had looked surprised, but said, 'That's good. Guilt is not helpful.'

Not helpful. In Alison's office, no matter what you unearthed, she had neat labels to cover every type of shame and failure. Instead of being 'wrong' or 'bad' or even 'evil', your worst doings were 'unhelpful', 'self-destructive', the result of 'cognitive dissonance'. That was the one in which you were torn between two versions of yourself: good witch, bad witch; good mother, bad mother. Neither could win but neither could lose.

Now, as she watched her daughter, Jessie's eyes opened behind the tangle of hair that fell over her face. She stared at Anna. 'What time is it?' she asked.

'After five, I'd say. The others have gone to book somewhere to eat.'

'How's Rudi's foot?'

'He's limping a bit, but he seems to have forgotten about it.'

'He cried so much.'

'It was sore.'

'I know, it's just, well, what's the point of making such a fuss?'

What indeed? Anna thought, when you had something to do it for you. A body to cry out when you couldn't.

'Are you enjoying the holiday?' She sat up, to get away from the edge of Jessie's stare.

'Yes.' Jessie almost shrugged, and Anna wondered why she couldn't leave those questions alone, as she had been told. Stop looking for reassurance, she tried to tell herself. Stop needling and picking at her, asking her questions that pretend not to be the question you're asking. Stop talking about food and how she feels. But she couldn't.

'Have you heard from Harriet?' she asked, well aware that it was the same conversation, just from a different angle. The conversation that begged: *Are you okay? What's going on with you? Talk to me.* All the things that couldn't be said.

'No. I'll see her when I get back.' It wasn't the answer Anna wanted, was still vague, but it would do, Anna decided. It seemed . . . casual. Relaxed.

And because of that, suddenly it was a good day. The kind they hadn't had in a while – she had almost forgotten that such days existed. Maybe it was okay not to talk for a while, not to analyse, explain and explore. There was so much talking waiting for them at home, and so much talking behind them. Words piling up, useless, distorted, a jumble of spaghetti letters lying in random heaps, glistening slickly at her.

I hate you. Jessie said it so often now that even those words had stopped meaning much, had become dull and blunt; simply the way she had arranged the wet spaghetti letters.

The look on her face the first time she'd said it – spat out during an argument – told Anna how shocked Jessie had been to hear the words leave her mouth. She had looked terrified, waiting for the world to fall in. When it hadn't, she had been even more terrified, stuck with proof that, after all, you could tear apart yourself and the person you loved most, and still the end would not come. If even the worst was nothing, what solid ground had any of them?

'Shall we do a bit of shopping before dinner?' Anna asked, trying to keep things light. 'I saw a couple of interesting places at the top of the village.'

'Okay.' Jessie brushed the hair off her face. Her hands were large and red, the knuckles knotted, as if she had been scrubbing floors. 'Help me up.'

She held a hand out to Anna, who grabbed it and pulled her to her feet. She couldn't resist a quick hug, and felt a lurch of joy as Jessie stayed momentarily within her arms. She breathed in the smell of her daughter, even as she noted the absence of her, the spaces where more of her should have been. The Mickey Mouse T-shirt was soft and worn against the knobs of Jessie's spine – Anna thought of holding a bird or tiny mammal in her hands. But Jessie did not flutter or pull away.

'I can help you choose clothes,' Jessie said suddenly. 'I know what's going to be hot for autumn.'

CHAPTER 4

Then

That was the summer I came into my powers. Like a witch.

Those months slip in and out of focus. Isolated moments burning like lanterns in fog, looming up, then fading, lost in a haze of many things. Drunkenness, drugs, desire. The light they cast is distorted – things loom larger, fuzzier, more grotesque than they should. But this is how I remember it.

I was twenty-five, and nothing in my life had hinted to me of the person I could become. But the second I got to that city, stepped out of the airport and into the heat of that June morning, I saw my new self and moved quickly.

I had wanted to go to Paris for the summer, not Brussels. I had been so disappointed not to find the things I needed in Paris – a part-time job, a language course, a flat I could afford – but that morning, instantly, I knew I was in the right place. My place. It was in the sound of the bus as it moved away from the kerb in front of me, in the shouts of the taxi drivers as they disgorged passengers and bags, and called loudly to one another. Most of all, it was in the way these things soothed rather than frightened me.

I knew who to be in this city, which was shabbier than I'd expected, a semi-precious place, rather than the hard, bright diamonds of Paris, Milan, Vienna.

Brussels, I realised then, has no glamour or reputation. It just is. But there was a whiff of explosion to it that I loved. Or maybe just the bit of it I found to live in.

Fate – I'm sure of it – led me to the little flat above the Chez Léon bar, owned by Jacques, whom Fate could not have invented. The place was small and the windows rattled with the passing of traffic outside. There was a bed on a mezzanine level, which was tacked so badly to the wall that I wondered would it crash down one night with me on it, and a strange little bath, stained algae-green in a trickle below the tap. The flat would be noisy at night – I saw that straight away – and hot, while the line of ancient, treacly grease between the cupboards and the floor hinted at the kind of horrors that would have had my mother on her hands and knees with bleach and grim satisfaction, but I ignored them.

I wasn't here to be the girl my mother had brought up.

I wrote to Jessie – the best friend I missed already, although we had parted only a day before – describing the flat:

It's like an afterthought in a narrow building, made up of bits of cupboard and hall, blocked off by flimsy partitions. It smells of traffic fumes from the road outside, but it's in the middle of everything. My bed is just a box with a mattress on

it, but big enough for you to share, and there's a hip bath. I
won't begin to tell you about the loo until I see you! Come out,
Jessie, please do. Get time off work and just come. X Anna

She had said, 'I might, if I can', and I needed her to say yes,
she would. We did everything together. I wanted her to do
this with me too.

I spent an hour unpacking, putting my clothes into the
few drawers and cupboards, marvelling at the way the place
looked exactly the same when I had finished, then went out
to walk and stare and wonder at everything I saw. The streets
smelt of rubbish from giant bins that sweltered on corners,
and urine. There were homeless people, mainly men, with
muscular dogs in doorways, and I began to understand the
kind of area, or *quartier*, as I reminded myself to call it, I had
landed in. There were rich smells of garlic and butter that
made me think of long, late lunches and crisp white wine. I
felt like a wild animal, tracking the story of the city through
nose and instinct.

Above the shops and cafés there were tall narrow houses
and windows with long wooden shutters closed against the
afternoon sun. I imagined them from the inside, dark and
cool, slanted bars of light pouring in around the wood,
making dusty patterns in the air. What were the people in
those dim apartments doing? It seemed impossible that they
would be working, preparing food, studying, cleaning, any of
the normal things that fill days. Instead, I thought they must
be writing books, painting, making love as a sophisticated,
creative act, not just an urgent fumble.

Eventually I found myself in a park lined with tortured trees, their branches twisted into a lattice that exposed and imprisoned them. They reminded me of a painting I'd seen once in a book, of Andromeda chained to a rock, straining against her ties, while beside her Persius fought the sea monster.

I sat on dry, yellowing grass and ate a sandwich I had bought, watching a fountain trickle dirty water into a worn stone basin. In the distance, I heard sirens. Within minutes I had been approached by two different men, who lied smoothly, told me I was beautiful and asked if I would go for coffee with them. When I said no, they didn't seem offended, or particularly disappointed. One even sat and chatted for a while, asking where I was from and advising me on how to negotiate the city. When he had finally gone, dispirited by my monosyllables, I lay back, even though the grass smelt of dry dog shit, and considered what to do with myself. I had nowhere to be until I started my so-called job on Monday in two days' time, and I wasn't sure I could last that long alone.

I had some introductions, people I could call. Like a heroine in a Henry James novel, I thought. Newly arrived in the old world from the new.

There was the friend of a friend who was doing an internship at the parliament, a couple of kids working in Irish bars, and a girl whose parents mine knew, because they had all been at college together; she had lived in Brussels all her life.

'They have a beautiful house, very big and central,' my mother had said. 'I'm sure you could stay there for a while until you find your feet.' She was nervous, didn't like the idea of me going away alone for so long. But I knew I could do it.

'I'll be fine,' I said, 'but I'll ring her.'

She seemed the most promising, because she had been there the longest, could be expected to know the best places to go. There was no way I was going to hang out in Irish bars. Bet – short for Elisabeth – invited me over that afternoon.

'It's so hot. Come and sit in the garden and get cool and tell me why you're here.' Her voice was deep, with what wasn't quite an accent, more a careful way of pronouncing her words that made her seem almost foreign. She sounded like the kind of girl I might have been a little afraid of if I had met her at home. But not here.

She gave me directions from the Métro station closest to her, and I set off to find the one closest to me, 'Parc'. The jerky escalator brought me down to a grey tunnel with dirty walls and a floor that was sticky and sweetish-smelling.

The air was so grubby, I felt I could have rolled it between my fingers and seen thin lines of visible dirt emerge like worms. A hot wind blew from the mouth of the tunnel onto a platform that was empty, except for backlit ads for supermarkets, and a man with no legs, who played the accordion vigorously. Beside him was a skateboard, his means of transport, I thought. I wondered how he managed the accordion, which was nearly as big as he was. Did he use the escalator? Was there a lift? Or maybe he had a friend, who came for him in the evenings and helped him home.

I saw the scattering of coins across the thinning red velvet of the accordion case and added a handful. The man began to roll his eyes at me in a way that was both funny and terrifying. I moved to the far end of the platform and was standing close to the dark mouth of the tunnel, watching the accordion player in the convex mirror fixed to the wall, when the train came barrelling through, drowning the mournful music. It came without warning and was as empty as the platform. Where was everyone?

Bet's Métro stop was far grander, with art-deco tiling and posters recommending exhibitions. There was one for Magritte that I swore I'd go to.

Her house was beautiful, exactly as my mother had said: tall, built of stone, as if it had been carved out of the street, sitting inside a small front garden behind wrought-iron railings. The door was huge, like something in a fairy story, and the girl who opened it was tall too – my mother would have called her 'a grand girl', which meant she was large as well as tall, with curly blonde hair to her shoulders and a wide mouth. She was wearing bright red lipstick, a kind of vintage peasant dress cut low, so I could see plenty of cleavage, and had bare feet. She had a cigarette and I wondered at her parents allowing her to smoke in the house. Beside her, I felt half-formed, half-sized and half her age, although I knew we'd been born within a few months of each other.

'Well, aren't you just darling,' she said, almost pulling me into the house. Her voice was rough like unsanded wood. The deliberate staginess of what she said shocked me, and I wondered was she being rude. She must have seen something in my face because she laughed then and said, 'Don't mind me. I've been watching far too many silly old black-and-white films. My parents are away and I'm on my own.' That explained the smoking, I thought, if not the rudeness.

Inside was cool and echoey, the height of the door matched by the height of the hall ceiling and the highly polished dark-wood stairs that curved up and up above us. Smells of beeswax, old books and dust drifted down to me.

Bet led me into a large room with a gleaming mahogany table, on which stood a shallow bowl of pinkish tulips, drooping gently and starting to shed their petals. The walls were panelled in wood, carved with knots of fruit and flowers. The ceiling, also of carved wood, was far above us, and one wall was glass, looking onto a garden below. More rooms led away from the one we stood in, blurs of pink and cream and gold. I wanted to explore.

'Let's get drinks and go outside,' Bet said, either unaware of or indifferent to the beauty of the house. Imagine living here, I thought. Imagine this being normal so that you didn't notice it, just walked through, grabbing food and drink as you went, thinking about something else.

She gave me a beer, warning me that it was cherry-flavoured – weird but delicious – and we went down a wrought-iron staircase into a garden that was deep and cool, like sliding into a green pool. Trees rustled around us and wood pigeons cooed above our heads. A woven roof of leaves shifted and swayed, casting patches of light here and there.

Bet flung herself into a garden chair, waving at the empty one beside her. Her toenails were painted navy blue.

'Where are your parents?' I asked.

'In Ireland for the summer.'

'And you're on your own?' Had my mother known that?

'Yes. My brother's in Italy. You could move in here if you like.'

'It's okay. I have a flat. Don't you go to Ireland with your parents?'

'God, no! Hate the place. Weeks and weeks in the countryside with nothing to do, no one around for miles, plus the rain and wind.' The way she put it, it didn't sound very attractive. 'So where's your flat? And have you really just this minute arrived?' Her eyes, I saw, were large and flat, like fish close to the surface of a pond. They were reflective rather than curious.

'Yes, just this morning. The flat is in a little square called Place des Pins, a couple of floors above a bar.'

'I know it. Which bar?'

'Chez Léon.'

At that, she threw back her head and laughed, like electricity crackling. 'I don't believe it! Out of nowhere, you pitch up and land right in the centre of the hornets' nest.'

'What do you mean?'

'Just that Chez Lé, as we call it, is where it all happens. Sit long enough in that place and everything you ever wanted, and dreaded, will come to pass. Have you met Jacques yet?'

'Who's Jacques?'

'The owner. No, you wouldn't have if you arrived this morning. Jacques doesn't get up until the afternoon, if he gets up at all. Depends who he has up there with him . . . His place is directly above the bar, so must be just under you.' She gave me a sly look. 'So, boyfriend?'

'Not at the moment . . .' I trailed off. I hadn't had a boyfriend in a long time – the last one I dumped when I invited him to dinner and he told me that it would cost more to get the bus over and a taxi back than it would to buy himself something to eat – or a serious one ever, but I wasn't about to tell Bet that.

'Good,' she said, to my surprise. Then, 'You'll do much better here if you don't have a boyfriend. You'll meet more people,' she added, when she saw my confusion. 'I can introduce you to lots of fun people . . .' She grinned.

'Are you working?' I asked, wanting to change the subject.

'Not really.' She yawned, raising her arms high above her head and arching her back. 'I'm still studying, apparently. It takes years in this country. You just do exams when you feel like it, and I don't often feel like it.'

'What are you studying?'

'Political science. But I don't go to many lectures. I'm thinking of dropping out. Where are you working?'

'Part-time at a law firm – data-entry stuff, boring. What was it like growing up here? Your French must be amazing.'

'Hmm.' She wrinkled her nose, yawned again. 'It's not bad, but you'd get by without it.' That seemed an odd and arrogant thing to say. 'Growing up here was cool,' Bet continued. 'Better than Dublin, I'd say.'

I felt defensive enough to begin spluttering, 'Well, actually . . .' I stopped. Who was I kidding? There was no way that our teenage rugby club discos and nights in the university bar could compare with whatever Bet had been used to. There was more promise in the few streets and squares, the dingy Métro tunnels I had seen so far than in the whole of the city I came from.

'How long are you staying?'

'Three months. Until the end of September. I'm supposed to go back then, get a proper job, but we'll see . . .'

'And what do you want to do while you're here?'

'All sorts of things. Work, practise my French, visit museums and little towns, go to bars, restaurants, nightclubs. And I want to make friends who aren't other Irish people just here for a while. Basically, I want to live here like it's my city.' I smiled, wanting her to understand that I wasn't just another drifter-through with one eye permanently on home.

'That's good.' She sounded surprised, but perhaps a little more interested. 'Why don't we go out this evening? I'll make some calls.'

'Great.'

She invited me to stay for dinner – which turned out to mean takeaway Vietnamese food from a place round the corner. We walked to the restaurant through streets that were hot and still. 'It's like no one lives here,' I said. 'Like the whole city is empty.'

'It's just the summer,' Bet explained. 'So many people go away, and those who don't, well, they close their shutters against the heat and stay indoors. This year especially, because it's hotter than usual. When it gets cool again in the autumn, they all pour out and take up where they left off. The summer is like a long pause. But it's good. There's more room for us.' I wondered was I now included in 'us'. I hoped so.

We reached the restaurant, up a flight of dirty stone steps into what seemed a house like any other. 'This place, they make their kids come in and say goodnight to all the customers while we're waiting for our food,' Bet said. 'Weird.' She rolled her eyes with relish. 'But the food is good.'

The food *was* good – tiny crisp rolls with beansprouts and shredded carrot, steamed pork dumplings with bits of chive, some other kind of dumpling with something Bet said was water chestnut – and we ate in the garden as the dusk fell. The wood pigeons flapped from tree to tree, chasing ripe cherries, almost too heavy to fly, while higher up, on thinner branches, tiny songbirds piped out a welcome to the cooler evening air.

Her phone rang again and again, a loud old-fashioned bell sound. Each time, Bet would push herself up from her chair and walk to the back of the garden with it. I could hear her chatting loudly, sometimes in English, sometimes in French, making plans for later, explaining who was coming and what we would all do. I began to feel a bit scared. I hadn't expected this. I'd planned on having a few more days to find myself in this new place.

'Really, I should have a butler for this sort of thing,' Bet said, smiling complacently, back after yet another excitable conversation. 'That was Marina. She's going to call over now and we can all go together.'

'Oh, okay.'

'You can borrow something of mine to wear if you like. Though I doubt it will fit.' She looked down at herself, then at me, and laughed. 'But the good thing is you can change when we get to Chez Lé. Just nip upstairs.'

'Do I need to?' I was wearing a short grey T-shirt dress and white Converse, my hair in a high ponytail that fell halfway down my back. I thought I looked fine.

'Well, I'm going to.' She brought me upstairs with her, past rooms with balconies and large windows, to the top of the house where a bedroom, bathroom and sitting room with a TV and heaps of fleshy pot plants were hers. 'I can go days without seeing my parents,' she said, with satisfaction, pointing out a small fridge plugged into a corner of the sitting room. 'Practically self-sufficient. Except for money.'

Her room had a built-in wardrobe with mirrored front that looked nothing like the furniture in the rest of the house, belonging instead in a mid-market hotel. Bet slid back the door with a flourish to show me a rail of dresses organised by colour. She grabbed something black and told me to try anything I wanted, then disappeared into the bathroom.

I flicked through the clothes, which were all far more grown-up than the things I usually wore. Dresses and long skirts, in silks and floaty cottons, with pleats and bold patterns. I usually went for a variation on jeans and T-shirts. I wondered did everyone in Brussels dress like Bet.

She came back in a tight black dress, very simply cut, which ended just above the knee, and a pair of flat black sandals with long ties that went halfway up her calf. She looked good. Sort of gladiatorial.

'Nothing?' She waved at her rows of clothes.

'Not really my style. I'm too small,' I said, then worried she would think I was hinting that she was fat. But she didn't seem to notice.

'Thought not,' was all she said. 'What about make-up?' She'd redone the red lips, added some black around her eyes. She looked years older than me.

'I'm okay. Am I going to need ID to get in places?'

'God, no. No one cares here. I don't think anyone's asked me for ID since I was fourteen.'

'Surely you weren't going out at fourteen.'

'Of course I was. Anywhere I wanted. My friends were older,' she explained. 'I went with them. Let's go back down.'

Marina arrived, nearly as tall as Bet but thin, with short, silvery blonde hair and a long, graceful neck. She was gorgeous, wearing a pair of jeans so tight and low-cut I could see the top of her thong above them and the jut of her hipbones. The thong was bright purple and studded with sparkly bits. Above that – far above, so plenty of taut midriff was on show – she wore a black mesh crop-top. I was definitely going to have to change. Brush my hair at least.

'So,' Marina said, 'you're from Ireland?' She pronounced it 'Ahhh-land', as if Ireland was somewhere silly and funny. She sounded totally English, although Bet had told me she was half-Portuguese and had grown up in Brussels just like Bet.

'I am.' I tried not to be defiant. After all, I was here to be part of somewhere new, not carry the old place around with me, like a grievance. 'I like your hair.'

It was the right thing to say. She smiled. 'It was long until yesterday,' she said, 'long to here.' She gestured halfway down her arm. 'I chopped it all off. Just like that!' She snapped her fingers. 'And, oh, the freedom!' She ran a hand through the neat blonde crop, making it stick up.

We had more drinks – gin and tonics – and I felt quite drunk. We talked about music and clothes and different jobs we'd had, all telling funny stories that became more absurd as the evening got darker. Marina and Bet looked at me sometimes and whispered a little bit. They said things to me and about me that I didn't quite understand. They were like the Fox and the Cat in *Pinocchio*, I thought, sizing me up greedily.

'Will she do?' Bet asked Marina at one point.

'She'll do.'

'Do what?' I asked, feeling twitchy.

'Nothing,' Bet said. 'Or maybe everything.' She laughed. At me? Or about me? Did it matter?

'We're just wondering how you'll get on with everyone,' Marina said kindly, adding, 'We think you'll get on very well.'

Then it was time to go, and Marina said she'd drive. Her car was small and dirty-white with a door that didn't work so you had to climb across the driver's seat to get to the passenger side.

Marina drove fast and we listened to Billie Holiday, which surprised me. I had both of them figured for chart-hit girls, but they sang along – Bet well, in a deep, booming voice, Marina badly – to Billie, with her track marks and bruises, lamenting her solitude.

I stared out the window, held captive by the burnt-orange streetlights and the emptiness of the city. I watched the roads and squares slip by, with their statues of kings on horses, grand boulevards giving way to narrow cobbled streets. This was the land that lay above the Métro line I had taken earlier. It snaked through the bowels of the city, ploughing a different furrow with a different imperative. Down there was for getting places; up here was for dreaming and wandering.

By the time we parked close to Chez Léon, the music had changed to the kind of club anthems I'd expected: tinny voices that sounded like electronic kittens, laid over throbbing bass lines. The mood had changed too. There was a sharper edge to everything.

'Come up with me,' I said. 'I'll get changed really fast.'

'Okay,' Bet said. 'Let's have a look at this flat. I still can't believe you live here.'

Up the narrow stairs covered with worn cream lino and in through the door that stuck at the bottom so you had to kick it. Knowing the exact spot to aim my foot made me feel that the place was mine.

'*Vous êtes les biens-venues*,' I said, waving my arms expansively.

'This place is amazing!'

'It's literally made out of a broom cupboard.'

'A brown broom cupboard,' Marina laughed, 'with a bed on a shelf.' She gestured towards my mezzanine. 'I wouldn't jump or roll around too much up there.' She gave me a laughing look, which thrilled me a little.

'You've got a window looking right down over Chez Lé. Lucky you. It's brilliant. And you can spend all the time you want at mine,' Bet said generously. 'Use this place as a wardrobe.'

'Which is what it so clearly was!' I laughed with them, marvelling and exclaiming too. Then, moved by Bet's spontaneous generosity and the impulsive way in which she had included me, I hugged her. Marina ducked in, too, so that the three of us were clasped together.

'Give me two minutes,' I said then, disengaging myself to open drawers and the spindly built-in wardrobe. I picked a pair of tight dark blue jeans and a red tank top that was worn and frayed, but so soft that it clung just as I liked it. With black wedges, the whole thing was casual but sexy, I thought.

The girls were rattling drawers in the kitchen, telling me I'd better remember to get to a shop or I wouldn't have anything to eat – 'Except some old couscous,' Marina said, plucking an ancient packet from the back of a drawer; someone else's forgotten fundamental.

'Chuck it. Let's go,' Bet said.

And we went, fizzing with the excitement of a night out, the promise of those hours of darkness that might lead to anything.

CHAPTER 5

Jessie

It was awful hearing Rudi cry this morning. And all those ghoulish old ladies around him, tutting, muttering and not helping. Poor kid, his fat squidgy foot all covered with blood. I love Rudi's feet: they're the cutest part of him. Mine are the worst part of me.

He'd stepped on glass. The beach is full of it. I don't know why more people don't get cut. Or why they don't clean it up. If we were at home, Miss Flynn would have us all out on the beach with black bags and sticks. She'd love it – 'Look, girls! Something *useful* to do' – and we'd all love it too, although we'd pretend not to. We'd moan and give out, but we'd be away from the classroom, away from the non-stop watching of one another in our appointed places. Rudi got a big bit stuck straight into his foot and he cried and cried, in a thin, screaming way, so that I wanted to run over and distract him.

He's the only one who isn't careful around me. 'Jess, play

41

with me,' he says. Like he believes I will. He's the only one who calls me Jess, not Jessie. It's hard to resist him, but I do. It's too exhausting, and I can't go back to being the person who runs around playing with a five-year-old. Not now that I've worked so hard to stop being her.

Sometimes I think she's chained up inside me, that girl, like in one of those grisly stories where some sick guy takes a girl captive and chains her to a radiator for ten years.

I wonder what she'll do to me if she ever gets free. Left there on her own, in the dark, she'll be so angry.

But maybe she's not on her own. Maybe Other Jessie is with her. Would that be better or worse? Will Other Jessie take my side and explain that I had to do this? Or will she turn the girl even more against me? I used to think Other Jessie was mine, to protect me, but now I'm not so sure.

'She's your namesake,' Anna used to say. 'A Guardian Angel whose name you can call when you need her.'

'What was she like?' I would ask, because I loved the answer.

'She was like the moment a *piñata* explodes, and things cascade everywhere. Or a clown, turning somersaults and pulling faces, with pure white skin and short black hair. And her eyes were so big and shiny, they looked like pieces of mirror. But she was serious too.'

I knew what she meant. I had a card with a donkey on it once, wearing a huge smile on one side and a frown on the other: when you spun the card fast enough, the faces merged into a normal one.

I imagined Other Jessie twirling round: solemn, laughing, solemn, laughing. Happy face. Sad face. Middle face. Which face would I get? I used to think it would be the happy one, but now . . .

When I was little, I didn't really understand about her being dead. I just knew that she wasn't around, but in a way that meant she was extra-with-us. I liked that. We didn't have enough people, I thought. No dad, until Maurice came along. I used to draw pictures with Other Jessie in them. Sometimes she had wings or a harp. Sometimes she sang to me. She doesn't sing now. She's silent.

Before, when I first got smaller, I couldn't tell what size I was. I got really slow and hesitant because I was afraid of bumping into things. When I wanted to put a glass on a table or counter, I had to move carefully because I wasn't sure when I would encounter the surface. I didn't know how long my arm was or where. It moved into my line of vision, but I didn't know where it came from. It wasn't part of me, although I could still tell it what to do, but only as a puppeteer can – by moving it deliberately.

When I was lying down, I couldn't feel my head on the pillow. It felt like a big round helium balloon bobbing above me on a string. Other times, I would feel I was whirling, weightless, through somewhere dark grey and misty, whirling down a never-ending tube, so that when I sat up, I would be surprised to find where I was.

The feelings were strange, but I miss them now they're gone. When you feel like that, you have to hold on to each moment very carefully. It's like you're on a thin, wobbly bridge: you have to put down one foot carefully, then the other, and not look down or ahead, just at your feet. It's easier in a way.

It's a process of adjustment, one of the girls at The Laurels told me. She said it snottily, like she thought I was looking for an excuse to cop out. Her name was Isolde and she was like her name, tall and straight, like an angry stick. She would poke at me with her intentions. I know she meant to help, but her help came with so many strings.

'How committed are you?' she wanted to know. 'I'm not going to bother with you if you aren't going to commit.' Snooty bitch. That was after I asked her how she was dealing with the trays of food, knowing that everything was a special high-calorie version of itself; 'secret calories', they called them. As if we didn't know. That's when Isolde said the thing about 'riding it out', which made sense. But she also said to be sure to do what you can, when you can. That was good advice too. I do.

My new clothes are great. Jeans. A white shirt. A stripy top that people here really do wear, even the men, as if they know how disappointed we'd all be if we came to Brittany and there were no Breton tops. Harriet has one like it, but mine is cooler.

The lady in the shop said Anna and I could be sisters, which is so stupid and awful and *French*. But Anna was cool and laughed and said, God, no, not unless our mother had been an elephant.

She said it in French, although the lady had spoken to us in English, and I could see the lady took us more seriously after that, and didn't bother saying that the things we tried on were 'chic' and suited us when they obviously didn't.

It was good fun, a bit like it used to be, and I don't mind that, because I understand that sometimes you have to 'ride it out'.

Dinner was the same. They tried hard not to stare at me and I tried hard not to let them see that I knew they wanted to stare, and we all talked to Rudi and let him make us laugh with his funny ways and the things he says. He must be delighted. Since all the fuss over me eating started, we pay much more attention to him when we're together, like he's the only safe one. And Maurice can pay him loads of attention and Anna doesn't give out to him for it or say it isn't fair on me.

She used to. Not in front of me, but when she thought I couldn't hear. She'd think I was up in my room but I'd be on the stairs listening to them because I would have seen in her face that she was annoyed, and that it was to do with me, and I'd want to know what it was in case it was my fault.

Usually it wasn't: it was Maurice's. Or she'd think it was. Actually, often it really was mine, but she didn't see that.

'You need to make more of an effort,' she'd hiss at him.

'I do try,' he'd say. 'I try constantly. She doesn't want me to.'

'That's nonsense. She does. But she sees the way you are with Rudi, and you're not that way with her. She's not stupid.'

The thing is, he's right – I don't want him to. Not any more. And it's nothing to do with Rudi. It's to do with me. I used to like Maurice so much. When he first came along I was just a kid, and it was amazing. It was like he came charging in with a bag of fireworks and presents and broke up the too-tight bits between me and her. He loved her so much – I could see he did, the way he looked at her – and he loved me but only because of her, and he made everything fun and grand the way it hadn't been before. I mean, it was fun, me and Anna, but there was never any money and we didn't do things, just stayed at home and hung out with her friends – funny old Marissa and Jayne and nosy Susie, who was nice too.

When he came along, we did loads of things. He wanted to take us places – we went to Lapland one Christmas – and if he heard there was a show he thought I'd like, we'd go. I loved it. I wish I still loved it.

But I started to see how embarrassing he was, getting all excited about kids' stuff, and once I saw that, I couldn't not see it. I stopped wanting to go with him because people would stare at him when he laughed too loudly or made some stupid joke. And then Rudi came and we didn't go anywhere much for a while, and that was better, but I could still see that he was embarrassing and, anyway, I began to see that he did all those things only for her, not really for me. Harriet said he was 'buying love' when they turned the attic into my bedroom and made it so cool. I know she was really jealous, but she was right too, and I wouldn't have minded except I realised it was Anna's love he was buying, not mine. That made me upset because I thought it was both of us. Anna said I was wrong about that, but I didn't believe her.

Or maybe he was just buying her approval. Because he's a bit scared of her too, I can see that.

Rudi's foot will be fine, Anna says. It's a bad cut, but no worse than that. It's nice when things are bad, but not worse.

CHAPTER 6

Now

Watching Jessie read a restaurant menu was like watching a gambler studying the field before a big race, Anna thought. The keen calculations, the minute consideration that brought together all the terrible new information on nutrition and calories she had assembled and deployed against herself.

At least interrogating the menu gave her some kind of enjoyment – it was so clearly her against it, and she took pleasure in working her way through it, so as to win: 'Hake, grilled, no sauce, with broccoli. No butter.' She looked pleased with her choice and sat back, menu closed, as though she had triumphed.

But only momentarily.

Once the food arrived, it became harder for her, and Anna tried not to watch as she cut it neatly into smaller and smaller pieces. Halves into quarters, into eighths, into bits so small and regular they weren't food. Tried not to see as Jessie pushed the bits carefully round her plate, or notice how she visibly steadied herself as she lifted each small forkful. She would pause, fork in line with mouth, and take a breath, closing her eyes, as if to draw strength for the next step. Anna found herself matching Jessie's breaths, pausing as the fork was paused, breathing again only when its load had been deposited. Jessie chewed carefully, doggedly, more times than you would think possible for a small piece of plain white fish, then laid down her knife and fork and sat, hands folded in her lap, before beginning again.

Anna tried not to count the forkfuls, or the time between them, but couldn't prevent herself. Once she got to double figures, she relaxed a little.

And all the while they chatted. Laughed, even. Jessie described the woman in the clothes shop and how she had said they might have been sisters, so that Maurice, mistaking her intent, gallantly agreed, raising his wine glass to Anna, who wanted to tell him not to be ridiculous. But she knew he meant it kindly so she held that in too, casting a quick glance at Jessie who, for once, glanced back, a look full of mischief that brought her face – schooled into a blank by the plate in front of her – to life.

Later, they walked back along the harbour to the tiny house.

'Who wants an ice-cream?' Maurice asked, as they passed the only place still open, although it was barely nine o'clock. It was the crêperie, run by the small dark man who had brought Anna the first-aid kit earlier.

'Me! Me!' Rudi yelled.

'Jessie?' Maurice asked. She shrugged, gave a tiny, indifferent shake of her head.

'Really? Remember how you used to beg for strawberry ice-cream? One summer, in Spain, we could get you to behave for an entire day on the promise of a strawberry cone after dinner. There was that place with a hundred different flavours, but you only ever wanted the one.'

Jessie shook her head again, more decisively, refusing the memory as much as the ice-cream.

Anna glared at Maurice and shook her own head, almost imperceptibly, but he saw and turned to Rudi, talking loudly to him about scoops and flavours.

The man from earlier was behind the counter.

'*Comment va-t-il?*' he asked, gesturing politely towards Rudi.

'He's fine,' Anna said, 'thanks to you. Once I put the plaster on and he couldn't see the blood, he was fine.'

'*Les enfants . . .*' He left it at that, but Anna knew what he meant. Children – so easily distracted, so easily pleased. And it was true, until it stopped being true.

Back in the *gîte*, Jessie offered to put Rudi to bed and read to him, telling Anna to sit outside with Maurice. 'Have a glass of wine. Listen to the frogs and the crickets.' It felt like an order, so Anna tried to work out what was behind it, but Maurice was already gathering wine glasses and a bottle, then scraping chairs across the wooden deck to position them close to the tiny stream from which the croaks and chirps rose.

Anna sat in a pose of ease, one leg crossed high above the other so her knee stuck out at a right angle. She leaned back and sighed loudly, contentedly, every bit of it pretence. Maurice started on some story about work and things that had been happening while he was away: he was following it, he said, but not contributing. 'It gives me perspective,' he said, 'knowing what's going on but that I don't have to jump in.' He worked for a bank, and Anna couldn't believe that after all these years he still tried to discuss what went on there with her. She nodded, said, Mm, but her mind was tuned to where she could hear Jessie reading *Fantastic Mr Fox* to Rudi. She read well, her voice lifting itself out of the monotone she mostly affected these days, as if even the energy of expression was beyond her. Rudi was laughing at Mrs Fox saying, 'Your father is a fantastic fox,' and Anna wondered could she switch off her vigilance for a while and drink her wine.

'So, should I go for the next step up?' Maurice was saying. He placed his glass on the table in front of them and began to expand, again, on the pros, making smoothing, circular motions with his hands as he spoke: 'More money – that's the most obvious one. More commitment but, actually, that's positive too. I'm ready for it. Against is largely the extra time involved . . .' He droned on, pretending to consider as he spoke, when Anna could tell that his mind was made up. Or as good as.

Jessie was in the bathroom now. Anna could hear the water running. What was she doing? Showering? Brushing her teeth? Vomiting, in the swift, efficient move she had perfected? One killer swoop of her index finger. Should she go and bang on the door, demand to be let in, or fake some need – a tampon – to gain entry?

Shifting uneasily on her chair, Anna wondered why she had thought it would be easier with just one bathroom. Maurice had been furious at the idea of a house so small. 'We'll be like cards in a pack,' he had said, 'bundled in on top of one another.'

But Anna had insisted, believing that proximity would bring intimacy, that Jessie squashed into a tiny space beside her – the way they used to be when she was small, after Brussels, before Maurice, when they lived just the two of them in a ground-floor flat with one bedroom – would be easier than Jessie in their now-home with her own bedroom, bathroom, walk-in wardrobe. But it wasn't. The distance between them had not been bridged. It was no better to stand outside the flimsy door calling than it was to stand at the bottom of the stairs, straining to listen.

'I don't think it's the right time,' she said to Maurice. 'There's so much going on already—'

'But if I do this, you could take a step back from your work,' he said. 'Be at home more. Go part-time.'

Had he any idea, Anna thought, how much that idea terrified her?

Once before, when Jessie was small and having trouble at school – 'I'm too shy to make friends, Mum,' she had said, face hidden in her pillow, mortified by her own understanding of her failure to be popular – he had suggested she cut back on work.

'We can manage on my salary,' he had said, unable to keep the note of pride out of his voice, even as he worked to hide it beneath concern. 'You could spend more time with her, even for a while, till she settles.'

Anna had refused – 'It's good for her, having a mother who works.'

'It's PR,' Maurice had said, trying to be jovial, 'not world peace.'

'That's not the point. I'm good at it and it's a positive message. Jessie will be fine. She needs to stand on her own feet a bit.' At the time, she had believed it – that Jessie could only benefit from having a mother who was busy and productive in her own life, and that there was enough of her to go round.

'I think about you every minute of the day, even when I'm at work,' she had tried saying to Jessie, holding the child's face between her hands at the school gate, as if that could compensate. As if her child was old enough, wise enough, for that to mean something. Jessie had smiled politely, said nothing. And after a while she seemed to settle. She made friends, not many, but enough to get by, Anna thought. And they were, until it all went wrong.

Anna had invited the friends often to the house, encouraged them to hang out there, after school, on Saturday afternoons, and then, when they got a bit older, before nights out.

She had done it, she told Maurice, 'because I want her to have the company, but also I want to know who her friends are'. But that wasn't entirely the truth. She also did it because she liked the way she appeared to herself in doing it: someone young, fun, full of suggestions on clothes and new ways to do hair. She felt that Jessie's friends liked her, even looked up to her. It's about being a positive role model, she told herself, denying the thrill she got from being Somebody in their watchful eyes.

She brought home make-up samples from work or launch parties she'd been invited to, and distributed them. Made sure the friends rarely went home without a little something, a lip gloss or eyeshadow. Some were mass market, 'no great shakes', as she would say, but sometimes it was 'the good stuff', meaning Chanel, Lancôme, brands they wouldn't get their hands on otherwise.

She knew that some of the other mothers disapproved of her being so easy about make-up when the girls were ten and twelve. 'But they're going to do it anyway,' Anna had insisted. 'What harm in giving them a head start?'

The friends confided in her at times – troubles with teachers, with their own mothers – and Anna gave advice that she felt was good: not too prescriptive, not too involved, designed to make them think for themselves. 'Those mothers should be bloody grateful to me,' she would sometimes say to Maurice, with a laugh. 'They have no idea how much hassle I've saved them.'

All of which was why, when the trouble between them and Jessie came, she felt betrayed just as much as Jessie had been. Rejected. Mocked. As if all her little gifts had been thrown back at her, a hail of lipsticks and blushers, in their cute packaging, bombarding her with a flurry of 'No's' that made her so angry she wanted to fling back, harder, faster, bigger – a hail of solid blows and curses that would hurt them as they had hurt her and Jessie.

Now she tried coherent arguments with Maurice: giving up work wasn't just a question of money, it was a career, an identity, an 'opportunity cost', and he pretended to listen and consider. What she could not say was how frightened she was. Because saying that would be an admission that she had been wrong all those years ago in refusing to cut back, but more – far more – because she couldn't begin to imagine what kind of fist she would make of it now. Would she walk with Jessie to school each morning, after her daughter had walked by herself for years? Pick her up at the school gates? Suggest hot chocolate in a café on the way home? What would they talk about in all those new hours when they no longer had enough to say that was safe to fill even the few they had?

She remembered Jessie running to her, maybe six years old, with a piece of paper in her hand. 'Read it,' she had said. 'It's my to-do list.' There, underneath 'Get drest, brus tef, hav mi brekfist' was written, 'Chat wif mummy.'

'Hey, I made it onto the list!' She had smiled at Jessie.

'So let's chat now,' her daughter had said, then poured out a ribbon of things she had noticed and wondered about. A complicated jigsaw where some pieces fitted and others didn't. Anna had marvelled at the spirit of conquest in which she had set about herself, the determination to make anything she could see or reach work for her.

When had she lost that? Anna wondered. When had the ribbon spooled out? When had she dropped it?

Guilt is not helpful. Alison's words came back to her.

There was so much. So many faces that leered at her when she looked back over her life, laughing, mocking, reminding, re-enacting for her the failures, the messes, the mistakes and the shame.

One day she would have to walk back through it, stare down each of the episodes that held themselves out to her, like poisoned delicacies: 'Remember,' they whispered. 'Look at this. Look.' Not yet. One day, perhaps. Not now.

Sometimes her daughter's face was there too. Jessie as a tiny baby, a toddler, scared, uncomprehending in the face of Anna's anger. Jessie, crying or pleading: 'I'm sorry, Anna, I'll stop. I didn't mean to.' Jessie's fists, small and desperate, hammering on the bathroom door as she begged to be let in while Anna sat as tight as she could, silent, trying to breathe her way out of the state she was in.

Because loving someone, it turned out, wasn't enough. Why had she ever thought it would be? Surely her own mother, so limited within her love, should have been proof of that? Loving someone wasn't enough to make them happy. Wasn't enough to protect them from the world . . . from yourself.

Having Jessie had shown her oh-so-clearly, but she had known it already.

She remembered a neighbour from where they'd lived in a tiny first-floor apartment – Jessie was a baby – an older woman with grey in her dark hair. She had stopped Anna one day. 'Is everything alright?' she had asked, sharp, but not unkind.

'Yes. Why?'

'I heard a lot of crying last night.' Her voice was precise. She was the kind of woman Anna associated with well-run charity shops and lots of dogs.

'I'm so sorry,' Anna had said, all smiles and charm. 'Teeth!' She gave a deprecating flip of her hand in the direction of Jessie, asleep in her buggy. 'I hope she didn't keep you awake.' She had pushed back against the recollections of the night before – herself desperate, deranged, shouting at Jessie, as if she was a creature of reason, someone to appeal to: 'I can't do this any more. I just can't do it.'

As if Jessie, then perhaps eighteen months old, might say, 'I'm so sorry, you're right. Of course you can't.'

How pathetic, Anna had thought then, looking to be let off the hook by the very person who kept you on it.

'Never mind that.' The woman seemed unconvinced by Anna's explanation, by her charm. 'Look, I know you're on your own, and I wondered do you need help.' She was the kind of woman to come straight to the point. 'I'm not here all the time – my daughter lives in Cavan and I stay with her quite often – but I'm happy to do what I can.'

'No, not at all, but thank you. You're very kind,' Anna said, gracious, desperate. 'It's a phase. We'll be fine.'

After that she avoided the woman, making sure to be in a rush, on her phone, occupied somehow, when they encountered each other. What if I'd said yes? she had sometimes thought. What if I'd said, 'Please. Please help.'?

The trouble at school, over a year ago now, was only the flag Jessie had chosen to wave – the first flag. Anna knew everything bad had started long before that. Perhaps it had been there from the beginning, in everything she and Jessie had ever done together, even the good things. In all the late breakfasts, making pancakes and squashed berries with maple syrup, all the walks through parks, kicking leaves and picking up conkers, all the kisses goodnight. Every bit of it just waiting to collapse on itself, give in to the rot that had started with Jessie's birth – at the wrong time, to the wrong person, with the wrong name; all the wrongs of Anna's life, piling up and up, after that summer that was a magnificent beginning, until it became a terrible end.

'Why don't I have a dad?' Jessie had asked, when she was about four, with the bluntness of her age.

'You do have a dad,' Anna had said, knowing as she said it that it wasn't what Jessie meant.

'Where is he, my dad?'

'He lives in another country.'

'Why doesn't he live in our country?'

'Because his home is in the other country.'

'Why isn't his home where our home is?'

How badly Anna wanted to say he was dead, had died in some honourable way, perhaps trying to save them all from disaster, but she knew she couldn't.

'You'll have to tell her the truth,' her friends had said, when she had first confided in them about Jessie's questions, the impossible whys of her too-rapidly growing world where understanding already outstripped the paucity of available information.

She had tried, telling a wan version of events that she worked on as hard as she could. She wanted to take the rejection out of it, a rejection Jessie knew was personal, even though Anna tried not to let it be. 'He never met you. If he had, there's no way he wouldn't be here with you. He would love you just as much as I do, but he didn't meet you. He just didn't understand . . .' But it was Jessie who didn't understand, and said so, plainly, so that Anna was lost for any response.

'I'm not quitting work,' she said now to Maurice. 'That is not what is required here.'

'Okay, but I'm taking that job,' he said, as she'd known he would. 'Turning it down is not required either.' And it wasn't, Anna knew that. Knew Maurice had earned his promotion, earned the right to say yes to it in the years of care he had shown them all.

Around them, the frogs croaked and the crickets chirruped into the damp night air. The sound of water from the bathroom had stopped and Anna went inside to check. Rudi was asleep in his narrow bed. Jessie was in hers opposite him, covers pulled up to her chin.

She smiled at Anna briefly. One smile, released from the store she now rationed because smiles seemed to pain her. She didn't smile, like a child – simply because she found something funny. She smiled like a puppet, from politeness or wariness.

Anna smiled back, resisted the urge to kiss her. 'She needs space, the right to own her body,' Alison had said. Anna had heard, 'Stop crowding her.'

She went back outside, sinking into her chair and picking up her glass of wine. She drained it and poured more, conscious that she did so far too often these days. When I'm back, I'll be strict with myself, she promised silently. After the holiday.

'Asleep?' Maurice asked.

'Rudi is. Jessie isn't, but she's in bed.'

'She seems in good form.' He said it tentatively: for all his years as her father, he knew he would now be the last to know what form Jessie was in, and that getting it wrong was the surest route to having Anna look at him in the cold way that said she couldn't bear his intervention.

'She does,' Anna agreed. 'For now.'

'But that could be it,' he continued. 'I mean, maybe she'll be fine from now on.'

'All back to normal, like it never happened? You'd love that.' Her voice shook.

'And you wouldn't?'

'Sorry.' She took a breath. 'Of course I would. I just don't see that it can be that easy.'

'But maybe you're anticipating problems that aren't there. Lots of girls go through this kind of phase and come out of it.' He said it gently, so she responded as close to gently as she could.

'Maybe. But you were there when Alison said that lots don't. Or they do for a while, then fall back in. And I can't help thinking Jessie is one of them. She's still so focused on how she looks. It's all she thinks about. I find her peering at herself in mirrors, in shop windows, even in the back of a spoon. Staring and staring at her reflection, like she's never seen herself before.'

'I thought the therapist said it wasn't about vanity and models in magazines.' He sounded confused.

'And it's not, or not entirely, but that is part of it. Do you remember when she used to say, "I'm not sporty. I'm bookish." "I'm in the middle, not fat, not thin." "I'm into art and painting"?'

'Yes.' Anna knew he didn't – why would he? His place was not to be the slate Jessie wrote her life on – but she let him off.

'All those "I-ams" . . . Every one of them was an attempt to become, to think herself into being. I understood. I really did. Because I remembered what it's like, feeling that every time you take your eye off yourself, you disappear. No wonder teenage girls spend so long in front of the mirror. If they can't see themselves, they have no idea who they are. Imagine that, hours at a time when you simply cut out, connection lost, drifting in the dark. You must remember rushing to the mirror to check you're still there, wondering who you are now? When Jessie looks at herself, she isn't being vain, she's trying to see who she is. And if she's still there.'

But Maurice said he didn't remember.

'Maybe boys are different,' Anna said.

That night, after more glasses of wine, he tried to make love to her, and when she said no, with the possibility of Jessie, a thin wall away, hearing them, he said they could sneak outside, to the back of the *gîte*, and lie on the night grass. 'Like when we were younger,' he said.

'It'll be wet. And I'm tired.'

Had they really done such things? she thought then, conscious of the huff with which he turned away from her. She tried to recall. Had they once snuck off, somewhere quiet and private, unable to resist each other any longer?

When they were first together, Maurice had admired her 'nerve', as he called it. The way she would whisper 'come on', at a party and lead him to a dark room or corner somewhere, teasing him and laughing softly if he hung back or put up a hand to stop hers as she fumbled with his belt. 'We can't,' he'd say, mortified and delighted.

'Oh yes we can,' she'd whisper, driven by the excitement of being with him, of no longer being alone, and he'd let her, encouraging her with his silence, the sudden new depth of his breathing.

But then they ceased. Because Anna, replaying fragments of these scenes the day after they happened, began to realise that she remembered very little. That they existed in pockets of oblivion because they happened only at a certain stage of drunkenness, and after a while the missing bits made her feel ashamed. It wasn't so much not remembering what she'd done – she could always have asked Maurice, he wouldn't have minded, would just have laughed at her – but, rather, how she'd done it. Who she'd been while she was doing it, how she'd behaved. Who was she, when she wasn't herself?

Mostly, her memories of such nights belonged with someone else, in a different time, a different city.

CHAPTER 7

Jessie

Anna said wasn't it lovely to be home, and I know she's happy not to be on that holiday any more – we all are – but she didn't mean it was lovely to be home because it isn't. The smell in my room was so bad I thought something had died in there. Anna said it was just that I'd left the curtains drawn and the door shut, but I think she's wrong. I think something did die in there.

She says she'll get the cleaner to do my room but I told her not to. I don't want her digging around and finding anything I've hidden. She'd show it to Anna. She adores Anna. Everyone adores Anna.

Especially other women, I've noticed. The Queen of Competence: that's what Harriet and I used to call her, both of us admiringly. We planned that when we were in Transition Year, doing work experience, we would work for her and 'learn how to be just like her', Harriet said. That was when Harriet wanted to be like someone related to me. But, even then, I didn't want to be just like her, though I did want to know how she made everything go her way. The Queen of Competence: it suited her. That's what she is – always on top of everything. She even says it herself. 'I'm resourceful,' she used to say, proud of herself. 'I can always come up with something.' Not now she can't. I've got her.

'Your mom's so glamorous,' Harriet used to say. She always says 'mom', like she's American. She's not American. She's the same as I am. Actually, I suppose she isn't because I'm half-French. Or half-Belgian. I'm not sure which because I know fuck-all about my real dad. Anna said he was French but he lived in Belgium, and he was clearly a jerk – although she didn't say that – because he didn't want to know about me. Well, I don't want to know about him either.

At first I loved it when Harriet said that about Anna, because it was true, and I was happy she'd noticed, and I thought that, in the end, some of Anna's glamour had to rub off on me, that it was hereditary and eventually I'd get it, like coming into a trust. Then I grasped you had to make it yourself, and I started to see all the ways that Anna did, how hard she worked at it and that it wasn't natural – she just made it up.

There's a photo of her when she was younger, maybe in her twenties. I found it in a drawer where she keeps her gloves. Pairs of leather gloves in lots of colours: pink, dark green, black, with fur. The cupboard came from one of those antiques places she likes buying stuff from, so it smells of dry wood and someone else. An old someone who used that perfume that smells like soap that ladies used to have. The photo smelt of it too.

In the photo, Anna's sitting on the stone rim of a fountain that sends up a spray of water behind her into sunlight so that it looks like a giant sparkling halo around her. She's tanned and young, and her eyes are huge. She's looking straight at the camera, but almost through it, as if something on the other side is more important. She's glowing and smiling and sort of pleased with herself. But not in an obnoxious way. Other Jessie is there too, in the picture, on one side of her, and a girl with wild curly hair on the other.

Other Jessie is smiling, but she isn't as happy. You can see it. Her mouth smiles, but she's tense. She's paler than Anna – Anna says she always was – and her hands are in her lap, as if she doesn't know what else to do with them. The girl with the curly hair is huge, bigger than either of them, and she's looming over them in a way that's protective, but menacing, too.

I asked Anna about the photo and she said it was taken one morning after they'd been up all night and had gone to a park because it was too hot to go home to sleep. She said they did that – spent days snoozing under trees in the shade – until it got cool enough to go home. I can't believe she was like that once.

She looked sad when she saw the photo and said, 'Everything was so clear in that minute. And then it went wrong.' She said something about 'the past being never really past' and I knew she was thinking about Other Jessie. I thought about Other Jessie too when I saw it, more than I usually did.

I suppose I realised then that she was an actual person, not just a dead person. It must seem funny that I didn't get that before. She looked nice, actually. Like someone I could have been friends with. I wonder was she very disappointed to die. All the things she wouldn't get to do. Maybe she didn't mind. I don't think I'd mind. You wouldn't get to do things, but no one would make you do things either. Like, they wouldn't make you sit beside them, and ask, 'What's wrong?' in that special voice, when nothing is wrong; it's finally right, because you've worked out what you have to do, if they'd just leave you alone to do it.

For the first time, you can see what you're about, what you're meant to be, and you know how to be it – but suddenly, they're all over you, trying to redirect you, like a farmer I once saw shooing cows into a field, waving his arms to distract them from where they wanted to go, pushing them towards the gate.

That's what they're like with me. Flailing around, trying to distract me. Sometimes they succeed and I lose sight of myself beyond them, the self I need to be, because they're so busy filling my plate and talking about things they think I might want to do. Bribing me, really. 'Maybe we can get a dog,' Anna said recently, because when I was younger I wanted one and she always said no. But I don't want a dog now. It would just be another distraction. And I don't want to be distracted. I need fewer things, not more.

The thing is, though, Anna in that photo isn't glamorous. She's pretty, but messy and kind of casual. Now she's always perfect. Her hair is shiny and wavy and sits on her shoulders in a bouncy way. Her nails are done, her make-up too, even on weekends, and her clothes are neat.

It showed me what you can do. What I could do, if I wanted. I used to want to, but now I don't any longer. It's too much effort and, anyway, it's the wrong thing: it's about making the best of what's there. My way, now, is to make what's there the best I can.

Anna must have put the photo away after I asked her about it because I couldn't find it when I looked another time in that drawer. I wanted to keep an eye on it – to measure myself. In case I was turning into her. In case I wasn't.

'You're better than me in every way,' she used to say. 'That's how it should be.' The thing is, it wasn't true. I knew it wasn't, because I could see the way she'd looked at me before, when I was chunky and wobbly. Sometimes when she hugged me she'd make a joke about me being so cuddly. I loved it.

I can't believe it took me so long to realise she meant I was fat.

And when I started to get rid of the fat, she was really happy. 'You look great,' she said, pleased and enthusiastic, about my hair, my running times, which had improved and improved. But after a while she stopped saying it.

I guess no one wants you to look too good, not even your own mother. People look at me more than they look at her now. It's me, not her.

When I was small, I always knew I was supposed to be something amazing; because she was amazing, so I had to be, to justify her, if that makes sense. It probably doesn't, but that was how I felt. Like I had to prove that she was the real deal or I'd be letting the side down.

The thing is, I did let the side down by being me, not someone else.

I always thought Harriet would be better at being Anna's daughter – she was so cute, like a little elf, with long blonde hair, and she was great at ballet. People talked about her like they talked about Anna – impressed. And they always got on so well together, in a way that I didn't get on with either of them.

Harriet's not so elfin now. In fact, she's quite fat. Anna says 'womanly', but I know by the way she says it that she's only pretending to think it's a good thing. Who'd want to be womanly at this age? At any age? Gross wobbly thighs, soft doughy stomach, and breasts that sag. I've heard Anna's friends talking about their stretch marks and how they got them from breast-feeding or being pregnant, and how they're the marks of experience and they're proud of them. Bullshit.

Harriet carries on as if her boobs are something we should worship. She's always grabbing them and waving them around. Once she even called them 'The Girls'. I heard her. So did Jenna. We laughed so much that she never did it again, just muttered that that's what her mother said, and we were just jealous because we didn't have any.

I went to see Alison yesterday. She asked me how the holiday was and I said it was fine. Then we sat in silence and she didn't say any more and I swore to myself that I wouldn't if she didn't, and I won because eventually she asked me to tell her about something that had happened on the holiday.

I told her about Rudi cutting his foot, and we had to talk through that. How I felt, how I'd behaved, what I thought about it. God, she's awful. I wish I could tell Harriet about her the way I would have before. She'd love this stuff. Or I could work it up for Zach, tell him in a way that would make him laugh and think I was cool, being able to deal with these people. But I can't tell either of them. I can't talk to them any more since what happened, and that's their fault, not mine.

But that doesn't matter because, now that we're home, I'm back on track.

Jenna was all 'Oh, you're so brown,' when I saw her in school, asking about the holiday and what I did. I can see she's trying and that she's sorry for what she and Harriet did, but it's not a good time to be friends again. Anyway, she's just being patronising because she doesn't think I have it in me to go the whole way with this. I'll show her I do. She and Harriet pretend like they're worried for me but I know they're jealous. They don't have the guts to do what I'm doing, so instead they go all concerned and say it's too much and I shouldn't.

I messaged Isolde as soon as we got back to find out if she was still in The Laurels or out. She hasn't messaged me back yet. She told me she does that, waits a few days, to see if she wants to respond, then works out what she wants to say. Isolde's very strict. She's the one who told me about waiting exactly one minute between bites. She was right – it's a good way.

School is so weird, these last months since I got out of The Laurels. Everyone there is careful of me, and we all act as if nothing has happened, but we don't do things like we used to: we don't just hang out any more.

I know they want to ask, but they don't dare. They want to know what it was like in there, what I did all day, who I met, but someone has told them not to ask. I know they have. I wonder was it Anna? Or did she make the teachers do it?

The last time things were this weird was after what happened with Harriet and Zach, just before The Laurels. Things went quiet then, too, like the bit in a horror film when the creature goes under the water or disappears into an air vent or something. It lasted only a few weeks and it all went back to normal when I didn't freak out in front of everyone.

Sometimes I wonder why I didn't freak out more. Mostly I guess it's because I don't even know how to freak out. How do people do it? Scream and throw things, I guess. But I didn't want to do that. People shouting and screaming scares me. I hate the way their anger takes them over, running down into their fingertips and blocking the usual person behind it. How can they let themselves be overruled like that?

I just wanted to go to sleep and stay asleep. But, also, it wasn't even that surprising. We'd done the same to so many other people, me and Harriet. Why was I surprised when it happened to me? Maybe things actually matter only when they happen to you.

'Mutually assured destruction' is what Harriet called it – she likes catchy names like that – and she said it would keep us all safe. She meant the stash of texts and snaps of messages we all kept on our phones. The bitchy things, the mean things we said about other girls, the private admissions we made about ourselves and wished we hadn't. 'It's like a nuclear deterrent programme,' Harriet said. 'I can't shaft you because you've got plenty to shaft me.' But then I lost my phone, with all my nuclear weapons, and I told her. I never, ever thought she'd use that against me. But once I didn't have any defences, she was quick and lethal, showing stuff I'd sent her to the people I'd written about. Bad stuff. Stuff I knew I shouldn't have said as soon as I'd said it.

'Never write anything you would be ashamed to show me,' Anna always said, in her endless talks about 'Internet safety'. And for ages I didn't. But after a while it doesn't seem new and exciting any more, and it's as if no one cares what anyone writes. Because everything everywhere is constantly full of a tide of shit – saying girls look like hos and sluts and bitches and fat and isn't she a cow. In the end you just add to it and it doesn't mean anything. It's just more words. Until Harriet shows it to the person you said it about. And then it does mean something.

I felt bad. I didn't mean those things, or not all of them anyway. I just said them, because Harriet was saying so much and texting all the time, and I had to say something back. And the girls she showed them to were really upset, mostly Emma, who said, 'I thought we were friends,' and was sad. Until she trashed me too.

Harriet knew exactly which ones to show around. She didn't bother with the small-scale stuff, just went right in for the kill. The messages about Emma where I said she has a fat back and shouldn't wear short tops. It's true, but I wish I hadn't said it. And all the girls said what a cow I am, even though they all do the same, all of them. And the photo I sent Harriet of the skin on my heels which was so dry it had cracked and bled and asked her did she know anything to put on them, and she showed those to everyone too and they all said how totally gross it was, like they never had anything like that. And it's true they looked really gross because the photo was so close-up but that was just the photo and they knew that.

Harriet only did it because she was so annoyed about Zach. But I suppose that's not the point. The point is, she did it.

So Anna sent me to stay with Gran for a few weeks. She said it would be good for me, for her too, to get some distance. From what? I wondered. From each other, it turned out. I could see she didn't know what to say to me, so she got rid of me.

At first I hated it because Gran's house smells of boiled meat and dusty carpets, and I felt I was banished because Anna couldn't stand the sight of me. But it turned out to be perfect because Gran doesn't watch what I do, like Anna does, so I could get into a proper rhythm, and her food is gross so it wasn't hard not to eat it. So by the time I came back home, I was well on the way. But then they sent me to The Laurels, 'for my own sake', they said. At first that seemed like a disaster but it turned out not to be because I met Isolde and learned so much from her.

I wonder would Anna let me go back to Gran's. She won't. I know she won't. And even if she did, Gran would watch now too.

Isolde just messaged me back. She's still in, but thinks she'll get out next week. Maybe we can meet.

CHAPTER 8

Then

After everything Bet had said about Chez Léon, and the way she had looked as she said it, it was disappointing. Small, mean, even, with one big window onto the street, glass a kind of yellowish-brown, stuck over with ads for cigarettes and chewing gum so that inside was dim and smoke-coloured.

A bar ran the length of the room, with a few spindly tables and chairs on the opposite side, and a smaller back room crammed with machines – an ancient pinball, a couple of those weird gambling machines old men seem to like, a jukebox that didn't look like it worked and had songs by Jacques Brel and Georges Brassens.

It wasn't modern or stylish. Neither was it old and traditional. It wasn't remarkable in any way at all. It was sad and neglected, I thought, a bar for old men and labourers coming off night shifts, for the lonely and disappointed. A bar such as you might find beside the train station in any European city, a bit run-down, a bit squalid, somehow keeping going although hardly anyone seemed to go there.

Looking around – the entire place could be taken in with one sweep, down to the flypaper, sticky and speckled, that hung beside the door – I felt let down, and wondered if I had been mistaken in Bet. Maybe she didn't really know anywhere interesting, just the same places anyone would.

'I'll get us drinks. No one's here yet,' Bet said, ignoring the few small groups bent low over their beers. Clearly, they weren't anyone.

The girl behind the bar was as magnificent as a tall tree in scrubland. Where everything in the bar was soft and brown and subdued, she was hard and black and shiny: a piece of coal, with a diamond inside. Hers was a face where everything was wide – wide-open eyes set wide apart over a wide mouth, with a gap between the square white teeth – and everything glistened.

She screamed when she saw Bet, a yell that was both recognition and challenge, and leaned over the counter to embrace her, kissing her hard on the lips. I tried not to stare, to keep listening as Marina suggested we play pinball, but my mind flew along startled lines. Was Bet gay? She hadn't seemed so but, then, I didn't have much to compare with. Maybe she was and Marina was her girlfriend. Or the girl behind the bar. What did that make her offer for me to stay with her? Kind, or something else? Or was this just how people carried on in Brussels? I was so careful not to stare, to look at Marina as she spoke to me, when really I was jingling with nerves at the newness of everything. I'd had so little time to accustom myself.

Marina fed coins into the pinball machine and said, 'Challenge?' She went first, cheating unashamedly by slamming her hip into the side of the machine so it tilted, sending the silver ball wherever she wanted it to go. I watched her, trying to work it all out. I wished Bet would hurry up. I needed a drink.

'Anna, come here,' she called then.

I walked over to the bar, trying to look insouciant, to feel less like a dog on a lead, jolted into action by its master.

'Anna, this is Cécile. You're practically neighbours. I'm sure you'll be seeing plenty of each other.'

Cécile looked me up and down with indifference. I didn't blame her. If I was her, that's exactly how I would have looked at me.

'Do you live upstairs as well?' I asked, not knowing what else to say.

'No.'

'But she works here most days,' Bet said kindly, trying to lessen the rejection. Then, 'See you later,' she said to Cécile, and 'Come on, I got you a beer,' to me.

In the back room, leaning against the wall, she said, 'Don't mind her. She's stroppy as hell. Jacques makes her work too hard. And her boyfriend, Jean-Paul, just got sent to jail.'

'Oh. What for?' The glamour of looking like she did and having a boyfriend in jail nearly toppled me.

'Dealing. But really it's totally unfair. It was only hash and he hardly had any on him.' Bet sounded indignant. 'He needed a good lawyer but, of course, he didn't get one.' The police, she explained then, only went after immigrants. 'I could carry a Santa bag full of drugs and they wouldn't bother me. I could probably kill someone and they wouldn't do much. It's really bad, but useful,' she concluded, with the arrogance of one who would always be somebody.

'Cécile must be very upset,' I said.

'So upset,' Marina said, 'that she chucked all his stuff out the window of their flat as he was being driven away by the cops. Except his CDs. She kept those. Apparently one of the policemen laughed and said a few months in jail would seem like a holiday after her.' She giggled, then added, 'Nico was there. He told me.'

'When did you see him?' Bet asked sharply.

'This afternoon.' Marina looked, I thought, slightly smug.

'Right,' Bet said.

'He'd dropped Aleah at the airport. He called by on his way back. We had coffee.' Marina said it like she felt an explanation – a full explanation – was necessary.

'Good.' Bet smiled then. 'She's gone for how long?'

'Nearly a month.'

'Better,' Bet said.

'The unexpected bonus of having all those relations in Morocco, or wherever it is,' Marina said.

'Who's Aleah?' I asked. 'And why is it good that she's gone?'

'She's Nico's girlfriend. You'll meet Nico tonight. He's great. She's a pain,' said Bet.

'She's Moroccan, and her family don't know anything about him, although they've been together nearly two years now,' Marina said. 'They'd kill her if they knew because she's not

75

supposed to go out with anyone, let alone someone who's not from her culture.'

'Where's Nico from?'

'He's French, but he's lived here all his life, so he may as well be Belgian,' Marina said.

'Not that he would agree,' Bet added. 'He makes a big deal about not being Belgian.'

'And why is she a pain?'

'She acts all precious and helpless but really she's hard as nails. But because the family don't know, and because they possibly would actually kill her' – Bet was so blasé, I hoped she was putting it on – 'she gets to do this whole *Romeo and Juliet* thing that forces Nico to be really protective of her. I'm sure they'd have broken up ages ago if she didn't have that hold over him.'

'Oh, definitely.' Marina's certainty made me want to laugh. They were so busy, the pair of them, ordering the universe around them exactly as they wanted it to be. They might as well have been playing with dolls, or paper cut-outs, shifting things this way and that as it suited them.

I couldn't wait for Jessie to meet them. They were the exact opposite of her – so definite, so full of an assertiveness that was all self-generated. Jessie, I had long discovered, was unable to pin anything down 'because things change from moment to moment and I don't know what bit to pin because it might be the wrong bit . . .' Instead she skipped along, following where she was led, always willing to be beguiled.

'I like people to tell me what they are, rather than me trying to figure it out, as if they might be lying and it's up to me to find them out,' she once said. 'I don't care about that – they can be whomever they want.'

'Well,' I'd said, 'that makes you a terrible judge of character.'

'I'm not sure it does,' Jessie had answered, rubbing the back of her hand across her nose, where dark freckles stood out against the white skin. 'I think the way people want you to think of them tells you just as much as snooping in their psyche ever could.'

'I don't snoop in people's psyches,' I had retorted. 'You make me sound so creepy.'

'The Psyche Sleuth.' Jessie had laughed. 'That's what you are.'

Marina and Bet seemed so much older than they were, so worldly, with a sophistication they wore heavily, while Jessie seemed younger than she was because she moved so lightly.

I guessed I was somewhere in the middle. Older than Jessie, younger than those two, really the same age as all of them. Funny that life made people so different, I thought. Just as the same number of eyes, ears and mouth added up to completely different faces, so the same number of years could give such a different finish.

'Here comes Jacques,' Bet said then, nudging me so that my beer slopped onto my T-shirt and the floor.

We watched silently as a middle-aged man made his way through the bar, stopping for a word here and there, inclining his head in gracious acknowledgement of the salutes that came his way. Cécile spat something at him that sounded vicious, which he took with a quiet smile as he made his way into the back room towards us.

'Elisabeth.' He murmured her full name, bending low over her hand.

This, then, was Jacques. Once handsome, perhaps, although his face was so battered you couldn't tell. Perhaps he looked better now, with those lines and grooves, than he had in his fresh-faced youth. Perhaps age suited him as youth never had – stringy off-blond hair, almost the same colour as his sallow, sunken cheeks. His hands, I noticed, were yellow too, stained with nicotine. The cigarette between his fingers was without any filter and the smell of black tobacco clung to him, weaving around his aftershave.

'Mademoiselle Marina.' He did the same bending-low, not-quite-kissing thing over her hand, then turned to me.

'*Une amie?*' he asked, looking carefully at me, not up and down, like Cécile had. '*Enchanté.*'

'Anna. She's living in the apartment above you.'

'*Une voisine, alors.*' A neighbour. 'How pleasant,' he said. Only then did he allow his eyes to drop, slowly, the length of me and back up to my face. I found myself blushing, knocked off balance by everything that look contained. Such a depth of understanding, of unasked-for forgiveness for all the sneaky, unworthy, shameful things I had ever done or would do, as if he knew exactly what they were. What they would be. All, he seemed to say, could be contained easily within his scheme; nothing was forbidden, nothing frowned upon.

'*Et les autres?*' he asked Bet.

'They're on their way. Nico dropped Aleah to the airport earlier.' A look, so smooth and slight it was just a ripple, passed between them.

Jacques moved on. Later I learned that he never lingered, gliding here and there, with just a word or a gesture that kept the wheels around him spinning in the way he liked.

'Another drink?' Marina asked.

'Okay, but no more beer.' Bet made a face. 'Whiskey?'

'Vodka?' I suggested. 'Just ice, no mixers?'

'Good plan,' Bet said.

'I'll get them,' I insisted. 'My turn.'

We knocked back the vodkas, then another round, and the bar slowly filled around us with kids in shiny clothes and hair of many colours. They were extravagant, flamboyant and loud, calling to one another, screaming, hugging, delivering explanations that were explicit and surely unnecessary of their days and weeks. There was so much greeting and kissing – I soon understood that Cécile kissing Bet didn't mean anything.

Bet and Marina introduced me to the many who came to find them, and stay beside them. Handsome boys, neat in jeans and T-shirts, with clean hair and white teeth. Girls in baggy workman's trousers, with tiny tight T-shirts, or jeans and slinky tops. Lots of logos – Chanel, Diesel, even Volkswagen. Marina, I realised, was wearing an exaggerated form of what was clearly a uniform. Bet, just as clearly, wasn't.

'This is Jean,' 'This is Albert,' 'Anna, this is Chantal,' 'Laetitia.' The introductions came and went, guys and girls with clear skin and good manners, telling me it was nice to meet me, politely enquiring how long I had been there, then sinking into the comfort of talking to one another about things they had done or that other people they knew had done.

I leaned against the bar, conscious of Cécile on the other

side, dispensing drinks roughly – glasses slammed down so beer spilled over the side, measures of spirits poured and shoved across the counter – and smiled, shook hands, offered my cheek for a kiss, while Bet and Marina, on either side of me, kept up a laughing undercurrent of comment in low voices: 'He was in school with us. Nice guy, boring as fuck'; 'I doubt she's been to bed since Wednesday night, look how she's twitching'; 'You'll like her, she's a laugh. Boyfriend is awful, though.' They had, of course, a definite place for everyone who was there, even those who didn't come to say hi, just waved or shouted over. It seemed they knew everyone in the bar, by now crammed and noisy.

'How do you know Jacques?' I asked then. Bet started to tell me – a story about a nightclub and somebody getting beaten up – then broke off to say, 'Here's Nico.'

I watched the two young men who walked towards us. One had broad shoulders and hair swept back from a face with a strong nose and brow, like the head of a Roman coin. He wasn't tall, but the arrogant angle of his head made him seem so. He moved with purpose, arms swinging, as if he was cleaving a path through the people around him. He slapped a few shoulders, accepting high-fives and fist-bumps. Beside him, his smaller, slighter friend, whose dark brown hair fell into his eyes, was slower, avoiding the greetings with a half-smile, winding his way around, not through, the crowd.

First, they stopped at the bar to greet Cécile, who leaned over and kissed them both, just as she had kissed Bet. She filled glasses for them with beer, refusing payment with a quick, decisive shake of her head and a nod towards Jacques, watching from across the room. The one with the Roman profile raised his glass to Jacques with a smile that said it was no more than his due, while the smaller one said something to Cécile that made her grin.

I wanted to laugh. They were so clearly the Young Prince and his valet – I couldn't believe anyone would accept the role the smaller one played.

I guess every friendship pairing has a lead and a support actor. With Bet and Marina, Bet was the lead. With me and Jessie, it was me. But we didn't make it so obvious. There was a dynamic; the impression, at least, of fluidity. This pair, I decided, were like caricatures, the comedy buddy combo in a bad movie. Nico must be a real dick to have put this together, I decided.

And then they were beside us. Marina and Bet were doing cheek kisses and saying hi, smiling as they introduced me. 'Anna, this is Nico. And Alec.'

'Alec.' I repeated it as she had said it, with the emphasis on the second syllable, putting a hand out to the smaller one. To my surprise, it was the guy with the Roman profile who stepped forward, took my hand and leaned in for a kiss.

'*Salut*,' he said, glowing, as if congratulating me on making his acquaintance.

'Nico.' The smaller friend, the valet, smiled at me, made no effort to shake hands or kiss hello, just looked. But he went on looking as Bet asked him about Aleah and the airport, switching his gaze away only when Alec clapped him on the shoulder and asked if he wanted another beer.

They found stools and drew them close to us, making space a moment later for a guy with a thin harlequin's face, who was introduced as Pierre. He was darker than Nico and Alec, the skin of his face stretched tight across rather delicate bones. His eyes, large and dark, were the most arresting part of that sad face.

At first I watched more than I spoke, the conversation flitting back and forth between them all, except the harlequin boy, who said almost nothing. Nico spoke quietly to him sometimes. Alec used him as the patsy in occasional jokes, in a way that might have been friendly or not.

Alec talked the most, loudly, with gesticulations. And he was funny, telling long stories in which he pitched himself as the blunderer and fool, but somehow emerged victorious in his anarchic brilliance. He repeatedly shook his hair off his face, I suspected to show off his classical profile.

The stories seemed to involve falling asleep a lot – at work, to be woken by his boss; at home, with a saucepan of water that boiled dry; on a park bench, in the sun, to be shaken awake by a mother whose child had pointed him out and told that he needed to get into the shade.

Silly stories, but tending towards a point, I realised. That Alec was of one ilk, the rest of the world of another. That he was intrepid and reckless – up all night, out, absorbed, invincible until exhaustion got the better of him by day – but irresistible too, so that his transgressions must be forgiven, even by those, like landlords and workmates, who had a right to be irritated.

And yet I began to see that, for all his assurance and arrogance, he looked to Nico for approval of almost everything he said. He touched him a lot, a hand on his knee, an arm around his shoulders. Once, he even brushed back a strand of hair that fell over Nico's eyes. Nico said little and his stillness, in contrast with Alec's constantly tossing head, was interesting.

Alec drew the attention but it was Nico who kept it.

We laughed and drank. They asked me about Dublin, about what I was doing in Brussels, and I found myself telling funny stories of my own. All the ways in which I used to be shy, awkward and cautious melted away in the humid warmth of that bar. In French, it seemed, I was different. I blessed again the chance that had made me choose to study the language at university, and the exchanges – in Lyon, Arles and Perpignan – that had helped me perfect it, and hinted at the person I could be in this language that so suited the shape of my tongue and of my most inner self.

CHAPTER 9

Now

'I'll be gone for the rest of the afternoon.'

Anna said it snappily, trailing her coat and bag behind her, daring anyone to look up or over. It was the only way, she knew: show no hesitation, allow no sliver of space into which questions could burrow. *Where's she going? What's she doing? Is it work? What kind of work?* Because that was how the rot would start.

Fitting the weekly sessions with Alison into her life was harder than she wanted to admit, but doing so felt like good faith, a demonstration of the efforts she was prepared to make. If Jessie wouldn't talk to her, then at least Anna could talk to someone about her. And if that was difficult, doing it might prove how much Anna cared.

By now, she knew how each session would go. Alison would ask how she had been, then sit patiently while Anna said 'Fine,' defensively, followed by an absurd 'Great' that came with a shrug. Then Alison would stay silent as Anna's own silence built, until finally Anna capitulated and added the 'Well . . .' that they both knew was coming. Then Alison would arrange herself into a carefully relaxed pose while Anna faltered her way through a description of her week, and Jessie's place in it.

'Well, I suppose life is back to normal, but it doesn't feel like it,' she said now after the preliminary hostilities of 'fine' and 'great' had been got through. Alison, she noted, was wearing a very fluffy cream jumper. Even the colours she chose were careful, neutral.

They had been back from France for weeks, and Anna was surprised to find herself still edgy, unable to settle back into the routine of work, picking up Rudi, tailgating Jessie's comings and goings. It was late autumn and her daughter had begun going to hockey practice, study group, the library, just as before, and seemed no more withdrawn and sullen than Anna could tell herself was normal. And yet . . .

She had known even before they came back that the holiday hadn't worked. She had known it on the night of the shopping and the restaurant. Whatever they had set out to do, and she had never dared to define it, hadn't been done. Her daughter was still silent, hostile. Anna was still the enemy. Whatever new kindness they needed to find between them had not been found. It was all yet to do.

'I'm not hungry,' Jessie said, again and again, sitting calmly in front of whatever dish Anna presented, hands folded neatly in her lap, no evidence of a struggle of any kind. 'I don't eat that' was another favourite, no matter what Anna prepared. She said it almost in wonder, as if astonished that anyone could eat it. Or, indeed, eat anything. Anna, who insisted Jessie still sit with them for meals, hoping to 'normalise' something that was already beyond normality, would catch her daughter staring at her in silent disgust, eyes following the fork as it dipped from Anna's mouth to her plate, loaded food and was raised again. Anna found herself seeing the process through Jessie's eyes and wondering too that anyone would consume bits of dead animal and vegetable. Would talk about it, think about it, write books about it.

The girl's silent judgement was enough to throw Anna out of her own careful stride, so that she had to bring herself smartly back with a reminder that the disorder was Jessie's, not hers.

That, she supposed, was Jessie's power. She was only picking up where the rest of them had left off – like the wren that hid inside the eagle's feathers, letting it do all the hard work, then popping out, energised, to go the final short distance. Because every table Anna had ever sat at had carried silent questions about the food consumed on it. It seemed to her that Jessie had just harnessed a disorder that existed in all of them already, and taken it a little further.

The very cunning of the disease astonished Anna – the way it could comfort those it afflicted with the slick sheen of superiority, even while it destroyed them.

'What do you feel?' Alison asked now, smooth, bland.

'As if we're on pause, waiting for something to happen. Something bad. I wake up at night and the words "We're going to crash!" scream through me. When that happens, I can't get back to sleep for ages. I'm shaking, my heart pounding like I've plunged down a roller-coaster. There must be bad dreams just before I wake for me to feel like that, but I never remember them.'

That wasn't true. She remembered many of them too well. They were contorted and obscure, but they were memories as well as dreams, and Anna could have put a pinprick in the precise moments they recorded.

What she didn't say, too, was that she had used the waking as an excuse to move into the spare room 'for the moment', saying that Maurice might as well get a decent night's sleep even if she didn't. He had looked sad, and said he slept better when she was with him, even if she was restless, but Anna had ignored the appeal. It wasn't any of Alison's business, she decided, although in one of the earlier group sessions they all went to, Alison had told them everything was relevant. No, Anna had decided there and then. Not everything.

'What do you think the waking might mean?' As usual, whatever she gave Alison came right back to her, just spun around. She felt sometimes as if the two of them sat there and played with knives. Anna would unsheathe something sharp and push it fast across the table, tip pointing at Alison, only for Alison to stop it dead and calmly turn the handle until the tip pointed towards Anna.

Dutifully, she took up the latest knife and spelled it out. 'I suppose I'm still on high alert. I haven't been able to relax. I don't trust that we can manage.' *I don't trust that my daughter isn't lying to me. I don't trust the ground in front of my feet to support me. I don't trust myself to keep on being the person who can do this. I don't trust myself at all.*

In the beginning, she had tried asking Alison questions – 'How long have you been working in this field? Where did you train?' She'd thought that if she could strike up an equal relationship with this calm-voiced woman she might get proper answers to the questions that thumped through her: *Is my daughter going to get better? Will she lead a normal life? Did I do this?* But Alison had turned out to be skilled at evading what might have been intimacy.

'Let's talk about you,' she would say, after the most perfunctory answer. 'Not me, not Jessie. You.'

And Anna, who tried never to speak of the self that wasn't a mother, a worker, the person she had made so carefully, gradually found herself weaving a course through parts of her that she no longer had words for.

She didn't, she felt, do it very well, but she tried.

'I feel so angry with her, and helpless. When I see her cutting a piece of chicken breast – that she has told me precisely how to cook – into halves, then quarters, then eighths, putting the effort into cutting that she should be putting into eating, I want to scream. Watching her pick up a tiny bit on her fork and bring it to her mouth as if it's literally a piece of shit makes me angrier than I would have thought possible.' She paused, drew breath, tried to compose herself, then gave up. 'I made that for her. I cooked it.' Considered it, bought it, prepared it, served it, all the rigmarole of care that went into the things that appeared on plates in front of Jessie, which she spurned.

'If I can't feed her, and she won't let me hold her,' she said now, 'how do I show I love her? That's what bothers me. I can't keep saying it – it sounds so trite after a while. "I love you, I love you, I love you." Those are just words, like any silly pop song. But she won't let me do anything else. The things I have to offer her – food and comfort – she rears back from as if they'll hurt her.'

'You'll need to find another way,' Alison said.

'That's very easy for you to say.'

Secretly Anna marvelled at the deadly accuracy with which Jessie had chosen her battleground, the sharp instinct that had led her to the place where she could do most damage simply by doing nothing. How had she discovered it? Anna wondered. Had someone taught her or had she just known? Had Anna herself taught her unwittingly? But she couldn't have, she reflected bitterly. After all, her way was not silent and inward, like Jessie's: doing by doing nothing. Anna's way was to do.

Alison pointed out that the equation of food with love is a cultural norm and said she understood why Anna must feel rejected. 'But we're still talking about Jessie,' she continued, in a monotone. 'Tell me about you.'

And Anna dried up because what was there to tell?

The session ended, as so many did, in a trickle of words with thin meaning. Anna spoke aloud her resolutions – made nightly, broken daily – to do better. To be more patient, less personal, to love Jessie in a way that was calm and reassuring and consistent, that asked nothing of her.

During the sessions with Alison, she had discovered that, as well as all the things she knew, so painfully, that she had done wrong with her daughter, even the things she'd thought she'd got right had been wrong.

All her responses had been immoderate, it turned out, not just the angry ones. She had shown too much love, been too full of praise and admiration. Ending conversations with 'Love you!' was wrong. Praise was wrong. Or maybe that was just the way she interpreted Alison's silences . . . as if they came with judgement and hostility.

So Anna felt foolish and hysterical. Her attempts to weave a safety net around her daughter with words of affection and encouragement now looked feeble and pathetic – the vain efforts of primitive man to block out terrors of the dark with firelight and stories. And even though no one had ever told her a better way to do it, Anna knew she had failed. And failed early.

Because what Alison didn't realise was that this had all begun at a time and in a place she couldn't tell her about: to talk about it would only make everything worse.

CHAPTER 10

Then

Later, much later, we moved on to a nightclub. Had I been at home I would have been tired, longing for bed, played out. But here, I felt – as they felt – that the night was just moving into its truest phase. 'There's no point going earlier,' Alec said dismissively. 'The place is too full, with people who are just there to drink. They aren't serious.' I began to understand that these people felt themselves to be a tribe apart, inhabitants of a night city that belonged only to them and existed quite separately to the business of the day. Later, I would realise that being in the city but not of the city also set them apart. They had become used to it as a backdrop, a pool into which to dip, but felt no responsibility for it. It wasn't theirs, although they liked what it could give them.

Outside the bar, we stood in a knot, working out would we walk or drive.

'You can come with me,' Nico said. He handed me a helmet

and nodded at a shiny black Vespa, silver mirrors and edgings gleaming against the graceful curve of its front. Beside me, I felt Alec stiffen.

'And us?' he asked, with a loud laugh.

Nico shrugged, swung himself onto the bike and gestured for me to sit up behind him. I sat, fumbling for something to hold on to.

'Put your arms around me,' he said. So I moved closer to him, wrapping my arms around his waist, bracing myself for the bump as he rolled the bike off the pavement and onto the cobbled street.

I looked behind me as we moved off. Bet was smiling broadly at me, eyes sparkling. She shouted something I didn't catch.

We wound through narrow cobbled streets with buildings so tall on either side of them that it seemed they must meet overhead. Past kebab kiosks and late-night corner shops selling cigarettes and cheap beer. Young men stood on street corners or outside bars, drunk, calling to one another or at girls as they walked by. There was a smell in the air of gunpowder, as if someone had let off fireworks only we had missed the flashes and bangs.

I leaned close to Nico, face pressed to the back of his pale corduroy jacket. I wondered would he point things out as we went, but he said nothing, and when he stopped the Vespa after only a few more minutes and got off, he still said nothing, just took out a cigarette and offered me one, then locked the bike.

But when I held out my lighter to him, he leaned in towards the tiny flame, then took my hand to draw it closer to him. That was all. His hand on mine, warm and steady, for just a moment. And I knew then what Eve had felt when she'd reached for Adam's hand after biting the apple. And all the ways his hand, which she must have touched a thousand times before and barely noticed, felt different.

We were silent as we walked, and then we talked, in a flood that could have been nerves or just astonishment. I asked about the place we were in, a grand and gorgeous shopping gallery of marble with a domed glass roof. The boutiques on either side sold things so delicate they could only have been hand-made: shoes, leather belts, glass beads. One shop sold toys, the kind you might find in a royal nursery.

'Surely there isn't a nightclub in here,' I said. The nightclubs I knew were in ugly places, sometimes rundown, always a little away from commercial centres.

'Why not? As long as we're gone before the shops open and the bourgeoisie arrive, no one minds. Sometimes we cross over,' Nico said, with a smile. 'We are high, and ready to sleep; they are just getting started.'

'Like a relay race,' I said, wishing I'd been able to think of something wittier. He smiled again.

'You're nice,' he said, and I felt myself flush so that I couldn't look at him. *Nice.* I loved it. Not sexy. Not gorgeous. Nice. It made me think he meant it.

The club was in an old cinema, florid with stained red velvet and curly gold-painted wood. 'Théâtre du Vaudeville', it said, in art deco lettering between two fat pillars. A crowd clustered in front, some leaving, more trying to get in but turned away by the four heavy-set men in black bomber jackets, who stood around chewing gum and eyeballing newcomers.

As we approached, one of the bouncers rushed from between heavy red curtains across the entrance, shoving in front of him a skinny kid in a black leather jacket, whom he pitched onto the hard marble floor. I bent down to see if the boy was okay, but Nico took my arm and pulled me up.

'Leave it,' he said.

'But he might be hurt.'

'Anna, leave it.' It was the first time he had said my name. Because of that, and the way it sounded as he spoke it, I let him draw me forward. We walked past the crowd, and the bouncers hailed Nico with claps on the shoulder and the kind of winks that could have meant many things.

The red curtain was held aside and we stepped into a sort of holding pen, with another set of heavy red curtains in front of us, a dimly lit velvet tunnel, with a booth to the side where we paid a girl with a silver ring through her nose. She, too, greeted Nico, leaning out to kiss him.

The music pulsed through the curtains, intensifying as we stepped into a large oval room with layers of tiered seating – red again – around the sides and a dancefloor in the middle. An ornate balcony ran around the room, and above it the ceiling was picked out in swirls and plaster shapes. Jessie, I knew, would love it because it was old and funny and had character. I began planning an email to her, describing everything: I knew that if I could do it properly, she'd definitely come out. She'd have to.

Nico bought me a drink, and then, as I settled back against the bar to talk to him, look at him, listen to him, he left.

The music was the kind that pounds and screeches and expands seamlessly to fill any number of hours. Bet and Marina arrived, introduced me to yet more people, most of whose names I didn't hear. Marina gave me a pill, shouting into my ear, 'They're good, not too heavy,' and we danced, for what might have been hours, together and separately. Sometimes Alec was there, moving with an assured self-regard, and Pierre, too, stayed close, although he didn't speak.

Occasionally I caught sight of Nico in the distance, with other people, talking, laughing, swigging beer. It seemed to me that wherever he was, the air was at its thickest and brightest. I saw Cécile too, with the same glow, the same sheen, as she had had behind the dingy bar at Chez Lé; a hot ember in all that red velvet. And Marina, at the bar now, running a hand through her hair and saying, just as before, 'I chopped it all off! The freedom!' to the guy beside her, who nodded approvingly. Jacques had made the pilgrimage from his bar: I saw him bent over a small girl, younger than me, with thin white-blonde hair and bad teeth. His soothing murmur wasn't audible, but the rhythmic stroking of his hand on her upper arm was hypnotic even at a distance. I thought about the yellow of his fingers, with their long nails, and shuddered.

'Come and meet Madame Pipi,' Bet shouted in my ear.

'What?'

'Come with me.' She grabbed my arm and dragged me up to the balcony, then along the back wall and into a cloakroom, where girls were reapplying make-up, smoking and chatting, some hoisted up to sit on sink edges and countertops. It was like being backstage at the theatre because of the many mirrors, the bare skin and smell of cheap perfume.

A girl wearing tiny powder-blue shorts, a shiny blue bra and a pair of huge white Yeti-style furry boots was dancing by herself, staring at her reflection in a full-length mirror. As I watched her, she leaned forward slowly and kissed her image, then resumed dancing, eyelids half-closed over dreamy too-black eyes.

An older woman with short canary-yellow hair and a tight black plastic skirt moved briskly in and out, between girls and cubicles, with a can of disinfectant spray and a cloth. Throughout, she kept up a running stream of commentary, her voice coming and going between partition walls and over the sound of toilets flushing. She seemed to be dispensing advice, asking questions and updating herself on the lives of the girls around her.

'Madame Pipi,' Bet whispered. 'Although she probably has another name. She's been working here ever since I've been coming. Some of these girls spend the whole night in here, chatting to her. She's like an agony aunt crossed with one of those Mafia wives. I once saw her chase a girl out onto the dancefloor and scream at her because she hadn't tipped. Come on.' She pulled me into a cubicle, just vacated by Madame Pipi, and locked the door behind us.

'What?' I asked.

'Ssh.' Bet took a piece of folded paper out of her bag, opened it and started scooping white powder on to the cistern lid. With a deft and practised hand, she chopped it into two lines, using a card.

'Are you nuts?' I hissed. I expected the flimsy door to buckle under furious hammering at any moment, then bouncers or even police to drag us out and into a waiting car.

'Hush. It's fine. No one minds as long as you're discreet.'

'It's hardly discreet, the two of us in here.'

'It's fine. Now, do you want some or not?'

'Okay.' If she was having some, I would too, even though it was a long time since I'd done drugs, had never really bothered with them much, and I could still feel the pill I'd taken earlier pulsing through me in heavy, undulating waves.

We each snorted a line, then stared at one another and burst into loud giggles. Bet ran her fingertip across the edge of my nose, wiping it clean, then put the finger into her mouth and sucked it. 'No telltale signs,' she said. 'Come on.'

We sauntered out of the cubicle, hand in hand. No one gave us a second glance, except Madame Pipi, who smiled as Bet handed her a folded banknote. I couldn't see how much it was for, but she seemed able to tell from its feel. She patted Bet's arm in approval and gave me a genial nod.

Back on the dancefloor, the DJ was finally playing the kind of club anthems I liked. We danced and sang along, waving our hands in the air and grinning.

'Isn't she cute?' Bet said to Marina, gesturing at me.

'She's cute alright.'

Alec was standing close behind Marina, arms around her waist so they swayed together. He leaned down and kissed the side of her neck.

At last the room was all but empty. The barman closed the metal shutters around his station with a clatter.

'Let's go,' Bet said.

'I'll go to the loo,' I said. 'See you outside.'

Madame Pipi was gone, the backstage chaos tidied away as if it had never been. I washed my hands slowly and for ages, staring as if I had never seen them before. My head was buzzing and hollow, and I felt a sudden slump of exhaustion.

The lights were off when I came out, the still and silent darkness of the empty oval room confusing me so that I walked the wrong way through it. The walls were so heavily panelled that I could see nothing that looked like a door, no chink of light to act as a guide. I began to push at the walls, frantic, in case I had been locked in, forgotten. My heart was thumping, I felt sick, and I was ready to start shouting, not caring how foolish I sounded, when something gave beneath my hand and I stumbled into the red velvet tunnel we had come in through. I was shaking, my legs wobbling with more than just the hours of dancing.

Ahead of me, two bouncers stood in front of the final layer of velvet that lay between me and the outside, where it must now be well past dawn. I hoped Bet and Marina would be there, because I wasn't sure I could find my way out of the covered gallery. Or perhaps there was more than one way out. I realised I had no idea what part of the city Nico had brought me to – but I told myself that of course the two girls would be there.

I walked up to the bouncers, debating whether to ask them where I was, how I might get to somewhere else, and stopped when they didn't move aside. They smiled, immobile, so I smiled back, waiting. They waited, arms crossed, one with a complicated tattoo of Gothic lettering running around his thick forearm. The letters, in deep navy, made me think of German army helmets. Exhaustion flickered at the corner of my eyes, like a faulty strobe. Still they waited.

'*Alors, on a bien danser?*' one asked, in a sneery way.

'Yes, it was great,' I said, relieved that the peculiar silence had been broken. I shifted my weight, ready to start walking, but still they didn't move. I looked behind me. I was alone in that dark red tunnel. My panic of moments before prickled at the back of my neck. Why was I still standing there? What didn't I understand about getting out of somewhere that now seemed sinister, not charming?

'You must be tired,' the other bouncer said.

'Yes,' I agreed. 'Very.' Still smiling: the pathetic indication of my good faith.

'You must be looking forward to going home,' said the first, leaning closer to me.

'Yes.' I was desperate now. 'I am.' I leaned back. Away. But they both moved closer. With the three of us in the tight tunnel, there was nowhere to go.

'Not surprised,' the first said. He began flicking my hair with the back of his hand, flipping it from side to side. I stayed still, heart thumping, wondering was there another way out and would I find it if I was to turn now and run away. The idea of going back into the dark, empty room, so far away from the outside world, which, after all, lay just beyond the weight of the curtain, stopped me. That, and the knowledge that they could catch me, too easily, if they wanted to.

Perhaps they were teasing me, I thought, a strange kind of joke. I lifted my head higher, trying to think of something relaxed, disarming, in French, to say to them, but my mind gave me nothing.

The hand flipping my hair crept forward to my face now, cupping my cheek. It was hot, and the thick fingers felt demanding. I swayed, leaning into the hand for balance instead of away, hating the instinct that made me do that. The hand increased its pressure, searching my face, learning it.

'Alain.' A voice behind me broke the spell, caused the hand to stop, to withdraw. I turned, unsteady, to see Nico just behind me. He put his shoulder against mine and I wondered if he'd realised I was about to fall. 'She's okay,' he said. 'She's with me. She's new.'

'No problem, Nico,' Alain said smoothly, stepping back into doorman pose so that the way through the curtains was clear.

Nico pushed gently into my back to start me walking and, as we stepped through the door, I saw him press something into Alain's hand, held out at a practised angle.

'Are you all right?' Nico asked, once we had walked a little way down the deserted gallery. A white early-morning sun poured through the glass roof. Of Bet and Marina there was no sign.

'I'm fine.' I drew a shaky breath. I didn't want to admit how scared I'd been. 'But I don't understand.'

'You have to pay them,' Nico said.

'But don't they get paid by whoever owns the club?'

'Not really. It doesn't work like that. They get paid other ways. Most of us give them money. Some of the girls do it differently.' He was silent then, and I began to understand. The threat had been real, not imagined.

'Shit,' I said. 'If you hadn't come when you did . . .'

'It would have been fine,' he insisted. Because he wanted me to believe it? Or because he believed it? Or because it wasn't a big deal to him? I don't know, but suddenly it didn't matter.

The bouncers, the fear, belonged somewhere else, somewhere I was happy to turn away from.

We stood in the wide-open square outside the gallery, with the morning sun slicing across the pointy tops of the medieval buildings around us, and I couldn't believe it was only my second day. I felt I'd been made brand new, forged in the cauldron of that hot red space and sent for the first time into the world on that shiny morning.

I looked at Nico, leaning against his Vespa, and smiled. 'What day is it?' I asked. 'Where am I?'

CHAPTER 11

Now

When her attempts at talking to Alison had dwindled to a halt, Anna went back to work. It was late afternoon and she let the door thud shut, lest anyone might think she was trying to slink in unobserved.

'Right, let's have a meeting about the Nord-Zee account,' she said loudly, a woman busy and important, but one who made time for all her duties. 'My office, ten minutes.'

That would give her time to check her email, get coffee and sit in silence for a moment.

She could see Andrew watching her through the glass wall of his own office, and knew that he could see her until she sat down, when she would be hidden by the computer screen she had angled for just that purpose: a screen behind which to duck, and hide. She entered her glass box with an air of faint exasperation but, once hidden, she sagged, too weary even to sit up straight. She knew she should eat. She had missed lunch to keep her appointment with Alison, and now badly needed something. She fumbled in her drawer for a protein bar and wished she had someone to laugh with about the irony. Wished, more, that she could ever have laughed about the irony.

Andrew rapped at the glass door. 'The Nord-Zee meeting?'

'Two minutes.' Her mouth was so full of dry, crumbly, chocolate-flavoured protein, she could barely speak. She grabbed a bottle of water, swigged, and said, 'Just let me send a couple of emails. I'll be right there.'

He smiled. 'Enjoy your lunch.'

Telling him had been a mistake, she knew that now. It had built an intimacy that he wanted more than she did, one she had tried to reduce. The knowledge, held between them, gave him scope to speak to her as a friend, an intimate, rather than as a colleague.

At the time, telling had seemed the only option, and a 'good' thing to do. Maurice had been in favour – 'You're going to need time off, sometimes at short notice, depending on what happens with Jessie. You have to flag this.' And Anna had wanted to. Apart from the practicalities, a small part of her had wanted to acknowledge the vulnerability of an Achilles heel that wasn't her own, maybe even wanted to foster the intimacy she also dreaded. She wanted to allow Andrew the opportunity to be better than she knew him to be, but also to test her standing in the company he owned and to which she was, she believed, indispensable – how much leeway would she be given?

Enough, as it turned out. Or enough, at least, for the first weeks of the crisis when Jessie was kept in The Laurels – so discreet and private – where they took over the business of feeding her at great cost, stepping into the vast breach left by Anna's failure; by Anna's hysterical shouting, through which Jessie had sat mute, outwardly meek, but unwavering, with the stubborn aggression of the habitually obedient. Anna squirmed when she recalled how quickly panic had replaced compassion in her, when she began to understand how resolute Jessie was, and how badly she herself had expressed that panic – in threats and recriminations, long, violent sentences that began with 'I can't believe . . .' and wandered through waves of 'always' and 'never', the very words Alison had told her not to use.

How easy it had seemed to be for Jessie. All she had to do was nothing.

'Right, the Nord-Zee account,' she said, iPad in front of her with any notes she might need. 'We have a client meeting next Wednesday, and we'll need to show the kind of activity they'll be expecting. Sally, what do you have?'

The meeting moved into its ordained rhythm, smoothly, like a car rolling down a hill and gathering pace. Anna guided it skilfully, engaging other members of the team to make their contributions so that they could feel they had indeed contributed, and Andrew could see her in full mastery of a situation she needed to be master of. If work slipped from her grasp, there was so little left.

Anna was good at her job because she was clever at remembering names and faces, and things about them. But she had discovered her greatest skill by accident: the ability to create a cosy sense of influence and access. Nothing so crude as name-dropping, just the right shading, at the right time. This, as well as an ability to put in long hours and her determination to earn what she called 'enough', meant that she was still there in an industry where the attrition of women was high.

At first she had done it because, with so little between her and Jessie and the cold whistle of an east wind, what choice was there? Then, after Maurice came along, she did it because she wanted to, and to prove she could. And, if she was honest, because it was hers and not his. Now she did it because what else was there to do?

Of the women she had started with, over ten years ago now, she was the only one who remained. The others had left, worn down by the long hours, the clients who were happy for women to do the work but continued to address questions to the men who sat beside them in meetings. Or they had children, and swore they would be back, but rarely were and never for long. Anna was the only one who had gone that distance, so that she was now respected even beyond her capabilities, which were many.

Stick around long enough, she sometimes thought wryly, and you will triumph. Victory, she had learned, was so often to be found in longevity, in simply staying the course.

Andrew began to speak, diffidently, with the nervous rush that caused the foolish to presume he was hesitant and could be driven, to mistake his covert ruthlessness for indecisiveness. Or, at least, fail to realise that one lay beneath the other. 'From the firm's standpoint,' he was saying, 'this needs to be mapped out in a way that is far clearer, that leads directly towards the objective of creating positive sentiment . . .' and he was off.

Secretly, Anna kept score – a kind of platitudes-bingo she played with herself. She gave herself a point for 'going forward', two for 'reaching out' because she hated it so much, and one each for 'multi-directional', 'creative content' and 'harmony of strategy'. It wasn't much, but it had kept her mildly amused in the past. Less so now.

The meeting wore on, past the stage where there was anything new to say, but Anna allowed it, knowing that everyone there needed to feel they had added their store to the heap. This was part of being 'good with people'. She stared at her hands, slender, knobbly with the rings Maurice had bought her to mark the big events of their lives – engagement, wedding, the birth of Rudi, anniversaries. You could measure out her moments in the hard bright gleam of diamonds. Maurice, she thought suddenly, had never asked her if she liked diamonds, had just presumed she did. In fact, she preferred the warmer sparkle of rubies, but she had never told him. Her hands, she decided now, looked like they belong to someone else. Someone older and harder.

For Jessie's birth there was nothing. Nothing to wink and flash and remind her of a time she would never forget.

She remembered all the fatuous promises, made by older relatives, the mothers of her friends, casual strangers: 'Wait until you see your baby', No feeling on earth like it,' they cooed, but not as if they quite believed it. Or, at least, not for her. They were nervous even as they spoke. She was 'so young', just twenty-five, she had no career, no money, no husband, little family support. Those women talked about the wonder of a new baby but cast worried glances when they thought she couldn't see them. As if the difficulties in her 'situation' would override the maternal laws they had known from within the safety and comfort of good marriages and secure standing.

When Jessie was born, Anna knew instantly, the great question of her life had been answered, and the answer was this: the resolute Yes of this squirming bundle of flesh and blood and warmth. The thousand-year-old eyes that looked into hers, and the way the child demanded that Anna be equal to this. The same eyes that later reproached her because she wasn't.

The meeting ended at last, at an hour that made it respectable for everyone to gather their things and leave. Except Andrew, who liked to arrive late and stay until long after everyone had gone.

They had kissed once, years before, at the end of a long and very drunken office evening out. Anna was already married, Andrew, too, had been with someone at the time, and neither had ever mentioned it again, but the memory of his tongue lurching around her mouth still made Anna squirm, especially if, like now, they found themselves alone in the office together. The way he still looked at her, so that she knew the memory was in his mind too, made her claustrophobic, but also excited, in a way that bothered her.

'Good meeting,' he said, leaning against her glass door. 'Sure you're okay? That everything's okay at home?'

'Yes. Thank you,' she said. Then, when he didn't move, she knew she needed to give more. 'It is still a delicate situation but I think it's starting to settle down.' She was as bad as him, she thought, with her obscure evasions, words that meant little, strung together so they meant less. But what else was she supposed to say? *I have no idea what is happening or what to do. My daughter is denying life and I am watching her do it, because I owe a life and sometimes I think it has to be hers.*

'Well, if you ever fancy a drink, or need someone to talk to . . .'

'Thanks, Andrew. That's very kind.' And it was. Or maybe it wasn't. Maybe it was something else. She was too tired to try to read the signs. 'I might take you up on that one of these days . . . You'll be sorry . . .' She tried to make a joke of it but he didn't laugh and neither did she. 'Better go,' she said. 'I'm meeting friends.'

The friends were in the kind of bar that served food and ten types of gin, and they were not to be put off any longer. Since she'd got back from France, they had been clamouring to meet and she had been stalling, for all the reasons that made them so insistent: Jessie, Maurice, herself.

These were friends who had never known Other Jessie, as her daughter called her, who would always be First Jessie to Anna. She had gathered them about her after that summer, after baby Jessie was born, drawing them from mother-and-baby groups, her first job, Montessori, because they had children the same age or walked the same beat.

She had needed new friends, because she could not go back to the group she had known before that summer, because they were friends of First Jessie too.

They were kind and generous, her new friends, especially in the matter of playdates and sleepovers, tiding her over the first hard years at work when every day felt like a thread pulled from a hem, the unspooling relentless and high-pitched. They were like honorary aunts to Jessie, strict and loving when Anna wasn't there. They were funny and smart and successful. And all of them together were not a match for First Jessie.

'Drink?' Marissa asked.

'God, yes. Anything. Red wine?'

'Are you eating?' That was Jayne.

'Yes, but mostly drinking.' They laughed at that, dutifully.

'So?' Susie was first to it, as Anna had known she would be.

'What?'

'The holiday?'

'Fine. Lovely, really.'

'By which you mean it was nothing of the sort.' Susie again. A waiter arrived with bottles, glasses, plates of cured ham, cubes of sheep's cheese, olives, roasted vegetables in oil, elaborately carving out space so they could admire his dexterity, the precision with which he placed a bowl of artichoke hearts.

'Was the weather nice?' Waiter gone, they returned to the attack, but more gently.

'It was okay. A couple of cloudy days, mostly still in the twenties, though, and a few really hot ones.' If only they could continue on the weather, Anna thought, then move to a play someone had seen, a film, a new restaurant. But, of course, they didn't.

'How was Jessie?' Jayne, the most direct, was also the most concerned, feeling the triumphs and pain of others almost as she felt her own.

'She was pretty good,' Anna began slowly, trying to gather herself, to talk to these women as she couldn't talk to Alison, whose neutrality was more judgemental for its insistence that there was so much to be neutral about.

'She was quiet – very quiet – and she clearly still has very little energy. She lay on the beach or in bed and did almost nothing with any of us. She wouldn't come for walks with me, or go shopping with Maurice, or even play with Rudi. She was like a lizard soaking up heat, sucking it deep into her bones. But she was polite, mostly. The nights we went out to eat, she came with us and ate some of what she ordered. She does that awful thing now of quizzing waiters about how food is cooked, is there butter in things, and can she have the sauce on the side.'

'Jesus. In France! They must have loved that,' said Susie.

'Exactly. It's France! There's butter in everything.' Anna laughed a little, the first slugs of red wine cheering and relaxing her, as they always did, so that she could begin to see her life as a play that might be made amusing, rather than simply pathetic, in the telling.

'And did she talk at all about what's going on with her?'

'Not really. She doesn't. I can see how much she hates being the centre of that. She said it was like being in the middle of a never-ending game of Chinese whispers, with people saying things to her that she's said to them, but saying them wrong so she doesn't understand. And, anyway, she still can't see that there's anything wrong with her. As far as she's concerned, the rest of us are the problem. That place she went to, they fed her up, which was good, of course, but they didn't persuade her that she needs to think differently about any of this.'

'But at least she's eating.'

'Yes, though still like someone chewing a mouthful of grit, no matter what I give her. And no sauce on anything, no dairy, no sugar, all that stuff. She has so many rules, as if that's the only way she can feel safe.'

'Half the world eats like that nowadays,' Jayne said, typically soothing. 'And it doesn't do them any harm.'

'No,' Anna agreed. 'If she keeps to that, it's fine. I mean, it's joyless and tedious, but I suppose it's healthy.'

'Better than us,' said Marissa, pouring more wine.

'Hmm, I wonder,' Anna said.

'Does she seem happier?' Jayne asked.

'I'm not sure,' Anna answered slowly. 'I mean, obviously it's nothing like as bad as it was before France, and before The Laurels. But she's still nothing at all like she used to be. And I don't trust it – any of it. It's like the calm after the storm . . . before another storm.'

They looked thoughtful, and Anna could see them – unwittingly, even unwillingly – turning over in their minds, for reassurance, the ways in which Anna and Jessie were different from them and their own daughters.

Anna was, she knew, although she did not want to be, the eldest in an uneasy tribe. Her friends looked at Jessie, looked at her and tried to learn fast, before it was too late, what not to do with their daughters. This, as much as concern, was the motivation behind their endless questions: why? how? what?

'It was that business at school that started it, right?' Susie asked. They had been over this so many times, moving from the rage of the early exposure – 'I'd like to kill those girls,'

Susie had said, 'actually kill them. Little bitches!' which was exactly how Anna had felt, although she had never said this to Jessie, had instead tried to be reasonable and measured about it – through long, detailed analyses of how and why and what the school had done, and finally reaching a sickened acceptance: this was what happened. This was what girls now did to one another. Sold each other into misery for a price that was safety, protection for themselves, a short-lived charm that kept them from being consumed by the fire they so eagerly fed. For a while anyway.

'I suppose so,' Anna said, 'although Jessie did once say that there were other things as well.'

'What other things?' Jayne asked. They knew the answer.

'Her dad, mostly. The lack of one.'

'That's not your fault,' Jayne said sharply, as Anna had known she would. This was what they did for one another – shored each other up, insisted they had all done their best, that the bad things that happened were not their fault. And, of course, they had only the version of the story Anna had told them, in which it certainly was not her fault.

'And she has Maurice,' Marissa added politely.

'She does,' Anna agreed, just as politely. They didn't really talk about Maurice, mostly, she guessed, because they thought they knew the story: that Anna had married him for stability rather than love, for the home he could give her and Jessie. It was a version they approved of, and that Anna had never contradicted, even though it wasn't true, not remotely, and she wondered at them for believing such a thing, and even more for tolerating her if they believed it.

She had never fully told them of her intense gratitude for Maurice's kindness – or just how wonderfully close to love gratitude can be, until it starts to wane and reveals itself after all as base metal, tricked out to look like gold.

He had come into their lives, hers and Jessie's, like a warm, bright explosion, determined to love them both. His way was to bring gifts, cook food, make plans, laugh at Anna's fears that it wouldn't work, and wrap them both with care and talk of holidays they would take, restaurants they would visit. He was a way back into a world that Anna had thought would never again be hers, and she had loved him for it.

And it had worked well between Jessie and Maurice at first. She was such a good child, Anna thought, and he was so eager. It was strange, but from the start he had liked the package: Anna and Jessie together. Unlike most men, his face hadn't fallen when she'd told him about her daughter.

'Great,' he had said, in a way that made Anna think he must be far more in love with her than she had suspected. Later, she realised it wasn't that simple. Yes, he loved her, and wanted her, so Jessie was not the deal-breaker she had been with other men, but Maurice also wanted something that spoke to his view of himself. That made him somehow different, more fluid and bohemian, than others he knew.

She had begun to understand when he had introduced Anna and Jessie to his parents, insisting that they come together that first time, although Anna had tried to say that perhaps it would be easier for them to meet her alone first.

'Nonsense. They love kids,' he had said, wilfully blind to

whether or not they would love a kid who was not his but, by then, was linked to him.

And of course they hadn't, Anna thought, recalling that first meeting in the large house so different from her parents' house; a house filled with people for whom her suburban semi-detached childhood was a matter of mild curiosity. But they had come round, had seen the real fondness between Jessie and Maurice, which had lasted throughout her childhood but fallen at the hurdle of her awkward years.

At first, aged maybe twelve, flushed with the excitement of change, Jessie had practised flirting with everyone. Tossing her hair, batting her eyelids, she walked and sat and moved quite differently, animated by the vivid contrariness of 'hide' and 'be seen'.

She had tried out her tricks on Maurice, who had repelled her with a bluff heartiness that Anna had known must hurt her daughter, even though she also knew that his options were limited. What was he supposed to do? Encourage her? And yet the rejection she could see in Jessie's shoulders and the tightness at the back of her neck told Anna that she didn't understand, saw only that he brushed her off in a way that clearly stung. There was no safe mirror in which she could watch herself.

Where had all the rot started, Anna wondered. With her, or with Jessie? Was it then, when Maurice grew so uncomfortable with the girl's early teenage vamping that he put up an awkward distance between them, hurting Jessie so that she turned against him? And had Anna gradually turned too, in solidarity? Or was it that Anna had already cooled and Jessie had sensed the distance, been animated to disrespect because he no longer had her mother's protection? Either way, it didn't seem that she could really blame Maurice for what was so far outside his control or understanding. And yet she did.

'Are we having dessert?' Jayne asked.

'I am,' Anna said. These days, she always said yes to dessert. It was a small act of defiance against the allure of Jessie's way. Suddenly, thinking again of Jessie's face as she watched the people around her eat, she recognised the repulsed confusion. It was the way Anna sometimes thought now about sex, with bemused astonishment. People did that? For pleasure?

She shoved it out of her mind. She and Maurice were just going through a bad patch. It wasn't surprising, with all that was going on. It would pass, as it had before. After Rudi was born, months had gone by, but back then, she had looked forward to 'normal service resuming', as she had phrased it to Maurice, with a laugh. Now, she dreaded the moment he might insist on talking about what was no longer between them.

Why, she wondered briefly, did the idea of touching him repulse her? He was the same man he had ever been. Cautious, decent, a little foolish; keen to be seen as more capable, more daring, than he truly was.

It was she who had changed; she knew that. As if Jessie had shaken loose the shelf of her life, tumbling all the things she had so carefully stood upright so that they fell, in a heap. She had found herself thinking about the past as she hadn't done for years, or not so much thinking about it as inhabiting it. And it made a contrast with the present that was no longer bearable.

At first, after Jessie was born, she had wanted to put distance between herself and that past, had wanted to run far away from the lazy, seductive irresponsibility of that summer, where night had been day, and day simply a series of hours to get through. Where wasted was normal, and the bargains one struck had different stakes, different prizes.

After First Jessie died, that had fallen apart and she had deliberately moved away from it, filling in the gap with regular hours, bills to pay, places to be, her daughter to mind, then Maurice, a house to run, Rudi. She had appreciated the difference between the new life and the old, believing she had buried one beneath the other, and that it was right to do so.

But it turned out that past life had been there all the time, not gone or forgotten. And it suddenly looked desirable again. Or some of it did; a memory of love that could still make her heart speed right up.

In the taxi on the way home, Anna stared out the window at the wet streets that slipped past, empty and furtive. She pictured the home that awaited her. The polished floors, the carefully chosen rugs and bland paintings. The house was furnished as Maurice wanted it – 'You care more than me,' Anna had said, wanting to be generous, to give him back some of what he had given her – 'You decide.' Really, it was his mother who cared, and whose love of what she described as 'Scandinavian chic' was reflected in the pale wood and stark barrenness. Only Jessie's room felt like somewhere Anna would have chosen.

She conjured up Rudi, asleep, breathing in and out gently,

the smell of hay that clung to him. Maurice, in front of the television with a glass of wine, would be waiting for her to come in, say goodnight and go upstairs before he swapped wine for whiskey.

Jessie, in her attic room at the top, listening for Anna's tread, for the sound of the door opening and Anna's question: 'Are you awake?' They did this every time, always had done. Once, Jessie would have been waiting, full of the story of her day, with questions and comments to chirrup at Anna until Anna called a gentle halt. Now, Anna knew, Jessie would stay still, breathing a lie into the silent dark.

'Here?' the driver asked, pulling in outside the front gate.

'Yes,' Anna replied, wondering what would happen if she said, 'No. Keep going.' Go where? To the station? The airport? And then what?

Her phone beeped. Andrew. She paused, hand on the taxi door, then sat back and hit reply.

CHAPTER 12

Jessie

I dreamed of Other Jessie last night. Not much of a dream. She was looking for me, to tell me something, but she was in the wrong place, or maybe I was, and she couldn't find me. But she's still looking.

I have bad dreams all the time now. This one wasn't the worst. I sleep badly too. I can't get comfortable, and when I do fall asleep, it's like I'm only ever waiting to wake up again. Like I'm covered with threads, and something jerks them, so I get pulled awake, fast and hard, and then I can't go back to sleep.

Sometimes I get in with Rudi. He's so soft and warm. I'm cold all the time. Anna asked did I want a hot-water bottle when she saw me shivering one night, but I said no. Hot-water bottles are for when you're sick and I'm not sick.

Other Jessie looked really worried, and in the dream I knew she'd been trying to find me for ages. She needed to tell me something.

I've read enough of those books about dream analysis and universal symbols to know that everyone in my dreams is me. But she didn't seem like me. That's why I remember her so clearly. I don't know if she seemed like herself, because I have no idea what she was like. Maybe she was like Anna.

Anna sort of talks about Other Jessie a lot, but doesn't say much about her. She never said how she died. Just that it was 'an accident'. And I never really asked her. I guess I didn't care. But I will now, because I do now.

If Other Jessie was me, in the dream, then what am I trying to tell myself? That's easy. I know the answer to that: work harder; be stricter; don't be lazy and pathetic. And don't listen to people who pretend to be friends but are actually jealous.

Isolde taught me that. Earlier I met her for a walk. She's out now. I didn't tell Anna. She wouldn't have approved. And I want someone who is just for me, someone she doesn't know about.

Isolde looked good, although she says she's still not where she wants to be. She's much longer at this than I am. She says her period started when she was twelve, and stopped when she was thirteen. Mine has come back. I asked her if that was a bad sign.

'It is what it is,' she said. 'Don't worry about it. Just keep focused on what you're doing, and why you're doing it. That's the point. Everything else is extraneous.'

Isolde is incredibly clever.

'If I was in America, they'd say I was a straight-A student,' she said once, in the dayroom at The Laurels with its disgusting green walls and pictures of meadows. Like that's going to make us all do what they tell us. 'They don't say that here,' she went on, 'because in this country we don't appreciate people making the best of themselves.'

I asked then if she was still getting straight As, because my marks are much worse now. I just don't care as much as I used to.

'Of course,' Isolde said. 'The point is to be the best.' She was a swimmer too, a good one, but she admits that she doesn't swim now. 'The water's too cold.' Instead, she runs, same as me, except farther and more often. She does ten kilometres most days. That would take me over an hour at the rate I go. How does she find time?

'You make time. It's just what you do.'

Isolde talks loads about that stuff – what she does, how she does it – but when I ask about her family, she says less. I think she doesn't like them much.

'What's it like being home?' I asked her yesterday.

'Can't wait to move out,' she said, making a face. She's only sixteen. How can she even be thinking of moving out? See what I mean about her being focused?

'The place is so untidy,' she said. 'My mother thinks she's so good at everything – "You try running a house with four kids and a husband who thinks shoes live under the sofa" – but she does a rubbish job. There's stuff everywhere and the cupboards in the kitchen are full of junk all thrown in a heap. Packets of crisps and biscuits and sticky spice bottles and jars of sauce with leaking lids.'

It sounded gross alright, but I wouldn't say Isolde is easy to live with. Her standards are very high.

She says mean things about her brothers too, three of them, all older than her.

I sort of know why she does it. You have to. You have to make them terrible and ridiculous so you can push them away, beyond you, and then you can concentrate on what you're doing. If they aren't terrible and ridiculous, you have to listen to them and then they might be right, because you're used to them being right.

It was easy with Maurice. I pushed him and he went straight away. He went easy. Rudi, I can't push him. I just can't. I know he's a weakness but I can't. And Anna won't go. I keep pushing, but she won't budge.

I can see sometimes that she wants to, though.

She's so petty. Even now. All she cares about is what things look like. What I look like. 'Let me see you eat.' Not 'Please eat' or 'Did you eat?' Let *me* see you eat. Me, me, me. Her, her, her. Eat, eat, eat.

How do people even do it? Eat so much more than they need? All day, cramming stuff into their mouths, chewing and swallowing, chewing and swallowing, over and over again. And they need only a tiny fraction of it. How wasteful. It's so easy to live on less, and know exactly what you're going to eat and when you're going to eat it. I'm so much freer than I used to be. Free of all that thinking and talking about food. It's so neat now, my meals: I know what I'm going to have and I have it. That's it. No more patrolling the kitchen – fridge to cupboard – the way I used to, a handful of this, a bite of that, cruising round, eating and eating. Peanut butter on top of cheese on top of a banana, some toast, a biscuit, another biscuit, more cheese, and on and on and on.

I think a lot about all the wasteful things I used to do, because I didn't know better. Like, I used to shout and yell at Anna if I wanted something she wouldn't give me. Not very often, only sometimes, but it never worked. Those times, she stayed all reasonable and sure of herself. 'I'm not going to do that, Jessie,' she would say, like she deserved a medal. Now I don't do anything, I don't even raise my voice, and I get what I want. I guess the difference is that what I want now is nothing. Or, rather, what I want is a non-something – to be left alone, to *not* do things, rather than do them. For people not to be on at me, saying why don't I do this, or go there. All the plans, making them and never being sure there weren't better ones? It used to do my head in.

I can't believe how easy it gets. At first it's hard, saying no to things, and people, and then what's hard is saying yes.

But still it's just eat, eat, eat, eat, eat, eat. I think if I have to hear that word many more times I'll choke on it.

I feel like it's written all over me. I'd do it, to shut them up, except I won't give them the satisfaction. It's a battle, I know that. It's me, and it's them, and I guess we're not on opposite sides exactly, it's just that I'm on my side, for the first time ever, and they aren't.

I was always on her side. The two of us together. That's what we used to say. 'You and me, babe, against the world.' Except now there's only one of us and the world is so against me.

But this is the best way I have of drawing a line between us. Of saying 'No' to her in a way that she can hear. Before, she turned all my nos into yeses, just by refusing them: 'Oh, you will,' she'd say. Or 'Go on, you might as well . . .' no matter what it was – a party I didn't want to go to, a sleepover, a project in school that meant I had to stand up in front of everybody.

Jenna got an exemption from doing that, or reading aloud or any of those things, because it stressed her so much, but Anna wouldn't let me. 'You'll be fine,' she would say, with the laugh that said how up for everything she was. 'Nerves are good. They make you sharp.'

I said no, she said yes: the same pattern, all the time. Until now. She can say yes all she wants now. It's still no. And the thing is, the difference is, I know why it's no. I can see what I want and who I want to be and exactly how to get there, and I won't let her stand in my way.

There was a party once, back before Harriet and I stopped talking, and she was trying to make me drink the gross stuff she'd brought with her. It tasted like cherry syrup but there was loads of booze in it, and Harriet, who swore to her mother when we were leaving that she wouldn't drink, was hammered.

'Come on,' she kept shouting at me, 'have a drink, for Godsakes.' Her speech was all slurry and she was holding on to me really hard, partly because she was squeezing my arm, trying to persuade me, but mostly because she needed to hold herself up.

She was really angry with me when I kept saying, 'No, thanks,' as if I was the one who was behaving badly instead of her. 'You're such a prude,' she said. 'Such a goody two-shoes. You need to let go. Live a little.' Like she was some sort of amazing free spirit instead of a drunken girl at a stupid party wearing a dress that showed how big her thighs were, all the way up to her knickers. She was holding the bottle of cherry stuff like it was a weapon, shaking it at me. If she'd broken it and had the sharp end pressed into my face, she couldn't have been more vicious about it. I looked for Jenna but she was snogging some guy from Zach's school.

That was one of the parties Anna said I 'really should' go to, because 'It might be fun, and if it's not, you can just leave. I'll come and get you.' Except that meant me texting her and admitting I was having an awful time. That I was a total failure at parties.

'For fuck's sake, Jessie.' Harriet was still going on at me, and I probably would have given in then, but Zach came along and took her off to dance, and when I watched the way she was falling around in front of everyone, twerking and shaking her hips, I was so glad I didn't.

She was so disgusting, so spread out and sloppy and undisciplined. Flopping and falling and wobbling. Standing there, watching her, knowing that I could walk without falling over and just get my coat and leave with perfect dignity, any time I wanted, I knew then I'd been right to say no, and that I'd carry on saying no.

The next day, Harriet said it had been worth it but she must have been lying to save face. It can't have been. That's just one of the things we all say – to cover up that we feel shit about something. *It was worth it*, when you get caught and get into trouble, or someone takes a photo of you looking disgusting and ridiculous and posts it, saying something mean. *It was worth it*. Just another of the lies we all tell.

I hate those songs about being a teenager: 'Sweet sixteen' and 'Young and sweet'. They have no idea. They think it's all smooth and shiny – skin, hair, smiles – but it's not: it's pitted and pock-marked and snarled and vicious, and if you get it wrong you're torn to pieces – and how can you ever get it right? If it ever looks like you might, they move the goalposts to make sure you don't.

I don't even know what the differences are – why Harriet gets it and I don't. We were the same when we were little kids, just messing and scribbling and playing with ponies, but then it was like she got called into a room and told stuff, and I didn't. So now she knows and I don't. She understands how it works and I don't.

That means she knows the rules and I don't. So I'm not cute and sweet and having fun and going to *pool parties* and *the mall*, like everyone is on MTV. And I used to feel I was letting everyone down by not doing that – all the people like Gran and Anna's friends, Susie and Jayne and Marissa, 'cause they'd ask what I was up to and I knew they wanted to think I was going out and spending hours getting dressed and being excited about everything, and even though I was, a bit, I wasn't really, because I always knew I was faking most of it. So I felt bad. Like I'd messed up.

I don't feel bad now, though. I don't care. They ask, and I just smile and say nothing.

Anna didn't ask that stuff or expect me to be giddy and giggling over boys and lip gloss, but she wanted things, too, just different things. She wanted me to be aloof and have 'other things' in my life. 'You need to know what defines you,' she'd say. 'You need your framework.' I used to think she meant like a signature perfume or something, same as the magazines go on about, but then I started to understand that she didn't: she meant, like, knowing who you are and what you stand for.

I don't stand for anything. Not a single thing. I tried being interested in Amnesty and gay rights and stuff, but I'm not. I don't care, really, so I stopped that. The letters and leaflets still arrive but I just bin them. I feel bad because it's always about people who are having a really hard time, in prison or a camp or being tortured, but I bin them anyway.

Anna doesn't do any of that stuff either, not like Harriet's mum, who's on loads of school committees and raising funds for refugees. Anna doesn't do it but she doesn't have to – she still seems like she knows exactly what she's about. Like she knows everything, and I know nothing. Like there's room for her and there's no room for me.

CHAPTER 13

Now

'Jessie, you'll be late. Hurry!'

Anna tried to keep her voice cool and neutral, without the twitch that threatened it, the one that said she was always, these days, the supplicant, Jessie the withholder. Sometimes now she felt like a bland robot, a carefully neutral wall of pastel beige that moved around Jessie's life, blocking one bit, then another.

There was no answer from Jessie, which didn't surprise her, so she went up the final flight of wooden stairs to the attic room with its dormer window through which the sea was just visible.

'You're the only one in the house with a sea view,' Anna had said, when they had converted the attic, painted it pale pink, even the floorboards, and moved Jessie out of the small room beside herself and Maurice.

'You should have it,' Jessie had responded immediately, coming close to lean against Anna.

'It's yours. All made for you.' Anna had seen she was nervous about moving so far from her but that, too, was a reason to encourage the step towards the independence she felt Jessie needed. 'You have space now for sleepovers with more than just one person. You could have a couple of friends over.'

Jessie had looked nervous at that, too, but had nodded. She understood the value of personal space. 'You're not welcome in my room,' she would say, when there had been some kind of dispute between them. She would say it, voice shaking, lip trembling, eyes imploring Anna to beg. And Anna, because she could then, did.

'Please let me be welcome,' she would say. 'I'm so sorry for shouting. Please don't turn me out.' And Jessie, who had so little power then, would relent.

Well, now she had more, and Anna couldn't plead her way out.

'Jessie,' Anna said now, 'you're going to be late.'

Jessie wasn't up yet, she saw with irritation, was still a messy lump in bed. 'What are you doing? Come on, hurry!'

The room, she saw, was carefully, precisely tidy, all Jessie's things either put away in drawers or ranged carefully on shelves and desk: little ornaments, a jewellery box, various objects found over the years and loved into significance. The parade of stuffed bears and rabbits was not yet rejected outright but had been banished to stiff columns on high surfaces, rather than tumbled into a cosy heap as they had been when she was a child, trying to fit them all into her bed at night.

'I feel sorry for the ones that don't fit,' Jessie had said, 'in case they're lonely.' She had looked anguished, so Anna had helped to devise a system, a rotation, that was fair and Jessie had adopted it, though Anna knew perfectly well it hadn't solved the problem, that she still fretted about those left in the toy box or doll's cot on nights when it wasn't their turn.

'I'm not going in.' Jessie's voice was hoarse. She barely poked her head above the duvet as she spoke.

'Why not?' Anna wondered if she had a free first class or perhaps she was sick.

'I'm just not. I don't feel like it.'

'Jessie, you have to go in.' Anna felt the panic starting, the knowledge so painfully learned that, against the brick wall of her daughter's 'no', she had no weapons.

'I don't and I'm not.'

'Okay. Why not?' Anna tried to keep her voice even.

'Because I don't want to.'

Anna took a breath and tried again. 'Jessie, you aren't allowed take a day off just because you want to.'

'Not a day.'

'What?' Anna checked her phone. She needed to leave if she wasn't to be late for a meeting with a possible new client, a group Andrew was very excited about.

'I said "not a day". I'm not going in tomorrow either.'

'Jesus Christ, Jessie!' Anna did away with the voice of reason, and allowed herself the sharp irritation she had been choking back.

'There's no point in shouting,' Jessie said, still barely raising her head from the pillow. 'That's not going to change anything.'

Anna felt she could have slapped her, shaken her, anything to get through the cold, smooth wall Jessie had put up around herself. She needed to get out of the room, fast, before she gave in to the desire to curse her daughter into some kind of reaction that wasn't this frozen hostility. It's like chipping ice off the inside of a freezer, she thought. 'We'll talk about it later,' she said. 'You can stay at home today. Only today. This is not me saying you can carry on staying at home, okay? Now, I have to go.'

'Of course you do,' Jessie muttered.

'You'll be on your own in the house,' Anna continued, as if she hadn't heard her. 'Rudi's coming with me now.'

'Good,' Jessie said, lumping herself even more tightly into her duvet.

Anna drove fast, faster than she should, holding back the urge to tell Rudi to be quiet as he chattered away behind her on his way to crèche. She made 'um' and 'ah' noises, as if she were listening, and tried to inject some brightness into her voice when he asked a question that had to be answered. But inside she burned with rage at Jessie and the casual cruelty of her careful silences and reluctant monosyllables, the way every bit of her screamed 'Help me!' even while she looked coldly back and insisted 'There's nothing wrong.'

The meeting went badly because Anna was distracted, although not so badly that she wouldn't be able to tell Andrew, truthfully, that the prospective client was thinking about joining the agency.

Outside their office, she sat in her car for a long time, staring through the windscreen with the radio on. The day was dirty with wet leaves, the exhausted grey of an early autumn when winter will be long. It still surprised her that, with no real ties, no anchor beyond Jessie, after everything she had seen and lived in Brussels, she had chosen to stay in this small, clammy country. That alone, she thought, said so much.

She thought of Jessie at home, in bed, and wished she could enjoy feeling that her daughter was snuggled up and happy. A snow day. A storm day. But it wasn't, and she knew Jessie would not be luxuriating in it as once she would have been.

'Let's both stay at home today,' Jessie used to beg sometimes. 'Stay in your bed and watch DVDs and not get out of our pyjamas for the whole day.' Sometimes Anna said yes. Mostly she said no.

'No can do,' she would say, trying to be matter-of-fact, trying not to let the anguish show. 'Model positive behaviour around work,' the books said. 'Don't let your child associate your leaving with distress.' And Anna had done what the books told her, peeling her daughter's icy fingers from her coat or bag, or trousers when she was very small, stepping brightly out, closing doors smartly behind her.

Later, she told herself, once I get settled, once I put some solid ground down for both of us, then I will take the time, stay in, wrap a duvet around us both and we can wear our pyjamas all day with the fire lit, eat toast in front of the TV and watch daytime crap.

But 'later' never came, and now Jessie changed out of her pyjamas as soon as she got up, dropping them daily into the laundry basket as if they burned her.

Anna had tried to make a joke about not being a washerwoman and could Jessie not wear them for a couple of nights, but the girl had looked at her blankly and said, 'That's disgusting.'

Often there was no real difference between her PJs and her daywear – a series of sweat pants and tops in greys and pinks, all too big so that they hung loosely on her bony frame, flapping a little like a scarecrow's clothes. The alternative was the stripper dresses, so tight you wondered how she could breathe, with shoes that had made Anna laugh with their desperate bid for sophistication.

Except that Jessie didn't wear them any more, no longer bothered with the false eyelashes and streaks of orange tan, had turned her back on the teen discos and house parties, because she didn't go out. 'They're pathetic,' she said now, turning a sharp shoulder when Anna suggested she might like to go somewhere.

It was a disease, Anna thought, of lines and edges. Of bones and tight skin and an attitude that became hard so fast it set like cement. First Jessie was plump and soft and lost, then skinny and hidden behind a hard, thin sheet, like Perspex. Behind it she watched but said little. Her body did the talking. The barbed wire of her spine. The smell from her mouth.

A leaf blew against the car window and made Anna jump. She realised she had been sitting there for too long, doing nothing.

Can you do lunch? she texted her mother, who would be surprised but would, Anna knew, say yes. She firmed up a story to tell Andrew – budgets had changed, the potential clients would be back to them, 'bit of a waste of time, really' – and made her way into the office.

The dining room at the Claremont Hotel was just the kind of obvious ornate that her mother appreciated – lots of white and gold, with squashy sofas and thick carpets – and with a menu that didn't challenge her.

The Claremont was her type of place – with waiters who almost bowed when they greeted you, and a maître d' who might remember her name. It was the place Anna had been taken to on special occasions: Holy Communion, major birthdays, graduation. The three of them sitting, shy, unable to settle on a topic. First the weather, then who had been at whatever the celebration was; later, when Anna was older, perhaps a political or financial scandal. It had been in the Claremont that she had told her parents she was going to Brussels 'for a few months', knowing as she said it that she didn't plan to return.

'This is pleasant,' her mother said now, cautiously. She was wearing her autumn coat, black cloth with a ring of dark brown fur around the collar and cuffs. She hung it carefully over the back of her chair. Anna knew that she was wondering why she was there.

They ordered – Caesar salad and a steak for Anna, pâté and roast chicken for her mother, whom she tried to call Mum, as she used to. She would have preferred 'Mary', but knew her mother would take it as more evidence of what she didn't actually call Anna's pretensions but only because she didn't have to: it was so obviously what she thought.

Her mother drank water. Anna, to annoy her, had a glass of white wine, conferring with the waiter about grapes and countries until she knew she had made her point – *I am not like you* – and despised herself for needing to make it.

'How have you been?' It was what her mother always asked. Not 'How are you?' which might lead Anna actually to tell her.

They spoke then in their own code, about Maurice, Anna's work, her father and his various ailments: the knee that pained him when it was damp – as if it ever wasn't damp, Anna thought – the lower back problems, the damaged teeth that made certain foods difficult.

Each time, she could see the placards of her mother's mind come into play, the same giant signs that were raised aloft day after day, year after year, which covered most of the eventualities of their conversation with simple, cut-throat responses.

'Knight in Shining Armour' said the placard when Maurice's name was mentioned. 'Career Woman' flashed up for Anna's job, which Mary always spoke of as if it were a hobby, or something that someone more powerful, a man, might take from her at any moment. The one that said 'Duty' was for Anna's father.

'What might you do if you didn't have Dad to look after?' Anna had asked once, years before, because she was feeling bitchy, and because she wanted to know. Her mother had looked terrified and told her sharply 'not to be talking like that'. But she had looked momentarily hungry too.

The placards obscured the contents of her mother's mind quite as much as they revealed them. They were a way of hiding, Anna knew, as well as reassurance – a flow of old positions that her mother could walk on, like stepping stones.

They ordered dessert – Black Forest Gâteau for Mary, which Anna hoped wouldn't be too deconstructed, pear and almond tart, then coffee for herself – and moved on to the health of various neighbours and relatives, none of whom Anna had seen in years.

At last, and exactly when Anna had known she would, her mother put down her spoon – the gâteau had been rich and reassuringly traditional – and asked, 'So how has Jessie been?' She sat back and folded her hands in her lap, to show she had finished eating and that she didn't intend to be drawn too deeply into a conversation about her granddaughter. It was the way she used to sit when Anna was younger, any time it seemed as though she would be required to do more than feed, clothe, drive or maybe lecture her.

'She's okay.' Contemplating the coming discussion, Anna suddenly realised just how much she hated the part of herself that kept going back to her mother, looking for a comfort she had never really known. She had invited Mary to lunch because she needed to be with her, in case she had overlooked something that might be there, now when she needed it most. But once they had gone through the thin rituals of their conversation, she knew that there was nothing after all, and she no longer wished to expose herself or her daughter. So 'She's fine,' Anna added, and shrugged. 'It's not easy,' because she had made her mother come to lunch, and needed to say something.

'It can't ever have been easy,' her mother agreed, pleased to be on sure ground. 'The early days. Just the two of you . . .' She had a way of dwelling on, almost gloating over, the perceived misfortunes of Jessie's babyhood, as if soothed by the satisfaction of unorthodoxy duly punished, Anna, reaping the whirlwind of her transgressions. 'Perhaps your father and I could have helped more,' she continued, 'but we felt . . .' She stopped, unwilling to risk disloyalty to her husband by continuing, unable to voice what exactly they had felt about this daughter who had 'disgraced' them. Because that was the placard that belonged with Anna's return from Brussels and Jessie's later birth: 'Disgrace'. The placard was swiftly unearthed each time the subject came up, although the word was never spoken.

But Anna wasn't ready for any of the ways in which her mother could have, should have, been kinder. 'Actually, you're wrong,' she said, fast, lying, but only a little. 'It was easy. It was tiring and there were always too many things in the day, and it was lonely too sometimes' – her mother stirred a little – 'but it was easy, because it was the two of us, me and Jessie. That was wonderful. We were a team. Now we aren't, and that's the bit I can't cope with. Being against her or, rather, her against me. Now it's lonelier than ever, and it's much too late for you to help.' She hadn't meant to bring her mother here to attack her, so she tried again. 'I'm sorry. It's just . . .' She shrugged and her mother sat, if possible, even farther back in her chair. She had taken the sleeve of her coat onto her lap and was stroking the fur, as if it were a small, docile animal.

'Tell me,' Anna said suddenly, 'did I cry much as a child?'

'As much as anyone,' her mother said.

'And what did you do?'

'Do? I left you to it.'

'So you let me cry it out?'

'I suppose. Is that what they call it now? Babies cry, then they stop, or they fall asleep. It's normal.'

'But did you ever feel, I don't know, as if the screaming was inside you? In your head? Going through and through and through you, like a saw, cutting and slicing?'

'No,' her mother said. 'I didn't.' She looked appalled, just as Anna had known she would, but when Anna didn't say anything, she rallied and tried again: 'I didn't like it,' her mother said, her voice softer now. 'It's hard to listen to a child crying, but I knew you were fine. That you weren't hurt, or hungry, so once I made sure you were safe in your cot, I just closed the door.'

Anna could see it perfectly: her mother calmly closing the door, then walking downstairs to the kitchen, certain she was doing what was right and normal.

Not for her the agonised back and forth between Anna and Jessie; the child's cries that seemed to voice Anna's own fear and lack of faith in the world, building until she found herself screaming back, drowning Jessie's yells with her own. It was as if Jessie's cries tripped an alarm within her that shrilled so loudly, it cancelled all calm and rational thought. Not always

– mostly she was exactly as she should have been: in control, master of herself and what she needed to do – but too often.

These were the things Alison wanted her to talk about, Anna knew. But she couldn't. Not yet.

She stirred sugar into her coffee. 'What's the worst thing you can say to a teenage girl?' she asked.

'I don't know.' Her mother looked astonished at the question. Astonished that such a question should exist. 'Um . . . that she can't do something?' she tried.

'No, that's fine. They get that. The worst is to say, "I understand. I know what you're going through." That, more than anything else, reduces them to despair.'

'But why?' Her mother seemed confused and uneasy. The stroking hand moved a little faster.

'Because if you – even you, their born-ancient mother – know, then it means they are indeed as pitiful and dreary as they fear. You have to pretend it's all new. That they are the first to know what any of it feels like.'

'Any of what?' The uneasiness was growing.

'Any of the things they feel. The confusion, the pain of being alive, the impossibility of happiness.' She kept her voice deliberately light, as if they were chatting about a bag one of them had seen, a pair of shoes they might buy. 'You have to let them believe that they are the first to all of it, even when you know – so exactly! – what they're going through. When you remember just what it's like to be strip-searched' – her mother flinched at the words – 'as you cross a road in your school uniform by drivers, pedestrians, the fathers of girls in your class. To have a lightbulb flick on over your head one day out of the blue, and for all men's glances to become heat-seeking missiles, drawn by your body, changed, inside which is your mind, unchanged.'

Her mother stayed silent, and Anna wondered why she didn't join her in silence, then call for the bill, leave with a polite 'How nice that you could come. Give my love to Dad.' But she didn't. Instead she ploughed on.

'Imagine dressing a child in a bodysuit shaped like Marilyn Monroe and a pair of fuck-me shoes and sending her out, in a blonde wig, to sit on a barstool.'

'Anna, that's disgusting,' her mother protested, concerned only with the crudeness of the image, not with the fundamental unfairness of what lay behind it.

'Yes,' Anna said. 'It is. And that's what it's like. You turn twelve, or thirteen, for some it's even younger, and suddenly you're right there, in the glare of nothing you ever wanted.'

'But you were a happy teenager,' her mother insisted, veering fast off topic.

'Happy enough,' Anna agreed. 'But not immune.'

'Well, I can't pretend to understand what you're talking about,' her mother said, proudly almost, as if taking a stand against yet more of Anna's pretensions, 'but I'm sure Jessie will be fine. She's a good girl.'

As if that meant anything. As if that wasn't precisely the problem.

And then, just as Anna was trying to catch the waiter's eye and call for the bill, her mother said, 'I wondered if . . . '

'Yes?'

'Well, if maybe . . . '

'Maybe what?' Anna was impatient, awaiting a request to spend more time with her father, to visit more often, already planning regretful excuses.

'If Jessie's father . . .' Her mother stopped there, knowing she had nothing to add to 'Jessie's father' because she knew nothing about him. Anna was shocked, thrown so far off her stride that she dropped the bag she had just picked up.

'What about him?' she asked sharply. 'I told you, back at the start, he doesn't want to know.'

'Yes, but . . . '

'But what?'

'Well, maybe that could change.' Somewhere Anna admired the fact that her mother believed in change of any sort, and was willing to reopen a conversation they had had, just once and very briefly, fifteen years before. But she knew she had to close it, fast, and keep it closed.

'There is no reason to think it can. No reason to bring any of that up again, when it can't possibly help. Anyway, I don't have any idea where he is now.' She slammed all the doors as firmly as she could, one after another. Leave no chink, no gap that could be widened.

Her mother stayed silent for a moment, then, 'People do change,' she said stubbornly.

Maybe, thought Anna, as they said their polite goodbyes to the maître d' and left, but that wasn't much good to her because the past did not change.

CHAPTER 14

Then

Bet and Marina were waiting at the entrance to the gallery, sitting on the kerb, smoking, with Alec and the silent Pierre. At first I was sorry to see them. I wanted it to be just me and Nico. I thought we could get coffee, talk, that he could walk me round the early-morning city and tell me things about it, about himself, he had never told anyone else, and I could listen to him in a way he had never been listened to before.

Even as I spun it, I knew it was a fantasy drawn straight from a film, and that it would stay there.

'Where have you been?' Bet asked slyly, getting up and pulling Marina to her feet. 'We've been waiting.' Suddenly, the fact that they had waited – for me – made me as happy as if it had indeed been just me and Nico setting off into the city together. I looked at him, to see did he register that I had been waited for, but Alec had taken him aside and begun telling him something with much gesticulation and loud laughter. Pierre, close by, listened too but looked at the ground, rhythmically kicking the corner of an uneven cobblestone so that his toe bounced off it at precise intervals.

I told Bet and Marina about the bouncers. They nodded wisely, in open enjoyment, far too blasé to be shocked.

'Alain,' Marina said, almost with approval, it seemed to me. 'Figures.'

'He's fine,' Bet said, with a dismissive wave, like one who knew how to handle him. 'You have to watch him, though.'

Just as they played down the incident, I played down Nico's role in it. I wasn't sure why. Partly, again, it was that I didn't want to seem pathetic, when they were so canny and streetwise, but partly, too, it was an attempt to hold back. There had been something complicated in Bet's smile when Nico put me on the back of his bike, in the enthusiasm of both girls for me and him going off together. For me in general, if I was totally honest with myself. I needed to pack that away for a bit, then think about it when I was alone, and sober.

'Let's get beers and go to the park,' Alec said loudly.

'And breakfast. I'm starving.' That was Marina.

'Good idea,' Bet said, taking my arm. 'I'll show you the best croissants in Brussels.'

'Surely you don't eat croissants.' All the girls I knew were on diets.

'I eat anything I want,' Bet said.

'If you dance all night, you pretty much can,' Marina said, seeing my confusion. 'Croissants, pain au chocolat, hot chocolate with whipped cream . . .' She gave a dreamy smile. I couldn't believe, looking at her hip bones, that she consumed any of those things.

* * *

Bet, Marina and I stood outside the bakery in a queue behind five or six older women, all with shopping trolleys and silk headscarves, in defiance of what was already a hot morning. Nico, Pierre and Alec were on the other side of the street, in the shade, leaning against the windowsill of a tall house.

'Goodness, people here get up early,' I said. My eyes felt prickly and sore and I longed to close them, even though my whole-body exhaustion of earlier had gone. Instead, I felt wide awake, even a bit twitchy. It might have been the drugs, or simply anticipation. 'It's barely seven. In Dublin, nothing would open till nine and even then, on a Sunday, there would be barely a soul around.'

'These women would be shocked by that,' Bet said, with a laugh. 'They think the world will end if they aren't outside the bakery when it opens.'

'And they have a point,' Marina added. 'In an hour, there won't be a thing left on the shelves and by midday the baker will close and go home.'

The queue moved slowly, with much chat between the ladies, who were very proper and correct, greeting one another with a kiss on each cheek and polite enquiries after each other's health.

'They do it every morning,' Bet whispered. 'The full twenty-one-gun salute of a greeting. Every single day.'

A car drew up then, small and red with dirty wheels. Three dark-skinned men, probably a couple of years younger than me, sat inside. The windows were down and some kind of French hip-hop poured out, loud, with a deep and dirty bass sound; music that smelt of petrol, that spoke of tall towers and burning cars.

The driver pulled in alongside, idling the car on the road in front of us. Bet and Marina started to dance to the music, rolling their hips in a parody of a million MTV rap videos. After a moment I joined in, the drugs from earlier making it impossible to hold still, to resist the magic of that music. I felt like the girl in *The Red Shoes*, bewitched, condemned to dance. The guys in the car whacked up the sound and leaned out of their windows, whooping. The old ladies looked deeply disapproving and, drawing closer together, began to mutter among themselves.

The guys were leaning so far out now that one, in a red Adidas tracksuit top, hoisted himself right up and sat on the window edge. They clicked their fingers and called to us, shouting and laughing as we danced. Then the one on the window got down and came towards us, clapping and smiling. He positioned himself in front of Marina, moving in and out as she did, back and forth. They were like a pair of cranes, or puppets swinging from invisible strings. Bet laughed, egging them on as the old women drew farther back in horror.

'Come with us. Let's go, we can smoke a joint,' the guy said, gesturing towards the car. His friends opened the door, moving up to make space, although there was barely room for one more in the back, let alone the three of us.

'Come on,' they shouted. 'Come with us.'

The guy in the red track top was making coaxing noises now, waving his arms towards the car, as if Marina were a nervous horse that needed to be gentled into a box or stall.

Marina laughed and carried on dancing around him but moved no closer to the car, so he reached out a hand and took hold of her bare arm.

That moment of contact was like an alarm shrilling. Marina leaped back, shaking him off. 'Don't touch me,' she spat.

The women in the queue behind us had reached a climax of complaint, the word 'disgraceful' chucked around between them like a rubber ball. I wondered whom they meant, Marina or the guy in the tracksuit top.

Across the road, Alec, Nico and Pierre, who had been watching with amusement, started quickly towards us. Pierre was the fastest, reaching Marina almost before she had finished spitting out her words. 'What's going on?' he asked, putting an arm around Marina. She moved in close to him.

The kid in the tracksuit top looked from Marina to Pierre, then stepped back, hands held palm outwards in front of him. 'I'm sorry,' he said smoothly. 'I didn't know she was yours.' He looked at me and Bet. 'And them?'

'No.' That was Alec, standing close beside me. Nico, I saw, was with Bet.

'No problem,' the kid said, stepping back, still with hands outstretched, palms up. 'No problem, man, no problem.' He made his way to the car, without turning his back on us, as if he didn't want to expose himself. The women in the queue were silent now, watching through narrowed eyes.

The car drove off, music louder than ever, and I saw a beer can flung from the back window as it turned a corner. The can bounced on the fat cobblestones, ringing loudly in the early morning.

'You did well,' one of the women in the queue said to Pierre, patting him on the arm.

'Who do those guys think they are?' Marina asked no one in particular, hitching at her low-slung jeans. I didn't understand. The guy had only been dancing. He hadn't done anything. And the girls had encouraged him, had laughed and danced along. At first, anyway. I didn't get it, but I didn't say anything. I didn't get, either, why it was something the guys sorted out between them, with Bet and Marina hanging back. They didn't seem like that to me, feeble and needing protection.

I tried to ask how it worked, but Bet just said, 'It's the only way they understand.'

'It's true,' Marina added. 'If you don't do it like that, they just pester and pester for hours. They won't listen if you say no. They need to see you have a guy with you. If you're on your own, nightmare!' She gave a theatrical shudder, all good-humoured again.

'What did the Moroccan guy say to the fourteen-year-old girl whose house just burned down with all her family in it?' Bet asked then, nudging Marina in the side, like a parody of music hall entertainment.

'Do you want to come to the cinema with me?' Marina quipped, then dissolved into giggles.

Either the joke lost everything in translation, or there were all sorts of ways in which these girls were different from me. I thought about giving a big speech about common humanity, the ugliness of casual racism, as Jessie would certainly have done – I hated the way Bet always said 'Moroccan' when she knew there were other Middle Eastern nationalities: Syrian, Turkish, Egyptian – but in the end I didn't. Didn't know how.

We bought croissants so fresh they were like pillows and piled back into Marina's car.

'Are you sure you're okay to drive?' I asked her.

'It's fine. There won't be any patrols on a Sunday morning.' That there might be people, other motorists, clearly didn't occur to her.

We headed back in the direction of Bet's house, past many of the squares I had first seen the night before. Pierre and Alec were squashed into the back beside me, Nico following on his Vespa. I had wanted to go with him, had hovered, croissant in hand, while plans for where, when and who was getting the beer were made, in case he said something, but he didn't.

We went to a park with a round fountain and a triumphant stone arch in the centre on which pranced four horses towing a chariot. Inside it, a mighty green-bronze woman shook her standard at the sky.

The grass was short and yellowing, except for a lush ring around the fountain where the play of water reached into the air, then landed beyond the stone rim, creating a thin strip of green. It looked cool and pleasant there, but the others kept on walking, Pierre and Alec with a crate of beer each, Bet with an Aztec-striped blanket and Marina with giant packets of crisps. I carried two big bottles of water. I had suggested them in the supermarket, and everyone had looked indifferent, but I had bought them anyway.

We walked through the park, which was almost empty, to an obscure corner beside another fountain.

'Will Nico know where to find us?' I asked, in a way I hoped was casual. Bet winked at me.

'We always come here. He'll know.'

I blushed, knowing I had not been casual enough, and busied myself with looking closely at the fountain. It was more of a deep stone bowl really. Where the first had been polished clean and full of water, this was empty, except for a few dried leaves and twigs. Large and semi-circular, the figures carved in relief against the curved back wall showed – but barely, so worn and filthy were they – soldiers in battledress, and semi-naked Africans bowing before them. The effect of the wearing and discolouring of the stone was to make the bowing figures more grotesque, as if they were melting, effacing themselves as completely as they could. In contrast with the rest of the park, which wore a pleased and prosperous air, the fountain jarred.

'Belgium's glorious colonial past,' Bet said, seeing me looking. 'Grateful Africans greeting Leopold's conquering army. Something like that.'

'It doesn't look very glorious,' I said. 'It's falling to bits.'

'Everyone's ashamed of that era now, so they're letting the fountain gently rot away. In a few more years, a few more bad winters, you won't be able to make out any of it. Job done.'

'Why don't they just take it away?'

'Because all the proud Belgians who fought in various wars, and are always looking for another fight, will be furious and make scenes about their *patrimoine*. That's their national heritage. They'll say it's being debased by hordes of immigrants.' Her voice was full of scorn and amusement. 'Better to let nature do the dirty work.'

'There's probably an old man who comes here early in the mornings with a wire brush and tries to spruce it up,' Marina said.

'And his wife, with a bottle of bleach, to clean the stains,' Bet agreed, laughing.

'Jules and Françoise,' said Marina.

'Albert and Nicolette,' countered Bet. 'Maybe they're on

their way now and we'll be caught defiling former glories with our very presence.' She was laughing harder now. I turned away so she wouldn't see how shocked I was. She stretched out on the blanket and grabbed a beer.

Alec was fiddling with some kind of speaker while Pierre sprawled beside him.

'He hardly says anything,' I whispered, gesturing towards Pierre.

'I know.' Bet rolled her eyes. 'He's so creepy.' He didn't seem creepy to me, just sad.

'Whose friend is he?' I asked.

'Nico's, really. They've known each other for ages. Pierre is like his shadow, always there, slipping in and out of places where Nico is, never speaking. Alec is horrible to him sometimes, but Pierre never seems to care. He's weird.'

Then Nico arrived, hailed and waved over from afar, so that it was clear we had all been waiting for him. Alec relaxed visibly when he saw him. 'I thought you'd fallen asleep,' he said, as if such a thing were a fine joke.

Nico gave no answer, just sat down on the blanket and took a beer. He had changed his clothes – white T-shirt, jeans – and smelt clean. His longish dark hair was wet. Knowing he had gone home, showered, changed made me conscious of how grubby I was. My hair was stiff and coarse, and my skin had the sweetish smell of dried sweat. I moved up slightly, away from him.

'Beer?' He held out a bottle to me and I took it. In daylight his eyes had flecks of dark green mixed with the brown.

'Thanks.' I smiled, hoping my teeth weren't disgusting.

'It's going to be hot,' he said then, and lay down so that he was closer to me. I lay down too, beside him, aware to a fraction of a millimetre of the distance between us; of the smell of his shampoo and the way the air between our two arms was denser than it was elsewhere. The sky, which had been a deep blue, was bleaching white, as if it didn't have the energy to put forth colour as well as heat.

Alec had got his speaker working and played music just loud enough to be faintly aggressive. We ate crisps, drank beer and chatted, at first loud and excited, gradually slowing and drifting into longer silences.

Bet talked the most, telling stories that were outrageous and funny. More than that, they seemed the tip of a rich store – more wonderful, more personal – and I looked forward to a time when I would know her well enough to hear them all.

Passersby tsked at us, skirting our blanket and empty beer bottles far more widely than they needed to, and I basked in the knowledge of their disapproval.

I had always been such an ordinary girl. Ordinary house, ordinary parents, ordinary hair even – a colour that was neither dark blonde nor light brown but somewhere in between, until the sun got at it and gave it a few strands of brighter gold. Everything I had ever done was ordinary until that summer. In fact, the only thing different about me was something no one could see, and that was my deep desire to leave behind me the place where I was born and learn about new ones.

In that city, though, I was new too. I was exciting, even dangerous, leading a life apart from other, everyday, lives. Staying up all night when others slept, drinking beer when they drank water, coffee, juice, with this strange band of noisy, arrogant, funny show-offs I had fallen in with, who felt, already, familiar. As if I had, at last, found my tribe.

The morning drifted into lunchtime and we ate hot dogs that Alec bought from a van, thick sausages with something called sauerkraut that I had heard of but never tried, and sharp, yellow mustard.

Bet and Marina went for 'a wander' that I was too lethargic to join them on, too happy beside Nico, who was mostly quiet but who asked me questions from time to time – where was I working? when was I starting? – that I answered eagerly, although my replies didn't lead to more questions, as I hoped they would, only to more silences that were then broken disjointedly, not the smooth flow of regular conversation.

Alec's speaker ran out of battery charge and fell silent. He was annoyed and I was secretly glad. Around us, only the distant hum of traffic smoothed the edges of the hot air. It was like being inside a warm cocoon, a hollow in the centre of the day.

Bet and Marina came back, wet, having splashed each other at the working fountain. It was so hot by then that I wished I had gone with them, wondered how they had resisted climbing right in.

'You're soaking,' said Alec. 'Your hair.' He sounded faintly appalled.

'It'll dry in a second,' Bet said, tossing her springy curls. 'It's very water-repellent.'

'Like African hair,' Alec said.

Bet gave him a dirty look. 'It's Pierre who should have

African hair, not me,' she said, with a look at Pierre, who might have been asleep, or might just have been lying there with his eyes closed.

'Look!' I called. A flash of emerald green, vivid, almost poisonous, against the dusty leaves above me, caught my eye. I sat up. 'It's a parakeet! It must have escaped from some house or apartment nearby. Maybe someone left a window open and the bird got out. I wonder can we catch it.'

'I wouldn't bother,' Bet said lazily. 'You'd be better off killing it.'

'What do you mean?'

'There are huge flocks of them throughout the city. They build giant communal nests and eat everything. They're bigger and stronger than lots of the native birds, so they kill them, or simply starve them by taking all the food. They're a real problem. Pests.'

'But they look so beautiful.'

'Maybe in ones and twos. You should see when there are huge flocks of them. It's freaky.'

'Surely they die in winter.'

'Nope. They seem able to survive anything. For all that they're aliens, they adapt much better than the local species.'

I watched the bird move from branch to branch, listened to its rasping call, until a second joined it, another flash of green, each with a rose-pink splodge on its beak. I watched as they greeted each other, shifting from foot to foot, then set off together, fast.

'Never two without three,' Nico said, looking around.

'What?'

'Never two without three,' he repeated. 'Find me a third.'

'Nico's superstitious,' Bet said. 'You should see him when a black cat goes by, or if someone breaks a couple of glasses. He'll smash a third, fast, in case something worse happens.'

'There's one,' I said, pointing out another flash of green in a nearby tree.

'Good,' he said, lying down again. 'That's okay.' Then, 'It works the other way too,' he said, eyes closed. I liked his voice: it was soft, for a guy's, and low, so that you had to lean a little towards him when he spoke.

'What other way?'

'Two good things in a row mean a third that is even better.'

Bet and I exchanged glances above his head: fond, a conspiracy of indulgence.

I dozed some more with a dry wind shifting the leaves above me into a scratching lullaby, shifting patches of light and shade across my eyelids so that it seemed at times I was back in the nightclub, with lights slowed to less than a heartbeat. When I woke properly, it was evening. The mess we had made was packed away, empty bottles back in the crate, rubbish in a plastic bag, as if we had never been there. Long shadows dropped across the empty stone basin, making the supplicant shapes even more grotesque. It was time to go.

'I'll drop you home,' Nico said to me.

'But, Nico,' Alec said instantly, loudly, 'you said you'd drop me. That you'd help me move the bed into the back of the apartment, away from the sun. It's far too hot to sleep,' he explained. But he didn't want help; he wanted Nico. I knew that because I wanted him too. I envied Alec the openness with which he could appeal when all I could do was wait and hover. And it worked. He got him.

'Fine,' Nico said, throwing a helmet at him.

'I'll get the Métro back,' I said, wondering would Marina offer to drive me. She didn't.

Going underground, alone, after the perfection of that day, was like the cutting off of all that was good. I felt like Persephone, dragged to the Underworld by Hades. The Métro smelt of anger and wet dog. The black rubber floor was stickier than ever, as if it wanted to hold me down there, and the train, when it arrived, frightened me, roaring out of its tunnel without warning. The stations flickered by, mostly empty. A man asked me for the time; then, if I would go for a drink. When I said no, he muttered something unpleasant in reply.

I got back to my tiny flat, starving. The room was airless and old. I couldn't face going out again, trying to find a shop, buying something, making a meal, so I fished out the couscous that Marina had thrown into the bin, cooked it and ate it, plain, with a spoon.

I felt lonely and lost. I opened the window as wide as it would go to let in the city, let it comfort me. Then I leaned out, looking down onto the street outside Chez Léon. The pavement was wet, as if someone had washed it, or spilled something. The latter was more likely, I decided. I remembered I hadn't rung my parents since I'd arrived, although I had promised to. I wondered would they be worried, then decided that more likely they would be cross, and feel vindicated in all the things they said of me – careless, thoughtless, headstrong . . .

And I felt suddenly sorry for myself; alone, ignored and

misunderstood, with no one to care if I was in or out, lost somewhere in the dark. I told myself it was no more than a long-overdue hangover setting in, but I could feel tears gathering and knew that if I started to cry I would find it hard to stop.

Then a loud whistle and a yell of '*hé-la copine*,' – hey, girl! – made me peer harder into the darkening air. It was Cécile, crossing the road below me, towards Chez Léon, glowing with all the fire of the night before. 'Come down for a drink,' she called. Her voice, hoarse on the evening air, rose effortlessly to me.

'I can't,' I called back. 'Work in the morning. My first day.'

'*Bonne chance*,' she said, with a smile, walking into the bar and out of my line of vision.

That she'd hailed me, like a friend, made my loneliness vanish.

I got into bed and wrote to Jessie, a long message full of garbled detail that I relied on her to sort out, and finished by asking, 'So, when are you coming?'

CHAPTER 15

Jessie

I couldn't believe she let me stay at home just because I said I was going to. I didn't even know I was going to say it till it came out of my mouth, and then I thought she'd do *something* to make me go to school. But she didn't. I guess she couldn't.

So now I know I have power over her. But I don't know what to do with it. It's hard to break the habit of being careful with her, protective, because I've had it for so long, but I damn well will.

She just left, and I was on my own. I was tired so I didn't get up for ages. I kept meaning to, then drifted off to sleep again. I didn't sleep much last night. Bad dreams, lots of waking up worried, like I'd forgotten something, or eaten in my sleep – gone down to the fridge and helped myself to handfuls of cheese, yoghurt drinks, blobs of butter, all the things I don't eat now. I had to calm myself, breathing slowly, like Alison taught me for the panic attacks I used to get, when I thought I'd choke on the size of my heart blocking my throat.

Isolde says the trick is to save something – a rice cake or a cracker – for just before bed because you sleep better, but I didn't yesterday because I ate the rice cake at lunchtime.

To think I used to eat five or six of them at a time, with cheese on them, relish, cucumber. Sometimes I'd spread a layer of soft cream cheese, then put a slice of Cheddar on top. That's so disgusting when I think of it now. Like, impossible.

Isolde says you can have warm milk before bed too, as long as it's within the plan for the day, but she doesn't because she never has dairy. 'Made by cows, for calves, guzzled by humans,' she says, like it's the most disgusting thing in the world. The way she says it, it *is* the most disgusting thing in the world. 'You might as well drink rat milk,' she says. 'Why a cow? Why not a horse, or a pig?'

Pig milk. Gross idea. I don't eat dairy now either.

I moved this diary again yesterday, changed the password, because I found Anna snooping in my room. She said she wasn't, that she was looking for stuff I don't wear for a bag-to-charity thing Rudi's school is doing, but I know that's a lie: she hopes so much that I'll wear those clothes when they fit again that there's no way she'll throw them out.

Now the password is Elongate. That's another word I like.

Harriet Snapchatted me late last night. That's partly why I didn't sleep. She was going on and on about Jenna: did I think she was flirting with Zach? Or did I think Zach flirted with her? It's weird. She used to do the same thing with Jenna about me. I know because Jenna told me. Except Zach did flirt with me, and he definitely doesn't like Jenna. And then Harriet started texting: *But OMG babes how r u? U so thn now*, and *How much furder u goin to go?* I was reading and re-reading the texts for ages, wondering what she really meant by them, and should I respond and if I did what should I say, and would she show them to anyone.

And then I realised it didn't matter what she said, or asked, or thought. She's not part of this.

The Jessie I used to be would have been upset and worried, would have had stomach cramps and begged Harriet to tell her what to do to make things okay.

I don't know what to call her, that other Jessie, because she's not Other Jessie, and she's not me either. Sometimes at night, when I wake up, I'm confused and I don't understand how many of us there are now, or what the differences are. I have dreams where Other Jessie is staring at me and she's gnawing at her fingers, at the cuticles and the flesh around the nails, eating them, so that her fingers are bleeding and torn, and I know it's my fault but I don't know which of the Jessies she is – the one who died before I was born, or the one I killed.

There are too many of us, too many girls locked inside my head and my body, sometimes in harmony, sometimes fighting. I don't know where they end and I begin, but I know they're angry with me. With one, it's obvious why, but Other Jessie, why is she angry? She says I owe her something but I don't know what.

There are nights when I wake up and she's there, hunched in a corner, just silent, but I can't breathe. Then I wake again and she's gone.

'Tell your mother I saved your life!' That's what we used to say to one another, as a joke, in the playground if someone was on a swing or at the top of the climbing frame. We'd push a bit, then hold on like we were saving them – 'Tell your mother I saved your life!' – but really it's a tease, a torment, not a saving.

Zach did it to me, on the balcony bit of the shopping centre. Then he kissed me. He didn't realise Harriet was below, looking up and waving. She saw us. Or, rather, she saw him, because I didn't do anything, just stood there, but she decided to see *us*, see me, in fact, not him.

I was on the balcony, above the fake waterfall, looking into the pool below, watching the gleam of gold and copper that should have been fish but were coins, thrown in to pay for wishes. What could anyone wish for in a shopping centre? The perfect pair of jeans? MAC make-up at a discount? I leaned over to call to Harriet, then started as someone put his hands to my sides. 'Tell your mother I saved your life.' It was Zach, pretending to push me over but pulling me into his arms and kissing me.

He didn't save my life, he ruined it, and later when he saw me in trouble and going down, sinking into all the horrible things they said about me, he just stepped neatly back and away, like he was never there in the first place, had never caused the trouble.

Tell your mother I saved your life. Other Jessie says it now, but she doesn't say it to be kind or to rescue me. She says it like it's a jeer, hissing it at me through the knotted dustsheet of her hair.

I remember something Anna once said about Other Jessie, that she was like a *piñata*, full of funny, surprising things, and that seemed a cute way to describe someone but now I wonder. I mean, you have to whack a *piñata* really hard to get anything out of it.

CHAPTER 16

Then

I woke early on the Monday morning and for a moment, lying in my high bed so close to the ceiling, I was afraid. Afraid in case the new and joyous feeling of the weekend had left me in the night. In case I woke to rain and grey skies, with a hangover and no sense of purpose, in a strange city where I didn't really belong. In case the weekend had been a dream and now I was myself again.

But it was no dream: The same joy was there when I got up as when I went to bed. The city felt fresh and expectant, and I was still humming with my own internal sense of excitement.

I dressed in the black skirt and plain pink shirt I had brought, with low-heeled shoes. My hair went into its ponytail just as it was meant to, and I ran down the stairs and out.

The shutters were down over the door and windows of Chez Léon, and the street smelt of disinfectant. I bought breakfast from a grubby kiosk on my way to the Métro, a chocolate croissant and a takeaway coffee, promising myself that I would shop properly that evening, fill the flat with food, replace the spent bulbs, buy soap and shampoo. That morning I walked every step as if I was in a film.

At the office – large, open-plan, over three floors – a bored woman in a charcoal suit showed me where I was to sit, what I was to do, pointed out the loos, and told me I could have an hour for lunch and leave at five thirty.

I smiled, astonished that anyone would be paid to do what she was asking of me. My job, it turned out, was to digitise dusty old files tied with yellow tapes, taking them off a stainless-steel trolley, tapping their numbers into a database, then returning them to a second trolley on the other side of my desk. I had no idea what was in the files – I never asked and no one ever said. I didn't care. Every couple of hours, she said, a man would wheel away the out-trolley and refill the in-trolley with more files.

'Great,' I said, 'no problem.' This, I had instantly figured, was all anyone wanted to hear from me, the dogsbody on a short-term contract, there to do very lowly work. I was right. She smiled, relieved, and told me I could get coffee in the kitchen.

Work, it was clear, would be easy and boring. Exactly what I wanted it to be, a kind of soothing beige background that would leave my mind free to turn over the important things: Bet and Marina, the places we would go to. Chez Lé and Cécile. Nico, and when I would see him next. All the moving parts of my new life.

The days soon fell into a routine, so that after little more than a week I felt myself to be an old hand. My co-workers seemed polite, mostly older than me, busy and indifferent. Some invited me to have lunch with them, but I preferred to work through. That way, I found, I could leave at five and sit in a park, turning slowly brown in the late-afternoon sun. The trolley guy made sleazy jokes – hesitant at first, increasingly bold when he realised I wasn't going to report him – and I smiled patiently at him until he lost interest.

I didn't care what he said, what any of them said or did, because work was just a place to go to during the day when the others were busy. To my surprise, my new friends also had daytime existences. I had imagined them only at night, in bars and clubs. Nico was an apprentice at a graphics firm, Alec had a job in a bank, Marina 'helped' at a knitwear designer's studio where I got the impression she made tea and read magazines. Only Bet, because she was supposed to be going back to college in the autumn, didn't have anything, and would sometimes meet me, either when I'd finished work or for a quick bite at lunchtime, a *croque-monsieur* or *salade tomates-crevettes*, which I loved – a fat tomato hollowed out and filled with shrimp and mayonnaise that, often, was all I ate in a day.

Mostly I liked to keep my days separate and distinct. Dull episodes that I moved through with automatic pleasantries and as much efficiency as I could muster. I was never late – no matter what time I had gone to bed – and I worked fast and methodically, always poised to leave because each day began only when work finished.

'See you tomorrow,' I would call from the glass door as I swiped my way out, energy and anticipation surging as I ran down the stairs and out into the muggy, slow-moving afternoon, knowing that everything was ahead of me.

At the flat, I felt like Rapunzel in my tower. Whatever I did there – slept, ate, changed, sweltered – I was always waiting to be rescued, for the call from the street. The cry of 'Anna, you there?' or just 'Anna!' that sent me running to the window, wide open always against the city's blanket of heat.

'I'm here,' I would call back, leaning out to see who it was. 'Come up!' or 'I'm coming down!'

Mostly I went down. There was nothing to do in my flat, no reason to be there. So we went to Chez Lé and drank bad coffee, or beer, or shots of whiskey or vodka. And each time, as soon as we walked in, we were enmeshed in the bitter little dramas that swirled around the place. People complaining, telling spiteful tales, spilling the painful circumstances of their lives.

Usually it was Bet or Marina who called for me, but slowly I made other friends as well. Cécile would shout for me at times, if she was bored and chatty. I can't say she ever showed me much fondness, but she bossed me around, almost motherly in an abrupt way, giving out to me for not eating and slamming the odd free ham and cheese baguette in front of me. 'Eat! You're giving me the creeps the way you're losing weight,' she would say. 'You look like a junkie.' She was wrong – I was thin, yes, and getting thinner, which I loved, but no junkie ever glowed the way I did then.

'Where do the sandwiches come from?' I asked one day, through a dry mouthful. 'Do you have a kitchen?'

'I make them upstairs in Jacques' place. That's why you don't get a menu. It's whatever's in the fridge. I'm not a fucking chef, or a waitress, but you look like a ghost, so I feed you.'

'Thank you,' I said politely, wishing she wouldn't, wondering what conditions the sandwiches were produced in, but far too in awe of her to say anything.

Alec would shout for me sometimes, but never if Nico was with him. He did it only when it suited him – if he had an errand to run in town and didn't want to do it alone. One day he made me wait with him while he got new keys cut; another time it was an appointment with a guy who was doing something to the tiles in his apartment. He was strangely houseproud, I discovered, always moving things around, buying new lamps or throws, talking about paint colours and floorboards. After a while, I began to understand that it wasn't so much that he was proud of his place as proud of himself and, by extension, of everything that belonged to him.

The only reason I went with him was because I was always hoping Nico would join us.

Alec was a flirt. He couldn't pass up an opportunity to wink and grin, brushing a hand against a bare arm, reaching out to knead a shoulder. He flirted with everyone – girls in shops, in cafés, boys just as often, sometimes with me, though he and I didn't really like each other. For all that he pretended, Alec was wary of me. I don't know why. At the time I thought it was because I was immune to him. He didn't make me laugh. I didn't find him attractive, interesting or even pleasant, and that, I figured, was why he didn't like me.

Now, I'm not so sure. There is another way to see it. I arrived in his world and disrupted it. I'd say the determination shone off me from that first night. I wanted in, and I made no secret of it. I wanted Bet and Marina as friends. I wanted their scene, his scene. I wanted Nico. I wanted them so much that I tried to take rather than share. But I didn't want Alec. He wasn't part of my enchantment. That must have been galling, and perhaps a threat too, although I never saw myself as having such power. But maybe we all have more than we think.

Once or twice it was Pierre who called, his mournful face raised up to mine. That was awkward, because he said so little, and I would find myself grateful for Cécile's curt interjections, or even Jacques' discreet, insincere enquiries into our health and well-being. Otherwise I chattered brightly over the tundra of Pierre's silences, and he nodded, sometimes even smiled. He seemed to find me amusing, but it was hard to tell.

'Oh, who cares?' Bet said, when I asked why Pierre bothered calling for me. 'Gives him something to do.'

'Does he work?'

'Not sure. Takes care of his mother, I think. Or maybe it's a brother. Anyway, someone who has problems or is sick or something.'

'Have you ever met his family?'

'God, no. They live in one of the immigrant areas. His dad is African.'

'Really?' I was astonished. 'He doesn't look it.'

'Maybe North African.' Her vagueness was insulting, deliberate – it said she couldn't be expected to care. 'The mother used to be Nico's mother's cleaner. That's how they know each other.' I was starting to understand that Bet, for all her easy-going bohemianism, lived the same circumscribed life as everyone else in that city, much as she affected to despise them and their rules. There were places she didn't go to, areas she dismissed as 'immigrant quarters', people who didn't matter as much as she did.

But I didn't pay much attention, beyond a faint curiosity about how Pierre had got so close to Nico, and why Nico brought him along where only a few were welcome.

I saw Nico almost every day. And every day I sank deeper into my longing for him. Quickly, so very quickly, he became the central point of everything I did, so that a blind person, reading my life by touch, would have found him immediately. Thoughts of him were a knot, a whorl in my mind. Every thought that did not begin with Nico, ended with him. And I made no attempt to resist, hold back or test the ground in front of me. Instead, I leaped, fast and hard and reckless. I didn't know who he was or anything about him, but I leaped. I had waited so long to be in love, had finally decided it didn't exist, and now this.

Wherever I was, I waited for him, certain he would come. Even to be in the same room as him was enough. To see him, to watch as he made his way, slowly but definitely, towards me. To stand beside him, shoulders touching, sometimes my bare arm against his, to breathe in the smell of him, clean and warm, share a cigarette or even a drink – 'Try this,' he would say, handing me a glass of flavoured beer or sticky liqueur – it was enough.

By the time I had been to Chez-Lé three or four times, I felt I understood how it all worked, and congratulated myself secretly on my oh-so-sophisticated acceptance of the permanent display of exploitation. Everyone there was after something, or someone. It was like a kind of souk in which traders and punters tried to disguise the transactional nature of what they did with banter and sleight of hand. I couldn't wait for Jessie to come over so I could show her how offhand I was about it.

'It's like a merry-go-round,' I said to Bet one evening. 'With everyone in a fixed position so you can see them, stretch towards them, but never reach them.'

'The cycle of desire,' she agreed. 'So, who is it you want?'

'Hey, I've barely arrived,' I said, all showy protestation. 'Give me a chance! I'm just observing. But what about you?'

I was more curious than I let on. I wondered a lot about Bet. She was proprietorial about Nico, demanding of him, but what did that mean? I wasn't sure, and I needed to be. I wanted to know who, besides the absent Aleah, was in competition with me for him. Because it wasn't just me. We all felt it, I could see that; Alec, Bet, Marina, Pierre, Jacques, even Cécile. Animals, particularly dogs, loved Nico, seeking him out, then asking no more than to stand near him.

Perhaps it was his habit of silence, or the concentrated quality of his attention. He had a kind of charisma that had nothing to do with his conversation. It was simply in him. In his smell, the feel of his skin, his dark hair that turned back the light, most of all in his habit of just looking at you. It can't have been just me he did that to.

But Bet wasn't ready for that level of confidence. 'Not telling,' she said. 'You try to work it out. And as for you, I'm not sure I believe you. I think you know very well who you want. And,' she leaned closer, 'I think it's a good idea.'

'What?' I hadn't expected her to be so direct.

'You know what I mean,' she said. 'I'm just saying I think it's a good idea. A really good idea.'

'But what about . . .' I didn't want to say Aleah's name, because it felt too familiar and because Bet had not named Nico.

'Never mind her,' Bet said. 'She's dreadful. She hangs out of him and she's needy and wimpy. It's so nice when she's not here. We see so much more of him. He's not always dancing attendance on her.' From which I understood some of what Bet meant – that she hated Aleah and wanted her gone, and thought I would be a means to that end. She knew my future there was negotiable, that my three months could run on, become permanent. And Nico with me would be more accessible to her than Nico with Aleah. I wondered then was it the heat or something in the city itself – the way it was arranged into factions, areas and races in conflict with one another. It seemed to boil with intrigue. Or maybe it was just this particular gang of people.

'Right.' I needed to change the subject. 'What about Marina?'

'She's going out with Alec,' Bet said in surprise. 'Didn't you know?'

'No.' I was astonished. 'No one said anything, and they don't act like they're together.'

'Well, maybe "together" is a bit strong,' Bet said thoughtfully. 'But they have something worked out. You know.' She shrugged. I didn't.

The way Bet and Marina talked about men shocked me a

little. 'I must have fucked him in every toilet here and in the Vaudeville,' Bet said, of an English guy she had been seeing a few months before, watching me from the corner of her eye as she said it. They seemed to have been with so many, often the same, men, and described one guy as 'a walking case of cystitis', then went off into fits of giggles. I had no idea what they were talking about, but I laughed as if I did. 'It's a size thing,' Marina said kindly, obviously well aware that I was at sea.

I looked at Alec then, trying to understand what Marina saw in him. He was down the other end of the bar, complaining that yet again he had been served a glass of beer with more foam than liquid. Jacques was so cheap: he had Cécile well trained to up the froth. Alec had already taken the beer back twice and asked for the glass to be filled properly. Each time it got the same treatment and was returned to him with no less froth, so now he confronted Jacques, who was sitting on a barstool, listening to one of the old regulars gripe. Soothingly Jacques took the glass and handed it back to Cécile with an audibly reproachful murmur. She refilled it properly and snapped something derisory at Jacques, although it could have been meant for Alec, who didn't bother to find out.

'My friend Jessie is coming over,' I told Bet. 'She told me today. She'll be here for a couple of weeks. She's saved up all her money from work. She's a receptionist at a doctor's surgery.'

'Great,' said Bet, but without enthusiasm, and I felt a sudden anxiety. How would Jessie fit in? And how would I fit with her, and with the others?

'Honestly, you'll love her,' I said, determined to convince us both. 'She's so funny and brilliant. And she speaks good French. Almost better than me.'

The thing with Bet was that she liked only the people who were in her life. She had no curiosity and little kindness for those who weren't. She had only to meet Jessie, I decided, and all would be well. Once she met her, knew her, she would be interested in her and then she would like her.

There were other places we went to – bars, poky little clubs, sometimes a café – but mostly it was Chez Léon. Or Bet's, where I stayed many nights and where she grew taller still under those lofty ceilings, her voice deeper as it bounced off the gleaming panels of wood 'from the Congo', she told me. 'The spoils of colonialism.' She said it proudly, not ashamed as she should have been.

Sometimes we would encounter a middle-aged woman cleaning and polishing, dragging a vacuum cleaner behind her so that she was tangled up in it and looked like a weary St George battling the long-necked dragon. Mostly, though, the house was empty and somehow unbreachable.

Because of that, and the heat, we usually kept to the garden, the woven fabric of green where at night the air smelt of jasmine and something Bet told me was tobacco flowers. I wasn't sure that was true because their perfume was so lovely. More intoxicating even, in those airless, shifting nights, was the cool wet scent of dew falling on soft leaves and grass. The feeling that, were I to burrow into the ground, I would find something that wasn't in the same dusty cycle of sun on stone, warm winds turning in hot squares and streets.

In that heavenly garden, birds sang so late that, as the evening cleared to pale pink from the thick yellows of the day, their final notes seemed answered immediately by the stars.

One particularly hot night, we left the windows of the house wide open and played music loudly so that it drifted out to us where we sat on plaid rugs, at the back of the garden, candles in jam jars, which provided just enough light to see, here and there, the bridge of a nose, a hand with a cigarette or joint, a forehead or chin.

We sang along with the music, told stories and laughed. Marina fell asleep and Bet threw a rug over her, saying, 'She'll be fine here. Probably better than inside. I'll leave the back door open so she can get in.'

'Won't she be scared if she wakes all alone?' I asked, because I would have been.

'Why?' Bet asked. 'She knows the house.'

I wondered if Alec would say he'd stay with her, and thought how glorious it would be if I was asleep and Nico stayed. Then everyone got up and moved towards the house. Bet said goodnight and began to drift up the stairs. 'You can have your usual room,' she called to me, over her shoulder. I lingered, in case Alec left, in case Nico stayed, and even after they were gone – Alec yelling loud goodbyes on the doorstep – I waited, in case Nico came back.

The next morning, as I was hurrying to work, closing Bet's door behind me, an old woman washing the steps of the house next door, water coating the grey stone so that it gleamed in the early-morning sun, asked, 'Was it you outside in the garden last night?'

'Yes,' I said. The smell of bleach from her bucket made my empty stomach lurch. I was ready to apologise, to explain that we had been carried away by the beauty of the evening, but she didn't give me a chance.

'*Canaille*,' she said, throwing the contents of her bucket down the steps and firmly shutting her door. '*Canaille*.'

Riff-raff.

I was shocked. There was a wider world after all, a life of the city that wasn't us, our strange hours and yen for shadowy spots: there were people who rose early and retired at decent hours. Who worked hard and hoped for a break, who cared about the value of their car, their house, their children's future, and hated us because we didn't.

CHAPTER 17

Jessie

I've never really been in the house on my own before, not for
this long. Before, if I was sick, Anna would stay at home with
me, or Gran would come in the middle of the morning so I
had only a few hours by myself. Now, though, it's just me, all
day. At first I don't know what to do. I can't go to the kitchen
because I don't dare. So I look at pictures of icebergs on my
laptop. I've been doing that a lot lately. I love them. They're so
beautiful – so white and clear and hard. So stately, above and
below the water, and all around them is cool and clean and
empty. I look at pictures for ages, of Greenland and the poles
with ice. Not snow so much – I don't like the fluffiness of it;
the way it moves around makes me feel anxious. It's ice I love.
I'd like to go to that hotel made of ice, and take the furs off
the ice beds and lie down on the hard, cold surface, arms and
legs stretched out, my cheek turned to the side.

I hate the pictures with people in them, small and scruffy and tawdry beside something so magnificent, people with their ropes, puffy clothes and furry hoods with strings dangling off them. The only way to be with an iceberg is naked and perfect.

I get dressed and walk around downstairs. At first, the house is better with no one in it, but after a while it gets creepy. It's so still. Nothing happens. No phones beep, no TV, no Rudi yelling and making weird noises. No pots boiling, no drawers being opened and closed. I feel like stuff is moving around when I'm not looking at it. I check a couple of the rooms, opening the door fast as soon as I've closed it, but I don't see anything.

I feel dizzy so I go back to my room and sit on the bed. I look through the bits of myself I like – my wrists and ankles and knees, my arms from the elbows down – and then the bits I don't like: thighs, stomach, upper arms. Then I go back to the bits I like to cheer myself up. I think about a time when my thighs will be the same as my calves and my upper arms the same thickness as my wrists. It's to remind myself why I'm doing what I'm doing.

Anna tells me it's not attractive to be as thin as I am. As if that's the point. As if she has any idea. As if she isn't lying.

That picture of her and Other Jessie by the fountain, Anna's so thin, thinner than I've ever seen her, and in the picture you can tell she knows and loves it. It's the way her legs are – apart but knees turned inwards towards each other, like they're a bit broken. I know that pose. I know exactly what she was thinking while she did it. It's the one that shows how spindly you are. I know it. I've done it.

She's been here before me but she failed, because look at her now! So she doesn't want me to succeed.

My mouth keeps chewing, even though there's nothing in it. It's more a sort of mumbling than chewing. My teeth chomp and move all the time, grating against each other because there's nothing else. Sometimes I find myself chewing the inside of my cheek, which hurts and even bleeds. I tried chewing gum instead, to give the teeth something to do, but that made my stomach hurt. Anyway, I want to get used to not chewing. You can only be free, Isolde says, when your body no longer expects or wants.

It's the same with vomiting. Isolde says you're stronger if you don't rely on it, that the point is to have the willpower not to stuff yourself in the first place. She says it's not just a body thing, and I get that: it's the mind, really. It's yourself you need to control, and the body is only the first part of that – to make it stop bossing you and forcing you to do things, making you eat, because it wants you to, when you *don't* want to.

Isolde has a tube up her nose now. It's what they said would happen to me if I didn't listen to them and 'help us to help you' in the clinic.

I wonder what the tube looks like. It goes up the nose and back down the throat into the stomach, a little rat run for food so it doesn't need to go through the mouth. Because you can't shut your nose. It's horrible that a doctor would do that to somebody – like raping them. And even more horrible that your parents would let them do it.

Isolde said it was like swallowing a chunk of boiling plastic: it's hard and burns as it goes up, in and down. She told me she imagines it like an enemy inside her. Or a bug to tell them where she is and what she's doing. She won't go out with the tube, so I haven't seen her, and she said no when I asked her to send me a snap of it. She said I was childish for wanting to see it. She said there are instructions online for taking it out and she's going to do that as soon as she can. As soon as she thinks they'll let her get away with it. *They won't win this*, she texted, with the punching-fist emoji.

My room is cold and I don't know how to turn on the heat. Usually it comes on automatically when I get home from school.

If I was in school, I'd have history now, and afterwards, when school's over, we'd meet Zach and the other guys because they finish at the same time as us on a Wednesday. We'd go to the shopping centre, and I'd have to put up with Harriet and Zach doing their great love affair all over the place.

Normally I like sleeping in the day more than at night because it's less lonely. You can go to sleep with all the noises of the house, wake up and they're still going on, so you know people are downstairs if you want to see them, with lights on and everything jolly.

But this time I do it wrong. I fall asleep when it's still light so my bedside lamp isn't on, and when I wake, in a fright, it's dark and the hard lights from the street are shining in, making everything dirty, and I don't know where I am and the covers are so heavy that I can't move them off me and I'm stuck in sleep, the last bit of it that I can't break through, to be awake properly, and I'm pushing and pushing but it's like I'm paralysed because nothing happens, except my heart feels huge and is thumping, and I can't remember how long I've been asleep and wonder why the house is still so silent.

Did they come back, then decide to leave again without me? Leave me behind, maybe forever? Or maybe there is no them. Maybe it's just me and always has been. In all the world, only me.

When I finally get through the last sleep barrier, I'm breathing heavily. I go down to the kitchen then and eat what I'm allowed that day. An apple. A rice cake. A piece of chicken breast from the part of the fridge where I keep my stuff. A glass of Diet Coke. I chew everything twenty times and wait one minute between bites with my hands in my lap and not looking at my plate.

And then I go back to my room. I was so afraid that, on my own, with no one here, I wouldn't be able to stick to the plan. But I was. I did. I feel so good.

I sit on the edge of my bed for a while, upright, because you digest faster that way. Then I put on a movie but I don't watch it. I'm scared to put in earphones, in case someone comes and I don't hear them. I think I'm like a girl in a horror film – the one who's in the shower, or has headphones on, and the killer sneaks up on her because she's not paying attention and you think, *How can she be so dumb?* But, of course, in the film she doesn't know there's a killer or a monster, she's just doing what's normal for her. You forget that.

A day with no one in it moves so slowly, like it has weights attached, dragging it back; a day without breaks made by meals, a day without little threads that lead you from conversation to conversation and tie you to people.

CHAPTER 18

Now

It was late when Maurice came home. The house was quiet and Anna was watching TV with a glass of wine she had already emptied and refilled twice more than she had planned. The fuzzy feeling the wine gave her was such a glorious contrast to the tight, rough edges of her day, but she knew that was a problem. Tonight was the last night, she swore to herself. Tomorrow, herbal tea.

She sat, legs under her, hunched into a corner of the sofa. The room was dark. She hadn't bothered lighting the side lamps Maurice had chosen with such care for their soft, pinkish glow, like the inside of a shell, and the overhead light was too harsh. Only the TV, flickering in front of her, broke up the gloom.

She heard the front door close quietly, then the sitting-room door open. She looked up. 'How was your trip?'

Maurice had been to Brussels for work. He had wanted her to go with him. 'Wouldn't you love to go back?' he had asked, curious. He, too, had spent time in Brussels, some years before her – in the scrubbed confines of the European institutions where he had done an internship after college. They had excitedly compared recollections, only to discover they had almost no memories in common. It was as if they had been to different cities. His had been the world of Irish bars and receptions at the Parliament with clever trilingual young people from across Europe, all politely banging at the gates of ambition. Hers – well, Maurice had described it as 'like something out of a cabaret show, some sort of sleazy demi-monde. He had said it dismissively, laughing at her naivety, and Anna had agreed enthusiastically – 'Yes, that was pretty much it!' – at the time, loving the differences between them, and the side she felt she was now on.

'Why don't you come with me?' he had continued. 'We could have a couple of nights together. My mother would love to mind Rudi.' Rudi, not Jessie, Anna had instantly thought, hating the reflexive defensiveness that still caught her off-guard.

'No,' she had said. 'Last place on earth I'd want to go.'

'Okay, I get it.' He thought he did – the bad memories, the dead friend – but he didn't. Or not all of it.

'It was fine,' he said now, taking off his tie. He smelt sweaty and somehow caged, as if he had been confined for too long. 'Bland hotels, meeting rooms. You might as well be in an airport. But I still can't get used to seeing soldiers with guns everywhere on the streets. It's disturbing. It makes the whole place seem so violent, so unlike it used to be. I don't recognise it any more. You wouldn't either.' He spoke with certainty, but he was wrong.

For Anna, that violence, now so very visible, spilling into the grand squares and elegant boulevards, had always been there. Squashed and denied, but there. Now, it was faced down by the threat of more violence, poked at by machine guns, jostled by riot shields, but it was nothing new, had simply migrated from the edges into the centre.

'How was everything here?' he asked.

'Hmm.' She made a face. 'Jessie refused to go into school the other day. Just refused point blank.'

'What did you do?'

'Nothing. It was awful. I couldn't think of a single thing. Nothing to threaten her with, bribe her with, cajole her with because there's nothing she wants from me. I realised how redundant I am in her life. It's horrible.'

'So did she just stay at home?'

'Yes. I had to let her.'

'Did you stay with her?'

'No, of course I didn't,' she snapped. 'I had to go to work. I can't just take days off at short notice.'

'I know, I know.' He tried to soothe her. 'I'm only asking. So what happened?'

'Well, I think she must have had a pretty boring time, because when I got back with Rudi, she came straight downstairs and stayed down, watching TV and chatting with him. In fact, she was sort of following me round the kitchen when I first got in, like she used to do. Like she wanted to be with me.' She smiled at the memory. 'She didn't talk to me, but she was there, at least.'

'So that's a good sign?' He was so eager, so desperate that something – anything – would be a good sign. It annoyed her. She took another slug of wine. He had sat down beside her, but at a distance that questioned whether he was welcome.

'It wasn't. The next day, she went to school and was right back to normal, ignoring everyone, marooned in her room, as if there's an outbreak of plague down here and she has to keep clear of us lest we contaminate her. Her friend Jenna called for her but Jessie made me say she wasn't here, even though I could see Jenna knew she was. And when I said that to Jessie later, she just shrugged and said, 'Whatever,' like a parody of a nasty teenager.

She was silent then, and Maurice was silent too. 'I don't know where any of this is going,' Anna said. 'We aren't getting anywhere.' It was an admission that made her heart begin a slow descent.

'What about Alison?'

'God.' Anna rolled her eyes. 'Alison. All we do is talk and talk about Jessie and nothing changes. She has no answers, only more questions: "Tell me about you, Anna."' She mimicked the therapist's slow voice.

'Maybe you do need to talk about yourself more,' Maurice said.

'Now you sound just like her: "How does that make you feel?" It's not about me, it's about Jessie.'

'But about you too, surely.'

She shot him a sharp look and he back-pedalled, fast.

'I mean, you're her mother, it must be about you to some extent.'

'That's not what you meant, though, is it?' she said nastily.

'I'm only saying . . .'

'I hate it when anyone says they're "only saying". As if it's any different from shouting it from the rooftops.' Then: 'You think this is my fault.'

'I don't.'

'You do. Of course you do. Anyone would. And maybe it is.' She acknowledged it because she wanted him to deny it. He did.

'It's not your fault.' He sounded impatient, as if she were trying to claim credit. 'I only think there must be things for you to talk to Alison about too.'

Yes, she thought, all the things you know I won't say to you.

He had tried, years ago, and again after Rudi was born when he had found her weeping quietly in bed one afternoon, flattened by exhaustion and ricocheting hormones. Rudi, in the nursery next door, had been crying loudly. 'What's wrong?' He had been alarmed, poised for action beside the bed.

'Nothing. I'm fine. I'm just so tired,' she said, wiping her nose on the sheet surreptitiously so he wouldn't see. Maurice didn't like things like that.

'And Rudi?' He still sounded anxious, edgy.

'He's fine. He's just crying. Babies do,' she had said. 'He'll fall asleep in a bit.' The funny thing was, Rudi's crying didn't disturb her in the way Jessie's used to. He cried like a baby, a cross, tired baby. Jessie's cries had clutched at Anna, like the skinny hands of beggars, nixing all reasonable response.

Was it just the pitch, Anna sometimes wondered, and not

after all some existential horror; just a particular tone that had agitated her? Did it even matter?

It mattered.

Maurice had rambled on for so long then, and she had been barely listening, so it took a while to understand what he was saying. That he wasn't suggesting she take more time for herself and maybe get a massage.

'You could see someone,' he had said. 'Talk.'

'I am talking. I'm talking to you. I'll talk to Susie or Jayne or someone tomorrow. Who knows? He might sleep a bit better tonight.' She yawned, wishing he would go away. Rudi had fallen quiet and she wanted to nap.

'I mean someone professional.' For Maurice, who regarded psychology with distrust, to suggest such a thing had been unexpected, and strangely embarrassing. She had remembered then the look on his face the first time he had watched her scream herself into an ugly rage, then an exhausted silence. The look had told her what she needed to know – that he had never seen such a thing before. That it wasn't normal.

'Why would I do that? I'm fine,' she said then.

'Well, in case things get out of hand.'

'What things? Your laundry?' She was being bitter and evasive. She knew it, but had no intention of allowing him to tell her how she had shocked him, or that Rudi, his child, was different from Jessie, her child, and must not be exposed to Anna's moments of rage as she had been.

'I'm only thinking of you,' he had said.

She had turned away from him then, the wet patch of sheet where she had wiped her nose clutched tight in her hand.

'I'm sick of Alison,' she said now. 'And I hate talking about myself.'

'You say "hate" a lot,' he said.

'What?' Her voice didn't attempt to disguise the impatience she felt: *What are you on about?*

'You talk a lot about things you hate.'

'So what? You'd prefer me to gush about what I love?'

'It's just that I've noticed Jessie does it too.'

'Does what?'

'"I hate this, I hate that, I hate her . . ." You're right, she sounds like a parody of a teenager. But she sounds like you too. I'm not saying you sound like a teenager,' he said hurriedly, so that Anna almost laughed. 'She sounds like both. My question is: does she do it on purpose or is it subconscious?'

'I don't know what you mean,' she said, although, actually, she did. 'Anyway, I don't see what that has to do with anything.'

'I wonder how much she tries to be like you, that's all.'

'I'm the person she hates most right now. I very much doubt she's trying to be like me.'

'She doesn't hate you,' Maurice said. 'If anything, it's too much the opposite. It's like she's obsessed with you. Besotted. Like it's a love affair.' He sounded uncomfortable, and Anna knew that only the most profound disquiet could have made him say such things.

'Maybe when she was little,' Anna said. 'We were definitely a bit co-dependent.' She used the word like a joke, a bit of therapist-speak to laugh at, but neither of them laughed. 'Not any more. Now, she can hardly bear to look at me. I make her sick, like everything makes her sick.'

'I don't agree,' he pursued. 'I think she feels exactly the same, only she's confused about it now. Frankly, I think there's nothing she won't do for you. Or because of you.'

'If that were true, this would be so easy,' Anna said. 'This whole thing would just go away, would never have happened in the first place. So, *ergo* – *idiot*, her tone said – 'it's not true.'

He didn't rise to the *idiot* inflection. 'I heard her the other day, with Rudi. He was annoyed with you for turning down that bloody awful laptop thing of his, and he said, "Mama's mean." Well, you should have heard Jessie. She flew at him. "She's not mean," she said, "You're not to say that!" She was furious with him.'

The idea of Jessie championing her gave Anna a glow so intense she knew Maurice would see it if she looked at him. She kept her eyes down. 'She must have been feeling contrary, just disagreeing for the sake of it . . .'

'Not the way she said it. She meant it.'

There was silence then and Anna was about to turn the TV up when he said, 'Where did you go the other night?'

'What night?'

'When you met Jayne and Susie for dinner, after work?'

'Like you said, I met Jayne and Susie and Marissa for dinner, after work.'

'But you were back so late, and I bumped into Jayne a couple of days later and she said you were all so civilised and must be getting old because you didn't stay out.'

Stupid city, she thought, that wove in and out of itself like a village so that everybody was always meeting everybody else and casually discussing each other, like a load of starlings on a tree. 'I went for one more drink with Marissa, and of course one more turned into several . . . We only decided it after Jayne had hopped into a taxi and gone. There was no point texting her to come back . . .'

'Oh, okay.' He wouldn't ask her any more, she knew. And he didn't. Instead, he said nothing, then, after a moment, took her hand, the one that wasn't holding the wine glass, and squeezed it. 'I'm off to bed,' he said.

'I'll be up shortly. Goodnight.' She turned her cheek up for a kiss. When he was gone, she poured herself another glass of wine. The bottle was nearly empty. She had seen him notice it before he left the room. The TV droned on, a low mumble to which she paid no attention.

Did Jessie try to be like her? She couldn't see it. Once, yes, but not now. She remembered how hard her daughter had once worked not to blame her for anything, no matter how bad she'd been. 'It's not your fault,' she'd say, staunch against any suggestion otherwise. 'You didn't mean it.'

'I didn't, you're right. Of course I didn't,' Anna would say, hugging her hard, still choking back her own shame, dizzy with gratitude that this small child would forgive her.

There was a sickly gleam to the recollection that alarmed her. Did nothing ever go away? And why was it all coming back now? It must be the stress of the last months, she decided. She was losing focus, losing grip.

The things of the past no longer obeyed her orders to stay down, stay away. The texts from Andrew clogged her phone, even though she'd deleted them.

You must really hate yourself to get into such a mess, she thought sternly. To walk right in. To be so feeble about getting out.

There was that word again, the one Maurice so objected to: hate.

CHAPTER 19

Then

That night, Marina was playing the pinball machine with many loud pings and small explosions. Through the darkening air, sounds floated in from the thriving streets: sirens, shouts, laughter and the smell of kebabs. I was watching the door, waiting for Nico. I saw him arrive with Pierre, and felt the now familiar shaky excitement rush through me, half-sickening, half-wonderful. Then there was an almighty crash.

Marina started it with her provocative pinball playing. Twisting and turning, writhing and gyrating to every vibration of the heavy machine, regularly slamming her hip against it for emphasis, she had excited an old man behind her to such a fever pitch that he leaped up and slapped her, presumably as relief from the intensity of his feelings. Then he sat down, muttering happily to himself. Marina was yelling and swearing, demanding to know who the hell he thought he was, and how dare he? The yelling brought Alec, who tried to master the situation with much confident gesturing, ordering Marina to stop screaming and the old man to apologise.

Instead, the man consigned us all to Hell, got up, and walked slowly towards the door. There, he paused. He leaned towards a group of young men at a rickety table and said, 'Do what I'd do if I was thirty years younger,' jerking his head towards Alec and Marina, still standing beside the pinball machine, and walked out the door, which made a loud shriek as he dragged it back on its hinges.

We were all silent then, lodged in the beat before normal life resumes following an ugly disruption. Except that, into the silent beat, one of the guys at the rickety table carefully, deliberately, picked up an empty beer glass and flung it across the room at Alec. It missed, but only just, hitting a wall by his head and shattering.

Marina screamed loud and long and began to curse them as sons of bitches. She picked up another glass from a table beside her and flung it, more at the floor than at the guy, but it was enough to move the row up another gear. Bet ran to her, but I stayed where I was, shocked.

I had never seen a fight before, never been close to one. I had never smelt the hot metal that was anger unleashed fast, or seen the speed with which shapes broke up and rearranged themselves into dangerous, jagged patterns. Marina's yelling continued and Nico and Pierre, with a couple of friends I didn't know, took up positions beside Alec as he rushed towards the table, bellowing 'Fils de pute!' and overturned it, sending the entire load of drink and glasses onto the floor.

Jacques, from somewhere mysterious, produced a short

man, with no neck and a large chest, who proceeded to dismantle the situation by systematically pushing people, hard, into the street. I noticed that no one tackled him. Instead, they went where he shoved them and saved their rage for one another.

The entire fight spilled outside and I slipped out after it. I wondered where the old man was, and thought of how much he would have enjoyed seeing where his slap had led. On the street, the action stalled. It entered a kind of standoff phase, with insults yelled back and forth, but the distance between the two groups grew larger. Really, it should have been all over then. The glass-throwers moved off, with much swagger, in a way that told me they felt their honour had been salvaged, except that Alec shouted after them a crude line about someone's mother, whereupon the smallest and skinniest of their group picked up something, I couldn't see what, ran back and, barely a yard from us, flung it into the knot that was Alec, Pierre and Nico.

Nico's arm, bare below the sleeve of his T-shirt, went up to shield his face, and then it was over. The street emptied of bystanders, and Jacques swung open the door he had bolted against us all, waving us back inside. 'Cécile, *encore des bières* . . .' he said.

I went over to Nico, to ask what on earth that had been about – he seemed to like explaining things, I had discovered – and saw that he was bleeding. The underside of his forearm, where he had raised it to protect his face, was gashed and the blood was thick.

'Shit, what was it?' I asked, reaching for his arm.

'I don't know. A stone maybe, a bottle.' He shrugged. It looked nasty.

'Come upstairs, to my flat. I'll fix it.'

He hesitated, muttered something about Jacques.

'You're kidding,' I said. 'Jacques will give you tetanus, or rabies, just by touching this. Come on.' I took hold of his arm, gently, and tugged him towards me. I knew we needed to move fast, before Alec or Bet saw us, or any of the others. He came towards me and we moved off together. Looking back, I saw Pierre watching us, but he didn't say anything.

Up the stairs I fumbled with my keys in the almost-dark while Nico leaned against the dirty greenish wall. My heart was lurching at being so close to him, and the prospect of being alone with him. I felt sick and excited so that my hands were shaking and I wondered how I could mop up blood and apply a plaster with them.

'This is your place?' he said, looking around. He had never been upstairs before, only seen me with my head out the window.

'Yes.' My voice was shaky too.

'It's nice.' He sounded surprised.

'I like it.' I cringed at the banality of what I'd said.

He took in the entire boxy room with its tacked-on bit of kitchen and the open door through to the dark bathroom, then asked, 'Where's the bedroom?'

'Look up,' I said, and he raised his head, saw the funny little mezzanine with my bed, unmade, on it, and smiled. 'Sit,' I said then. 'I'll get disinfectant in case whatever hit you was dirty.' I tried to sound cool and efficient but knew I didn't. He sat up on the counter of the tiny kitchen and I leaned against his knees as I wiped away the blood, by now smeared across most of his arm, with a tea towel that I knew wasn't clean, then dabbed on the cut a cheap blue liquid antiseptic I had bought. He flinched and made a hissing sound through his teeth, then laughed at me when I apologised for hurting him.

'You're sweet,' he said, and the sound of him saying it caught in my throat so that I did the bravest thing I had ever done. I knew if I didn't I'd regret it always. I reached up and put my arms around his neck. He allowed me to pull him down from the counter, then leaned against it as I kissed him. We were almost the same height and our bodies fitted together without any awkward bumping of noses or chins, as if we had been sketched in one fluid line. I was so scared that he would turn away, or kiss me for a moment, to be polite, then say we'd better be getting back and his arm was fine now. But he didn't. He kissed me as hard as I kissed him, wrapping his arms around me.

'Anna.' The way he said my name was a spell. But whatever else he wanted to say, I didn't want to know. In case it wasn't yes. So I shook my head, and put my mouth back on his.

We went so fast, both of us then, with no hesitation. There wasn't a moment when I resisted or pretended I didn't want this as much as he did. More. I fumbled with his clothes and found I was still shaking as I took off his T-shirt, then my own. I couldn't undo his belt because my hands made a mess of everything except touching his bare skin anywhere I could reach it and burying my face in his neck. He smelt as I imagined amber must smell – deep and warm and golden. Beach sand on a hot day.

Before, I had always felt self-conscious and fake with men,

showing off and trying to act out the kind of stuff I had seen in the brief bits of porn I'd watched, posturing and pouting in a way I thought they'd like. Not this time. I wanted him so badly, I didn't have space to think about what I looked like, only what I felt. His skin against mine, his hands on my back, in my hair, at my waist. Within moments we were both naked, still in the little kitchen, our clothes in a puddle on the floor, and then he picked me up and carried me, my body crushed against his, to the sofa because there was no way we were going to make it up to my bed.

No junkie on a first hit ever recognised themselves so profoundly in the moment of giving up as I did then with Nico – or knew as surely that none of what was lost mattered in comparison with what was gained. And no junkie ever cottoned on so quickly that you don't just fall. You have to jump too, or at the very least let yourself go. I let go.

Afterwards, we lay there, entangled, silent, catching our breath and knowing that everything had changed 'forever'. I felt I had caught a fabled beast – a unicorn or manticore, something other people talked about, which I had presumed didn't exist, or not so that I could see it. Now I knew it did. I knew what desire was, why people wrote books and songs about it, killed for it. I knew need like a dark pit that could only be emptied further, never filled. I knew the purpose of my life and it was Nico.

He didn't say anything but, after a while, he leaned away from me and looked at me for a long time. He brushed a few strands of hair off my face and smiled, but he looked embarrassed too. I liked that. I smiled back, trying to think of

Emily Hourican

something to say, wondering if there was really a need to say anything.

And then the buzzer went, twice, in rapid succession, and a shout came up from outside. Alec.

'Anna, are you there? Is Nico there?' I stayed silent, perfectly willing to pretend that I wasn't, that Nico wasn't. I wanted to stay, just the two of us, but Nico sat up immediately and went to the kitchen for his clothes.

'We're coming,' he shouted from the window, once he was half dressed. 'Anna has been fixing up my arm. I'm wounded because of you.' He laughed and Alec laughed too.

'You're wounded because you don't know how to fight properly. I'm not hurt, and nor is anyone else! Hurry, we're going on.' I looked out and there he was, swaggering, blustering and making macho boasts. Mercutio, or a drunken soldier.

'All he needs is a pair of tights and a tin dagger,' I said.

'What?' Nico said.

'Never mind.'

'We should go down,' he said. Duty, his duty, clearly called him. And because of that, I had to take all my new discoveries, only just unearthed, and bury them again.

'You go. I'll be down in a minute.'

'Are you sure? I can wait.' He was tying the laces of his trainers.

'No, honestly, go, or Alec will just keep shouting!' I smiled, to show it was a joke. 'I'll be quick.'

And I was. I didn't wash, although I could have quickly half-filled the hip bath, so obviously conceived for exactly that purpose, and dunked myself. I wanted to keep the smell of him

194

on me for as long as possible. I wanted to go down there with some claim on him, something that Alec and Bet and anyone else might recognise with the subconscious understanding that he was mine now, just as I was his.

Back in Chez Léon, I felt like Oisín, home from Tír na nÓg, but in reverse. As if a thousand years had passed for me that were just minutes for everyone else. They were all still talking excitedly about the fight – who had done what, said what, and why – while I felt that the entire world had changed and couldn't understand why it didn't look any different. Only Cécile noticed me come in, and looked me over with a raised eyebrow.

I sat on a barstool beside Bet and Marina, who turned briefly to ask where I'd been, and listened to her explaining how she had felt when the old man slapped her, the fright she had got when the glass sailed past her head – far closer in the retelling than I had seen it. That she had had any part to play in the outbreak of aggression seemed not to occur to her, or to Bet. I listened and nodded, but really I watched Nico, standing with Alec and Pierre, so that every time his eyes rose to mine, they were there, waiting for him.

'Why did no one call the police?' I asked.

'What's the point? It was just a fight,' Bet said.

'But surely that's what the police are for, to prevent fights and break them up.'

'Not here. There are too many. If the police got involved every time, they'd never do anything else. And it was hardly a fight.' She made a flicking motion with her fingers, dismissing it. 'Those guys weren't serious.'

'So what happens when someone is serious?'

'Knives, broken bottles. People here fight dirty.'

'I saw a guy take his belt off once,' Marina broke in, 'and wrap it round his hand, so that the buckle was dangling down, and whack someone across the face. The buckle took a chunk out of the other guy's cheek. Nasty,' she said, with satisfaction.

We went on to a club – a new one, smaller and plainer, a grey box with rather vicious music – because it was a Friday, and because the idea that anyone would go home simply because of a fight, a cut arm, or tiredness was unthinkable. I went because I had to. As if Nico had hooked something to me when he was inside me, or unspooled something from me: I had to be where he was.

We didn't talk, no more than the odd remark. Alec scored, dispensing pills with his usual lordly self-congratulation, and I watched as Nico looked at me, for a time, before taking the pill, making sure I took one too. So I did.

They were strong, those pills, with a hard greyness to them, like the club walls, so that for a time I wasn't quite sure where I was and needed to lose myself, hide in the distraction of repetitive movements. I couldn't talk – the pills had slackened the muscles around my mouth and jaw so that I was slurring and mumbling. Instead, I danced for hours, only dimly aware of where the others were, waiting for the dreadful numbness to pass. When it did, I felt myself raised up, high and happy, on a wave of delight.

I found the others outside, a small backyard with whitewashed walls on which were stuck posters demanding a socialist republic. A brazier was burning logs, and Bet, Marina and Alec were standing around it, flicking ash from their cigarettes into the flames. Alec had an arm around Marina, but causally. I still couldn't see anything that held them together.

'There you are,' Bet said. 'Come and tell us where you've been.' Her eyes were huge, her pupils dilated, and her tongue was flicking in and out of her mouth as she spoke, like a serpent moving across a jungle floor – appearing and disappearing, between shadows and sunlight.

'Nowhere, just dancing. Those pills are so strong,' I said, by way of explanation.

'They're trippy alright,' Bet agreed, with a strange vehemence. Her hair, I saw then, was also like snakes, a nest of them, curling round each other, hissing occasionally with tiny mouths that hinged wide enough to swallow us all. I shook my head a little, to clear it, and the snakes settled down reluctantly.

'Cigarette?' Alec held out his packet and I took one, although I didn't want it, and looked around for Nico. 'He's not here,' Alec said, gleeful to pass on information he knew I wanted.

'Huh? Who?' I faked confusion.

'Nico. He's gone home. His arm was hurting. He left about half an hour ago, while you were dancing,' he said, self-satisfied.

'He said to tell you,' Bet said, placatory, patting my shoulder a bit too hard.

'Oh.' I shrugged a little, as if the news was trivial, as if I couldn't understand why they had felt the need to say anything, but Alec smirked before turning back to Marina.

He was wrong to smirk, though, because I knew what Nico had meant. I knew why he had told Bet to tell me. And I knew I needed to get away, get back to the flat, as quickly as possible.

I forced myself to wait and not fidget or betray myself, and after enough time had passed, I took Bet quietly to one side and said, 'I feel kind of sick. Like I might throw up.' I put the back of my hand over my mouth as I said it, to convey urgency.

'You poor thing,' she said. Then, knowingly, 'It's probably the pills. They're pretty strong.'

'Probably. I'll be grand, but I might just slip away. I don't want to mess up anyone's night.'

'Do you want me to come with you?' she asked, which was kind because she clearly didn't want to.

'No, I'll be fine. I'll sleep for a few hours and ring you when I get up. I'll come and join you wherever you are.'

'Okay.' She gave me a quick hug that was far more than the drugs talking, so that I hugged her back happily. 'Go on. I'll cover for you.'

I slipped out, making sure to have cash for the bouncers, which they accepted as if it mattered nothing to them, while cheerily teasing me about going home alone. I reflected on Bet saying she would 'cover' for me, and how funnily accurate it was, even though she'd meant it as a joke. There were rules even to going out as we did. You had to commit. If you weren't going the distance, you needed a good excuse or you would be scorned, then dismissed. Really, feeling sick wasn't enough of an excuse – that was being a lightweight – but I'd get away with it this time.

Outside it was still dark, but with the feeble, wavering quality that said it soon wouldn't be. The sky was like black lace, breaking in patches that would join together in larger patches, then finally a new dawn. My taxi driver was surly and disinclined to chat, which suited me perfectly because I was in too much of a fever to make idle conversation about the night I'd had, the day ahead. I stared out the window, watching charcoal clearing to moth-purple as we drove, willing the ancient Mercedes to go faster.

But what if I was wrong? Or if I was right but too late? How long since Nico had left? Everything was guesswork: 'About half an hour,' Alec had said, and I had waited about fifteen minutes, which meant an hour, at least, had gone by. Would he have given up? Or maybe never gone to my place? But he had. I knew it. Knew he would be there.

And even when he wasn't, I still knew, so that I made no space within me for the sickening sight of an empty square, empty doorway, shutters down across the window of Jacques' bar. By now, the air around me was silver grey with a thin ring of pink at the edge of my vision that might have been the sun coming up, or the pill I'd taken. Buoyant with belief, I went up the stairs and into my flat. I filled the bath, sat in it and washed my hair so that when the buzzer went, just as I'd known it would, I was ready, wrapped in a rough and faded towel, which was all my mother had been willing to part with.

'Can I come up?' Nico asked, his voice hoarse through the intercom, drifting to me in stereo through the still-open window.

'Of course.' I buzzed him in, then went to wait, leaning against my doorframe, watching him up the dirty stairs.

'So?' he said, when he reached the top.

'I knew you'd come.' I sounded triumphant. Because I had triumphed. I held out a hand to him, which he took, and we climbed the rickety ladder to my bed below the ceiling.

Outside, it was well and truly dawn, a wash of pink thrown recklessly across the sky, like bleach on a dirty street.

CHAPTER 20

Now

Harriet's mother rang as Anna was getting out of the car and Anna, conditioned now to take any call that might concern Jessie, answered, even though the timing was bad – she had a boot full of groceries, Rudi demanding she listen to a song he had learned at school, and very little time to make dinner before Maurice came back.

'Anna, it's Siobhan. I hope it's not a bad time,' Harriet's mother purred, as if there ever could be a bad time to hear from her. 'I thought it better to ring . . .'

'Siobhan, hi. No, it's fine. Is everything alright with Harriet?'

'Harriet's fine.' Of course she was. Siobhan took a deep breath. 'It's about Jessie.' Of course it was.

'Right.'

'Well, I was looking through Harriet's phone – I do that sometimes. It's one of the rules of her having one.'

Anna didn't care what the rules for Harriet's phone were,

and could hear the complacency Siobhan tried to hide, at how well she was handling all these new dangers in her daughter's life. 'Okay.'

'I check her Snapchat.'

'I thought you couldn't do that? I thought the whole point of Snapchat was it disappeared after a few minutes.' Anna knew she was being irrelevant and stalling but she couldn't stop herself.

'Well, I mean I check her photo stream. They take pictures of the important messages and save them, you know.'

'Oh.'

'And there are messages from Jessie that Harriet has saved, presumably because she's worried about her.'

'Presumably,' Anna said, trying to keep her voice light. Trying not to layer it with all the things she wanted to say, things like *Well, if she's worried about her and cares what happens to her, why is she such a bitch? How can a girl my daughter has known nearly all her life, who spent as much time in my house as in her own, turn like a cornered cat and lash out at her?*

'And I thought I should tell you . . .' Siobhan's words came out in a rush, and Anna could hear the faint strain of embarrassment, of knowing that her daughter was the aggressive party in a sad, circular squabble that none of them seemed able to get to grips with. 'Well, in one of the messages Jessie says she's going to take it "to the next level." Those are her words, and just, you know, given everything that's happening, well, I thought you should know.'

'Thank you. That's kind of you.' Anna made her voice clipped and polite, the way she did when she needed to set herself quite apart from the person in front of her. Make them feel small and gauche because she didn't like what they were saying. 'But Jessie is just fine. She's doing much better. I don't know what those messages were referring to' – here, she allowed a tiny note of disbelief to creep into her voice, a note that cast subtle doubt on Harriet's motives, Siobhan's ability to understand them, the very existence of the texts – 'but, fortunately, Jessie is in great form.'

'Oh. Right.' There was nowhere for Siobhan to go except backwards. 'Well, if you're sure . . . I mean, that's great she's doing better. If there's anything I can do . . .'

'I'll let you know. And thank you.' Anna hung up, opened the boot and began unloading bags, calling Rudi to follow her. She had been rude, she saw that, but only to stop herself from being ruder. To stop herself shouting accusations at Siobhan about Harriet, linking her nastiest, most intimate observations of the girl's character back to how Harriet had been raised, back to Siobhan and her failings as a parent.

She had sworn she wouldn't do this when it had all kicked off a year or so before. 'I'm not going to be that person,' she had said to Maurice, when she had finally realised she needed to discuss it with him. 'I'm not stooping to their level. It's a fight between teenagers, who have known each other a long time, and they'll get over it. I like Harriet,' she had said, with brisk conviction, even though it was no longer true and hadn't been since she had discovered Harriet's betrayals. 'These things always work themselves out,' she continued. And she had stuck to that, even though every bit of her faltered on 'always' because they didn't. Not always. Or not the way you wanted them to.

But she had remained true to that oath, refusing to meet Siobhan for the long conversations the other woman had wanted. 'It's between them,' she had said loftily. 'And I trust them to sort it out.'

In fact, she was scared to get involved, terrified of the murderous rage that swept through her when she thought of Jessie being upset, humiliated by Harriet, because Harriet's asshole of a boyfriend didn't know how to behave. Of Jessie alone and shunned, exposed on the bleak hillside of teenage cruelty, to be pointed at and whispered about, the subject of a thousand nasty comments. Most of all, she was terrified at what she would do to those self-possessed teenage bullies if she were to engage with them. So she had stayed on the outside, pretending this was a deliberate policy and not a beaten retreat.

'Don't let it get to you,' she had said to Jessie. 'It will pass.' She had hoped the unruffled surface of her approach, lie though it was, would show her daughter that this was nothing serious, was manageable and minor in the scheme of things.

Now she knew just how wrong that had been. Her calmness had made her look as if she didn't care, didn't understand the impact, when really she understood far too well.

She had always tried so hard not to be like her own mother, who gloried in an indirectness that she must have believed was impenetrable but that, in reality, Anna had been able to deconstruct since she was a child. 'You'll catch your death of cold going out like that' was not, never had been, a comment on the weather but rather her mother's appalled reaction to the bareness of Anna's arms and legs, the audacity of flesh displayed and not hidden beneath layers of subdued underclothing and tan tights. 'Aren't you a great girl!' wasn't a compliment or even an observation: rather, it was a reaction to her shock at the amount of space Anna seemed determined to take up in the world – the lack of self-effacement that her mother might have half admired but instead mistrusted.

With Jessie, Anna had tried to be open, direct, call things by their name. 'Vagina,' she had said firmly, the first time Jessie had asked 'What's that?' refusing to allow her own squeamishness at saying the word aloud transmit itself to the child. Refusing the vagueness of 'down there' with a feeble sketch of hand gesture, which was the only way her own mother had ever been able to acknowledge that part of Anna's body. 'Breast', 'nipple', 'bottom', 'desire': with all these words she had sought to create a strong and open framework in which Jessie could grow. No net curtains of shame draped over entire sections of body and mind, no fluttering distractions of modesty that was really disgust.

But she had failed. Although she had named the bits of herself and her daughter that Jessie had asked about, she had not, could not, name all the things that transpired between them, the angry moments, the bits of her own past that had been brought forward into the present, that would not stay down where she had dumped them.

Instead, when the trouble with Harriet started, she had packed Jessie off to her grandparents. 'To give you some distance,' she had said, and that was a lie too. Because it was she who couldn't cope with the rising level of drama, the way it was intensifying and whirling faster and faster, sucking everything into its vicious, swirling centre.

She had moved Jessie into her old bedroom in the house at Sycamore Park where she had grown up. Given her the same view, the same smell, the same bed, with faded stickers of ponies on the headboard. Had given her into the care of two people she didn't trust, whose view of the world was everything Anna had tried not to allow her own to be. Since Anna could remember, her parents had looked with suspicion at anyone who did not live as they lived, always waiting for them to fall. And when it was Anna, their own daughter, who had fallen, they had done for her the little they could get away with. True, they had not actually cast her out, but neither had they entirely let her in, so that she had felt as though she and her daughter were left standing in the porch, unexpected, unwelcome visitors.

They did the minimum, and did it without joy, lest the neighbours, or whoever it was they imagined watched them, interpret even that sketchy decency as enthusiasm. And they waited for someone, a man, Maurice, to lift Anna up again.

So Jessie had gone to them, a little shadowy but resolute, and come home a wraith, in baggy jumpers, like layers of disguise. Anna had had to peel them off one by one to discover the extent of the misery that lay underneath – an archaeological dig in which the prize was the arrangement of bones beneath the covering earth.

And, worse, the fault wasn't theirs. It was Anna's own. She had sent her. She had failed her. She was still failing her.

Because Siobhan was right, of course. Jessie was worse. Anna knew it, even as she was opening the front door, grocery bags balanced between knee and forward-thrust shoulder, stepping into a house that felt empty, even though it shouldn't because Jessie was there.

In the old days, she would have had lights on, music blaring, something rubbish and pop that Anna would sing along to, marvelling that she knew the words. There would be the smell of toast and maybe buns, if Jessie was baking, and their days to discuss and dissect. Now, whatever time Anna came home, Jessie was in her room, perched on the topmost rung of the house, lightly, uneasily, a frail bird seeming always ready for startled flight, as if only tethered there by old-woven ropes of love that she was busily unpicking one by one.

As Rudi barged in behind her, kicking off his shoes, throwing his little satchel onto the floor, Anna, instead of telling him to tidy up, was grateful that he filled the house with his things, his chatter, his requests. There was altogether too much space around them these days.

The uneasy truce they had all lived with for the last few months – 'These foods, no others, in these quantities' – had been disrupted just as Anna had felt she could begin to rely on it.

It seemed that every day now Jessie was finding new things to deny herself – 'I don't eat red meat', 'I don't eat nuts', 'I can't eat eggs'. She was adding now, constantly, to the list of the forbidden. 'It makes me feel sick', 'I've always hated that' or, simply, 'No thanks'. Repeated more and more often so that the words themselves prevented battle, because you couldn't fight on all fronts, so Anna, after flailing around for a while, attacking small fires here and there – coming home with new possibilities: 'What about tofu?,' 'Try this, it's made from quinoa' – had finally accepted that these were just skirmishes in the bigger war: that Jessie planned to eat only a barest minimum, enough perhaps to keep her out of the clinic, but no more.

Every day Anna had woken thinking that maybe today something would change, something would get through to her daughter. Then after a while she didn't: she woke to the same burden of Jessie disdaining their offers of help and pulling in the opposite direction to the rest of them.

They carried on as normal, going places, doing things, shopping, cooking, working, and in the middle of them the slow whirlpool that was Jessie dragged them all down, added weight to their heels, so they lagged, slowed, nearly stopped but didn't.

Because of the new rules around what and how, Anna had moved her efforts at interaction from meals to walks, just as Alison had suggested. 'Find something else,' she had said recently, 'something that doesn't come with negative associations. Move away from food.' So –

'An evening walk,' Anna had proposed. 'Daily. A chance to catch up.' And at first Jessie had said yes, drawn more by the prospect of exercise, Anna suspected, than her company. They had done laps of the local park, at a pace that was scarcely comfortable, too fast to talk, as if Jessie was dragging her mother along in her slipstream. There was no easy flow of chat between them, only halting sentences that were bits and fragments, never a full picture, and all the more terrible for that, like a mouth with broken teeth. But because there was so little else, Anna persisted.

Now, when Anna had switched on the TV for Rudi and finished unloading the food, stacking the shelves that were no longer raided, she climbed the stairs to the flight below Jessie's attic.

'Jessie,' she called, 'are you there? Let's have a quick walk before dinner.'

'I'm not coming.'

'Why not?' Anna tried to keep her voice smooth and neutral.

'I'm going for a run instead. You walk too slowly.' It was an accusation, all the more bitterly made because it was so trumped-up.

'I can run with you,' Anna suggested. 'That would be great.'

'No,' Jessie called, as Anna had known she would. 'I like running on my own. It clears my head.'

'You aren't supposed to run in the evening,' Anna said then. 'They told us that. In the clinic. It disrupts sleep, and you need to sleep. Couldn't you run in the morning and we could have a walk together now?'

'No.'

'Right.' What else was she supposed to say? 'Well, come down and have a cup of tea with me before you go. I want to tell you something.' That was a bluff, a ruse. She had nothing to tell, but Jessie would be slow and that would give her time to think of something.

'So what is it?' Jessie sat on a high stool, making it plain that she was there only for the 'something', not for companionship or tea.

'Siobhan rang me – Harriet's mother.'

Jessie was picking at the dry ends of her hair but looked up at that. 'Why?'

'She'd been going through Harriet's phone, looking at photos of texts, or Snapchats or whatever you call them.'

'Yes, she does that,' Jessie said, wary.

'There were some from you that she wanted to tell me about.'

'Fucking Harriet.' The weariness in Jessie's voice was enough to stop Anna, and cause her to reroute. Suddenly, she couldn't bear to confront her daughter, not when she was so nervous and spiky, like a small cornered animal with the pathetic defences of teeth and claws.

'That's what I said.'

'What?'

'Well, not "fucking Harriet",' she laughed, 'but that Harriet had no right to be photographing texts that weren't intended for keeping, and that Siobhan had no right to read them and ring me about them.'

'Really? You said that?'

'Yes. A bit more politely, I suppose, but that was it basically.' The lie cost her nothing, didn't even feel like a lie, because it was so necessary.

'So you don't know what was in the texts?'

'No, and I don't want to. If you have something you want to say to me, or that you think I need to know, you'll tell me. I know you will.'

Jessie looked at her then, a mix of desperate gratitude and the same wariness. 'Thank you for not letting her tell you,' she said, evading the rest of it.

'It's fine. Happy to.' Anna smiled and Jessie smiled back, a small, tight smile that didn't show her teeth. 'But, Jessie, I'm right, amn't I? You'll tell me if there's something I need to know?'

'Yes.' She said it so slowly that it couldn't be true, but Anna, having heard almost nothing but 'No' from her for so long, decided to let 'Yes' be.

'You know I'd do anything for you, right?' It came out, even though she knew it shouldn't, that not doing this – not throwing out lures, hoping Jessie would catch them – was part of what Alison called 'making space' between them. And she wondered, even as she asked, why she bothered because Jessie had begun to edge away from these protestations long ago. In fact, Anna thought, they were almost the first things to go: rather than demand proof of her love, her protection, as she had when she was small, Jessie had taken to dodging, ducking under anything Anna might say, embarrassed, almost disapproving.

'I love you bigger than the world and everything in it,' she would say as a child, arms held wide. Then: 'How much do you love me?' And they would try to outdo each other with the grandiosity of their affections, extravagant claims piling up – 'bigger than the universe', 'deeper than all the seas put together' – until Jessie had stopped playing the game, abruptly, about a year before. 'I love you plenty,' she would say, a little weary, as if Anna were petitioning for more than was reasonable.

Anna had tried joking; 'Who are you – Cordelia? "I love your Majesty/According to my bond; no more nor less."'

Jessie, even though she knew the play, had refused to engage, just shaking her head a little.

Now she stayed silent a moment. Then, with what was clearly an effort, she said, 'I know you would,' which was better than nothing. Then, in a rush, she added, 'So, Jessie – Other Jessie – you never told me how she died.'

'Didn't I?' Anna was startled, at the lack of preamble, at the places Jessie's mind was turning to.

'No. You just said she died and that it was before I was born but that she would have loved me.' She said it not with affection but with mockery, as if Anna had made up some silly story about fairies and princesses. Perhaps she had.

'Well, it was an accident,' Anna said. 'So unexpected and terrible.' The hopeless platitudes tripped out, just as they always did. 'It happened while we were in Brussels that summer.'

'The summer you got pregnant with me?'

'Yes.' Anna felt her heart speed up. Why was Jessie asking these questions now?

'So?'

'Well, Jessie, I don't really like talking about it. It upsets me . . . It was a terrible accident. Even now, I don't know exactly what happened . . .' She put as much appeal into her voice as she could because she hoped it would close down the conversation, but Jessie was indifferent to her mother's distress.

'Other Jessie says you do know.'

'What?'

'She says you do know. You know what happened. You were

there and you saw it and you know. I see her in dreams,' Jessie said. 'She talks to me.'

'Well, I've always thought she's a kind of guardian angel to you.' Anna felt she was back on safer ground.

Jessie rolled her eyes. 'She'll tell me how she died. I can see she's building up to it. We have an understanding.'

'How do you mean?'

'I mean she gets it. She's on my side. In this.'

'In what?'

'Everything I do.'

'Well, I'm sure she is. I mean, that's the point of a guardian angel, isn't it?' Anna was flailing. She was missing something, and she knew it, but could only dimly see what it might be. The way Jessie was talking about someone she'd never known gave her a weird shaky feeling. As if First Jessie was escaping the walls Anna had put around her. As if she was putting her fingers into cracks between the bricks and tearing them away one by one.

'Jessie was lovely,' she continued.

'Was,' Jessie said. 'Exactly. And you have no idea what she's like now.'

'Well, of course not, but how could she be any different?' Anna asked. 'She's dead.' She still hated saying the words. Still found she had no connection to them. They belonged to someone else. They had to.

'But not gone,' Jessie said then.

'No, because the people we love are never gone. They are still in our hearts, for as long as we want them to be.'

Jessie gave her a pitying look. 'Riiiiight,' she said, drawing it out with unexpected insolence. 'That's not what I meant, obviously.'

Obviously, Anna thought.

'I see Jessie,' her daughter went on. 'She talks to me. In dreams, and not in dreams. Sometimes when I wake, she's there too. I know stuff about her, and you. And I'll know more.' She looked sly but something else as well, something Anna couldn't interpret. 'I'll know everything.'

There is no 'everything', Anna thought. There never is.

'Jessie would have loved you,' she said again, because it sounded soothing, and she was at a loss for what else to say, but trying to hold tight to a fixed point. Something was changing there, in front of her, and she didn't know what it was.

'I know you miss her every day,' Jessie continued, propelled by the store of rage within her that she kept burning so carefully, as though she feared it might go out, and leave her with nothing. 'I know, because you're always saying it. And you try to say I'm like her, just to bring her back, because you want me to be like her, and I'm not. I know I'm not. Every story you tell about her, the way you describe her, I'm nothing like that. And, anyway, she told me I'm nothing like her.'

'Who told you?' Anna, distracted, checking her phone – another text from Andrew – expected to be told that Gran had said this, because it sounded so very like the kind of thing her mother would say. Sort of pointless, but destructive too, in a small way. She planned what she would say in response: that Gran had never really known Jessie or understood her. Hadn't really been that interested in her until she died and even then had been more curious than interested. She readied herself to say all this, but Jessie was still talking.

'Other Jessie did. She said I'm not like her at all. That I'm like you. And my dad.'

'Jessie, what are you talking about?' Anna's phone pinged as a message came through – Andrew, again. Was her daughter mad as well as thin? Or was the thinness sending her mad?

But Jessie just huddled deeper into her hoodie, her shell. 'Who's texting you?' she asked, because she had seen Anna read whatever was on her phone, then press delete. 'Is it him?'

'Him' was how she usually referred to Maurice, but the vagueness was an invitation Anna did not refuse.

'Yes,' she lied. She knew who Jessie meant.

Her daughter gave her a sharp look, then slouched off, hands drawn up inside her dangling sleeves, a cartoon teenager. She barely had the energy to pick up her feet, Anna saw, dragging them along with her as if they were iron-shod.

Why had she looked like that? What was she on about, that 'Other Jessie' had told her? That she would tell her 'everything'? Anna started to feel a queasy anxiety.

CHAPTER 21

Then

Into that warm caramel summer, Jessie arrived. The day she came, I went to wait for her at the Central Station, where her train from the airport would terminate. I sat outside, even though it was far too hot – the kind of thick heat that squashes your energy – because inside smelt terrible, of piss and dogs and dirty blankets. At night, the place was practically a homeless shelter. The floor was stained with beer and chewing gum and what was probably blood, although it might have been rust.

Jessie emerged, so pale I could almost see through her to the filthy cream-tiled walls beyond.

'You're the whitest person I've seen in weeks,' I said, hugging her and grabbing one of her bags.

'I'm always the whitest person anyone's seen in weeks,' she said, laughing. 'My skin repels sunlight like a mirrored surface. So?' She stepped back and held me away from her. 'You look pretty much the way your letters made me think you'd look.'

'And that is?'

'Insanely thin, brown, totally frantic.' We both laughed. 'Seriously, Anna, you seem to be living forty-eight-hour days. Or, rather, nights. You're like someone possessed.'

She was perfectly right, of course. I was possessed, driven forwards and backwards by my obsession with Nico. When he looked at me, I lived. When he didn't, I waited. And burned. And knew. That he was mine. That I just had to wait longer, more completely. I split myself in two, one part a puppet, sent out to dance and talk and flirt and drink, the other, keeping still, inside, watching, planning, burning. I consumed myself with the waiting. I started with the stuff that no one but I would much notice – all my interests that weren't him, my sense of humour, my curiosity about the world, went into the fire. Then, it was every bit of me that wasn't needed: I got thinner and thinner, more bitten, driven and hollowed out. But the fire needed more fuel, so I had to keep going, finding new things to burn. I burned through my love of family and friends, my ability to read a book or newspaper, to attend to any conversation that did not have Nico in it. I managed to continue working, because there I was uninterrupted in my thoughts. When I met Bet and Marina, I quickly turned the conversation so that his name might enter it. When I was with him, I was happy; when I was without him, I waited.

And him? He did nothing. Nothing beyond the ordinary run of chat, anyway.

I looked at Nico and saw love. I will never know if it was there or not. If it was, it didn't last, but maybe it was never there at all. No more real than the reflection of a reflection. A love made up of the dazzle of early-morning sun on old buildings, a strange city, lack of sleep on top of drugs and drink, the need to be a different person in a different time. Perhaps I fell in love with a city, with the possibility I suddenly saw in myself, and he just happened to be standing there.

I don't suppose it matters. Just as it doesn't much matter who he was, really – a man I barely knew, who had so quickly put a torch to me. At this distance, I'm not even sure he wasn't quite stupid: maybe those silences, which I always thought were enigmatic, or a sign of his refusal to respond to whatever I had said because it was idiotic, were because he couldn't think of anything. Now I realise I didn't even know his surname. He never told me. I never asked. Not until much, much later.

That first night had been our only night. We had fallen asleep as one person, and woken up as two. Distinct, separate and awkward so that the flat was more claustrophobic even than the hot, airless afternoon outside. All the certainties of the dawn had fallen from us, and I tried to bring them back by suggesting coffee, a walk, breakfast in the park. He said he couldn't: he had to meet Pierre. He had left almost immediately, saying he would see me later. He did, but only because I was where he was, and not because he had tried to see me. He left nothing behind, not a cigarette butt, not a scrap of paper, not even a smell. The sheets, which should have held some trace of him, of us, carried only the familiar smell of the flat.

At first, when we met that evening in the bar and he did so little to acknowledge that I was there, I thought I must be mistaken, or that he was shy, uncertain what to say to me.

Then I decided he didn't want the others to suspect. Perhaps, I thought, we would do the same as the night before, and sneak away separately, to be together. How clever, I thought, how exciting. Much better than letting Alec and the rest in.

But I was wrong. He didn't come that night, or any of the next nights.

But he would. I knew he would. I just had to wait, and not allow myself to become distracted. I felt like a handmaiden, charged with a sacred duty, tending a perfect flame no one else could see.

'Come on.' I grabbed another of Jessie's bags. 'We can walk. It's not that far, and you'll get to see some of the city. Oh, Jessie, I'm so glad you're here!' And I was, so happy I could have skipped out my excitement on the street beneath my feet, except the bags were heavy and I knew Jessie would laugh at me. She laughed anyway.

'So am I. I've missed you! Your letters were so packed, but it's not at all the same as being with you. Dublin without you is very, very boring.' She began telling me about various friends, people I could barely remember, as remote as if they were characters in a TV show, whose lives ended when the screen went black.

'Never mind them,' I said. 'Wait till I tell you about Bet, and Marina, and this incredible girl called Cécile, and there's the weird quiet guy, Pierre, who seems nice but it's hard to tell, and a guy called Alec who's such a jerk.' I couldn't say Nico's name to her, not yet, because I knew she would know, just by my saying it, that he meant more than the others.

'You've told me loads about them already,' she said, perhaps a little wry. 'It's almost like I've grown up with them.'

I started telling her more, about what we'd done, places we'd been, jokes we'd made. I was rattling, walking and babbling, her bags over my shoulder, pointing things out rapidly as we moved past them – 'Look, that place does amazing crêpes, filled with anything you can imagine' – throwing out stories about people and places she didn't know. I couldn't stop myself. I needed to fill in the mosaic very quickly so that I could get to Nico. Because I knew that Jessie would help me, that, with her, I would get him. Once he saw how vital I was to her, understood who I was in her eyes . . . I worried that I lacked any context for him, that I was just a girl who had drifted in and might drift out again. I needed him to know that I was a real person, with other people who looked to me, admired me, wanted me. Jessie would do that for me. She would be the setting by which he could better see me.

Outside the flat I dithered for a minute. 'I don't know whether to bring you upstairs or into the bar,' I said, waving frantically at Cécile through the window.

'Flat,' Jessie said. 'I want to see your platter-bed.' So we went upstairs and she laughed as hard as I had known she would, at the hip bath, the tininess of the place. 'It's exactly as you described,' she said. 'Except a bit more brown. It even smells brown. Okay, imagine you're an estate agent. How would you sell it?'

'Bijou?'

'Too ambitious. Compact,' she countered, 'with original features.'

'Yes, if the original was a wardrobe.' I laughed. 'In need of modernisation?'

'Flexible space. Would suit—'

'Doll. Or midget.'

'Or someone who clearly doesn't spend more than twenty minutes a day at home,' she said, opening the fridge. 'Seriously? Not even cheese?'

'Well, I don't eat here much.'

'You don't eat anywhere much by the look of you.'

I knew it was true, but I still loved hearing her say it. Jessie had always been the thin one, and now it was me. I never got tired of admiring my newly gangly legs, the bony bits where knees and hips protruded, the way my wrists looked barely thick enough to support my hands. These things were my armoury in the battle for Nico.

A loud whistle came up from the square below and I ran to the window.

'Hi!' It was Pierre, who said he was going for coffee and did I want to come.

'Very *Streetcar Named Desire*,' Jessie said, laughing. 'Or maybe *Cat on a Hot Tin Roof*,' as I was dancing excitedly up and down.

'We're coming,' I called down to Pierre. 'Give us a minute. Come on,' to Jessie, 'you can unpack later.'

'I didn't bring much,' she said.

Chez Léon was deserted at that hour, dust drifting aimlessly in beams of tobacco-coloured sunlight. I introduced Jessie to Pierre, sitting at the bar, and Cécile, who was doing something tricky with a beer tap.

'You're very pale,' she said to Jessie, looking her over.

'And you're very dark,' Jessie said instantly, but without any antagonism, so that Cécile, after a silent moment in which I wondered would she try to choke Jessie – I had seen her do it once to a girl she said had been 'impolite' – threw back her head and laughed.

'You're cute,' she said, patting Jessie gently on the cheek. 'Have a coffee.'

We sat and drank coffee, then beers. Jessie and I chatted about home and Brussels. Pierre and Cécile played chess, with pieces clumsy and ancient like chunks of driftwood, then Cécile went back behind the bar before Jacques arrived.

'So what about you?' Jessie asked Pierre, and, to my surprise, he told her anything she asked. That he didn't have a job because his mother was 'fragile' and needed help. That he was with her by day, with the odd hour off when a friend called in; a brother, who worked in a furniture shop, stayed in the evenings. 'It's why I go out at night,' he said. 'That's the way the time works for us. Otherwise I would live like everyone else,' he said, with a sad smile. 'I would be up in the morning, and go to my work, come back in the evening and stay at home.'

'Sounds rubbish,' I said, without thinking. 'So dull.'

'Hardly,' Jessie protested. 'Most of the world lives like that.'

'Dull,' I insisted. 'Who wants to live like most of the world?'

'I do,' Pierre said.

I felt embarrassed to be making a triumphant virtue of what to him was painful necessity.

'You sound like Alec and Nico,' he continued. I wasn't sure he meant it as a compliment.

'How do you know Nico?' I asked. Just as I had known she would, Jessie looked at me when I said Nico's name, drawn as surely as if I had twitched an invisible thread. Pierre looked too, I thought, but maybe I imagined that.

'We grew up together,' Pierre said, staring at the tabletop. 'My mother worked for his mother when I was very small. I spent many days at Nico's with him when we were children.'

'So what's he like, this Nico?' Jessie asked.

'He's a good guy,' Pierre said. 'Not always the most reliable,' he smiled his mournful harlequin's smile, 'but when you are in trouble, he is there, and when you are the focus of his attention, it is a very strong attention. Like the sun. But just like the sun, there is day and there is night.'

'And what's he like with his girlfriend?' I couldn't resist, even though I had already asked Bet and Marina. I needed another perspective. But that was too much for Pierre.

'I don't know,' he said, and fell silent, head down. It was already the most I had ever heard him say, and revealed a sort of awareness in him that I hadn't imagined. I looked at Jessie with affection and pride. I had been right: her particular kind of magic, that of a kind heart and a quick wit, with something mischievous and encouraging that danced in her brown eyes, was as potent here as it had been at home.

Jessie was always the one to coax confidences out of people. It was a way she had of being interested, but more than that. It was like she trusted you blindly – trusted that your innermost self, as you revealed it, would be worthy. That you would not, exposed, be less than she had imagined. But it was also that, in her own funny, sweet way, she didn't care. She didn't judge you, even in the light of your confidences. It was as if she accepted that this was what you were like in that moment, but believed you could be something else in another. It was reassuring to know you weren't pinned to whatever shameful admission you had made. That she would never again consider it unless you wanted her to.

So people told her things, all sorts of people, all sorts of things. I told her everything – I always had – about my parents and how bewildered I felt by them, how hurt by what I took to be the deliberateness of their distance from me, about all the lonely hours at home with no brothers or sisters, my failures and triumphs in school, in college, in my limited working life, my ambitions – vague, formless, no more than yearnings – to be more and better than I was, in ways that weren't yet clear to me and that I worried never would be. She said to trust myself, that she trusted me, and it would all be fine. Out with friends, when we met groups of drunken guys, one or two of us might come home with a conquest, or a funny story, but Jessie would always have learned something surprising: that the brashest and most confident-seeming was actually terrified he would be dropped from his team or that the quiet one's mother had cancer. Jessie learned because she asked and listened.

'So who's Nico?' she asked later, when we were back in the flat, eating takeaway Turkish kebabs.

'I knew you'd ask that . . .'

'Well?'

'He's this guy I met.'

'Duh!'

'Okay, he's a friend of Bet, Marina and Pierre. He's French but he's always lived in Brussels and, Jessie, he's amazing.

Gorgeous, but you wouldn't think so at first because he doesn't look it, but once you get to know him, he's just . . . It's like he's the concentrated essence of everyone else. Smaller, slighter, but sort of denser, so that everyone else seems stretched out and pointless by comparison.'

'Wow.' She paused, stared at me. 'Seriously?'

'Uh-huh. Very seriously, in fact.' Admitting it out loud was quite different from carrying it around inside: I wanted to cry, because of the impossibility of ever describing how I felt.

'Shit. Okay. And . . . can I ask?'

'What?' I knew very well what.

'Well, does he feel the same?'

'Well, sort of. Or not. I don't know. He stayed here, one night, last weekend, and it was amazing. The way they always say it will be in films and books, like fireworks exploding under your skin. But since then, I don't know what's happening.'

'He has a girlfriend?'

'Jessie, he's *mine*. I know he is. I know it with every single bit of myself. He has to be, or I will burn up into ash and be gone.'

'Jesus, Anna.'

'Yep.'

We stayed up late and drank wine and talked more. I told her everything about Nico. I listed almost every single moment between us, from our first meeting. The way he looked, how he moved, what he did. I told her how little he spoke, how I knew that he wanted me, even though he'd never said it.

'It's difficult, with the girlfriend, but we'll work it out.'

'But what happens in the autumn, when you leave?'

'I'm not leaving.'

* * *

Jessie said she would visit museums and galleries – 'anything free' – while I was at work the next day, then meet me afterwards. I drew her a map, complete with landmarks I knew she'd like – an amazing stationery shop where paper came in every shade of cream, white and pink, and every possible thickness; a row of trees with tortured branches; a café called La Puce Qui Ri, the Laughing Flea – and told her the right Métro stop. 'All you have to do is get off. I'll meet you there.'

'I can manage that.'

And she was already there when I arrived, reading a poster advertising a circus, with a photo of an elephant standing on a small tub while a girl in a sparkly dress smirked beside it. 'Poor thing. I can't believe they still have these.'

'Bet says they're all Albanians, the circus people, and they bring animals in illegally and treat them so cruelly. She says you should see the bears they have, with sores and broken teeth.'

'That's horrible. Why don't the police do anything?'

'Bet says they don't bother, because the real crime is the Moroccans bringing in drugs and the Congolese trafficking people.'

'Bet sounds quite an authority.'

There was a dryness to Jessie's voice, but I didn't pay any attention, just grabbed her hand and said, 'Don't be jealous. You'll love her, I promise.'

And I believed it as I said it, but it turned out I was wrong. Jessie didn't love Bet, or Marina, and they didn't love her.

We walked around the streets, went to dinner in an Italian restaurant that did a type of creamy pasta I knew Jessie would love, and she told me about her father who hadn't been himself and they feared it might be dementia. 'His concentration is bad now. Remember how he used to read the newspapers for hours?' I did. It was one of my strongest memories of Jessie's house, which I much preferred to my own because of the noise, the chatter, the jollity, the lack of crochet chair covers and polished fake mahogany; her father silent, absorbed in *The Irish Times* and the *Independent*, while around him his four children and wife laughed and gave out and teased one another. 'These days, he barely reads a paragraph before he's shouting at my mother that he doesn't know what these fellas are on about.'

'He shouts at your mother?' Jessie's father never shouted at any of them, and certainly not at his wife, whom he adored for her piety, her anarchy, the spirit of cheerful selfishness that allowed her to run a house, a husband, four children, a busy social life of card-playing and baking without ever slipping into the martyr role that my own mother, relatively unencumbered, so thoroughly inhabited.

'Yes, that's new too. He shouts at all of us now.' Jessie's eyes gleamed wet for a minute and she dashed at them with the back of her hand. 'That's why I wasn't certain I could come and visit, even though I had loads of holidays saved up at work. I didn't want to leave Mum, but she insisted. She said I should get a couple of weeks away, and that nothing terrible will happen in that time. She says that if it is dementia,' she choked a little on the word, 'then it's going to be a marathon run, not a sprint, and we all need to pace ourselves.'

'Shit, Jessie, I'm so sorry!'

'It's okay.' She tried to smile. 'I just feel so bad for him. He knows something is going wrong, but he can't figure out what it is. Sometimes I look at him and see such terror on his face. And then, when someone goes near him, he hides it with a big smile that anyone who knew him would see right through.' Jessie's dad, I knew, wasn't a man for big smiles. His kindness was absolute, but he didn't beam it abroad. He spoke little and smiled only sometimes, but there wasn't a thing he wouldn't willingly do for his family and the many others they brought home.

'Do you remember how he was always the one to collect us from town, or parties, when we couldn't get a taxi?' I asked.

'Yes, and he used to say, "I was up anyway", and never give out, even though he was only up because I wasn't home.'

Jessie's dad adored her in a way that made me sometimes sad and jealous, but mostly hopeful because even to see such love existed was to make me feel I might one day have it. 'It's because I'm the only girl,' Jessie used to say, but I thought she was wrong. He adored her because he could see how unusual she was, this little piece of quicksilver in his life, and he couldn't quite believe that he had produced anything so funny and so precious.

'Let's get another bottle,' I said.

'Not for me. I've had plenty.'

'Oh, come on, don't be boring.'

For the time we were in that restaurant, going through old memories and talking through a difficult future, I almost forgot about Nico, Bet and the others, but as soon as we left, I felt rising up in me the same sickening excitement – *This might be the night.* I was impatient to get to Chez Léon – we were late, by my usual standards – and irritated that Jessie wanted to change her top because it had a splash of pasta sauce on it.

'I'll only be a sec,' she said, outside the door to the flat.

'You're fine,' I said. 'Seriously, no one cares.'

'I care.' She laughed. 'I look like a toddler who spills food down herself. Just give me the key. I'll meet you in the bar. I can hardly get lost.' She made a wry face. I knew I should go with her, wait with her, chat while she got ready, be at her side when she came to meet my new friends for the first time, but I couldn't.

'That's true,' I said, pretending that getting lost was the only reason anyone might stay. 'You could probably let yourself fall out the window, and land on the steps of the bar.'

'You should get a rope,' she said, 'or a zipline. Cut out the stairs altogether.'

'Fine,' I said, too itchy even to pay attention to the jokes we were making. 'I'll go. Take your time. You don't want me hurrying you along, so come down when you're ready.'

'There you are,' Bet called, as I came in, waving her arms at me in a way that was chiding and proprietorial at the same time. 'You're so late!' It was an accusation and an interrogation all at once.

'Sorry.' I sat down on a barstool she pulled up for me, already scanning the room for Nico. It was crowded, the usual Friday-night fever starting to hum and thrum along its edges.

'*Où est La Petite?*' Cécile demanded. I knew she meant Jessie. *La Petite*, The Little One. It suited her, but I was astonished at this mark of favour from Cécile. Perhaps Bet was too. She looked surprised, then annoyed.

'She'll be along in a minute,' I said.

'The childhood friend from Dublin?' Bet asked. 'How's that going?' As if it must be a tedious imposition. I was about to answer, to say it was lovely, and they would all love Jessie, when she came in.

She'd changed into a clean white T-shirt, and taken her hair down from the straggly bun of earlier so that it bounced around her shoulders, springy and shiny, a dark contrast to the pale, pale face so that she looked like a cartoon kid, manga maybe, with big eyes and a pointy chin.

'Over here.' I waved at her, then realised Nico was standing beside me and I was distracted, saying hello to him, breathing in the smell of him that made me feel all over again that it was just him and me, and that he would kiss me because how could he resist? How could he not hear and feel the call of my blood in the same way I heard and felt the call of his? But he didn't; he just smiled at me.

'Hey.' Jessie reached us then, and I introduced her. She greeted Cécile and Pierre warmly, kissing both of them on the cheek, and said hello to everyone else, then told them to stop staring at her because they were making her nervous.

'It's like the first day at school,' she said, laughing, 'or a performance. I feel like I should do a dance or something.' They all laughed at that, except Bet, who just stared at her, then asked Alec and Nico if they'd heard anything from Cécile's boyfriend since he'd gone to prison.

Alec answered her, and began expanding on various theories of how Jean-Paul might be getting along. Nico stayed quiet, then asked Jessie how long she was staying.

'Just a couple of weeks. My dad isn't well so I have to get back to help my mum.'

I was astonished at her openness, at how she didn't try to present herself in any particular light, just told things as they were. It was what she always did, but I somehow hadn't expected it there, where everyone was so much more knowing and sophisticated than the people we knew back home. I thought she'd try for more attitude, like I had.

We finished our beers and ordered more. Around us, the bar filled with the usual glittering Friday-night parade of the colourful, charming, silly and shifty, mostly the same people who came and went every week, some a little more ravaged than when I had first seen them, a few others noticeably missing: this wasn't a scene where everyone lasted. The pace was too furious.

Many of them came to say hi to me, ask how I was, make a joke here and there, and I was proud that Jessie should see how completely I was knotted in after so short a time.

Bet, for some reason, had become very grand, talking about restaurants and hotels she'd been to with her parents, exotic holidays they'd had. 'Don't say you haven't been to Cuba? You'd better go, fast, before it changes. When we were there . . .' She launched into an anecdote about a guy on a moped who had led them down some dark alley so they were terrified but it was all fine because . . .

'She sounds like a dowager empress,' Jessie whispered to

me. I snorted, trying to hold back a laugh. I liked Bet, very much, but I wasn't above laughing at her with Jessie.

I remembered when I'd first met Bet, listening to her stories and thinking they were just the tip of a wonderful iceberg, with deep reservoirs of more and more fascinating tales. Now I realised that the depth had never come: the stories were either the same, or very similar, vaguely rambling, self-regarding, immune to alteration or progression. And I understood, with some sadness, that the best of her had come immediately, not in subtle layers of revelation. But I didn't want to think about that. It's fine, I told myself, because she's enough as she is. I don't need there to be more.

I tried to join in with the flow of her conversation, chucking in my own stories and observations, where I thought they roughly dovetailed with hers, working to make the conversation more general, less boastful, but after a while I gave up because Bet ploughed on through whatever I said. Jessie didn't say anything at all, and even Marina looked a little surprised.

Nico, after a while, started chatting to Jessie about Dublin, asking her what she did there, what it was like. I thought that was so polite of him, to make the effort, or maybe he was just stuck for something to say. He'd never done that with me – I'd made sure he never had to, by soaking up the details of his life, or the public bits of it anyway, as quickly as I could. From the start, he and I had talked – in as much as we did talk – about him, about Bet and Jacques and the places we all went to, not about my work or where I came from. I didn't want him to think of me as someone from elsewhere, who might go back there. I needed to be his present and his future, not something temporary, a summer distraction.

Usually he didn't talk much, but with Jessie he clearly said enough to encourage her. She was chatting away, telling him things she and I had done when we were younger – the good stories, I noted and silently blessed her; the stories that showed me in the light I needed, as someone intrepid, admired, rebellious.

I smiled at Jessie and she smiled back. I could see she was relieved: clearly she had been worrying about meeting these new friends. I understood then the insistence on changing, the moments alone in the flat, steeling herself. And I knew her apprehension had been for my sake as much as hers. That she hadn't wanted to let me down by being less than I needed her to be. And I loved her for it.

'Let's go,' Bet said, yawning stagily. 'It's so boring here this evening.'

We went to the Vaudeville and, when that closed, to a dirty bar by the station where the owner's large dogs, crosses of many breeds, lay at our feet, panting in the early-morning heat. Nico patted them, letting them rest their heavy heads on his knees, stroking their ears steadily, almost meditatively. Even that didn't disgust me, although I hated dogs.

We drank and continued drinking. Bet, Marina and I did more pills. Jessie said no. Pierre, Alec and a couple of guys I didn't know played a complicated gambling game on something that looked like a giant bingo machine, and the bar owner shouted at us every once in a while for spilling drinks or banging the toilet door so that the dogs growled, but he did it more from a sense of duty, it seemed to me, than any real antagonism.

Although who knew? I had seen enough by then to know that violence lurked in many corners in this city that couldn't acknowledge its past or the truth of its present; a place that was civilised and savage at the same time. Hot rage, it seemed to me, bubbled beneath a veneer of manners and courtesy, of gently intoned *'De rien, Madame'*, and *'Bonne après-midi, Monsieur'*, formulae assembled to be equal to all situations but that couldn't hide the many ways in which they were redundant.

Around and outside the careful formalities there was a kind of patchwork chaos, pockets of aggression, mainly picked out by area, age and ethnicity. Young men fought one another in gangs; mothers slapped their children; men hit women. Even girls beat each other up, solving disputes over men and money with their hands and feet. I saw Madame Pipi drag a girl out of the loos at the Vaudeville, because the girl – undoubtedly desperate, and as skinny as a stray cat – had taken a few coins out of the tips saucer. Madame Pipi pushed her so she fell down the stairs in a bony heap. Bet, who watched with me, had said cheerfully, 'What an idiot. Last place you steal is here. She should stick to shops.'

Once I noticed it, I found it everywhere. In the whispers of violence in the currents of hot air that rushed up from the Métro tunnels, in the chewing gum that melted on the streets and stuck to the soles of my shoes, in the flocks of dusty pigeons that clustered desperately around any pool of water. There was something rotten, which leaked into me, like ink on an onion skin, staining down through all the layers.

'I think I'll go back,' Jessie said, yawning hard. 'I'm wrecked. Surely it's bedtime.'

Outside it was daylight, another in the unbroken run of sticky, sultry days so that by now the entire city smelt sweet and greasy, like the bottom of a bag of popcorn. Everywhere the grass was parched, the trees exhausted, their leaves beginning to slump, drifting down towards hot pavements.

'You can't go,' Bet said. 'We're just getting started.' Her speech was slurred, a lazy running together of words, as if she couldn't be bothered to articulate properly, which made her sound both drunk and insolent.

'I'm not used to this.' Jessie tried to joke. 'I need time to acclimatise.'

'Don't go,' I said, but half-heartedly. As long as there were so many of us, I knew Nico would continue to ignore me. That anything between us could come only when we were closer to being alone together.

'Who's going?' Nico looked up from the dogs, dragging himself away from the silent communion of man and beast that he did so much better than man to man.

'Jessie is,' I said, willing it to be a done deal. But it wasn't.

'Let's all go,' Nico said. 'This place is crap. It's a beautiful day. Let's go to the park.' He couldn't really think it was a beautiful day, I thought, looking at the straw-coloured glare outside. But I agreed enthusiastically.

'Good idea,' Bet said instantly. 'We can stop and get beers. Alec, we're going.' She began to bustle and plan, Marina in her wake.

'You don't have to come,' I said to Jessie. 'We could drop you home.'

'No, no, she must come.' That was Alec, who heard everything, malicious beneath the bonhomie. 'She's hardly seen the city yet, just the inside of bars. This is an opportunity.'

'Do come,' Nico said, looking at Jessie. And although she should have said no, insisted she was tired and wanted to sleep, she smiled and said yes, and I told myself that it didn't matter, everything was fine.

We went to the same park with the decaying fountain, carrying almost the same things – beer, crisps, water – as on my first day, but where that had been a day on which we had floated gently, harmoniously, this time there was a fractured spikiness to us all that the park's shade could not absorb. Or maybe it was just me. I don't know.

I showed Jessie the fountain with the faded, corrupted figures of grateful Africans and watched her expression of disgust as she took in the meaning. 'You forget,' she said.

'Forget what?' Bet was on the conversation fast, like a duck snapping at mayflies.

'What all the grand buildings and broad streets mean.'

'What do they mean?' Bet was hostile.

'Exploitation, basically. Other people's misery.'

'You sound like a student Marxist,' Bet said, all worldly loftiness.

'Meaning?'

'Naïve. Childish.'

'Well, you sound like a total bigot,' Jessie said, but she said it quietly and Bet – thank God – had walked off, calling to Pierre to come with her and get a can of Coke.

I tried to explain. 'It's not that she's actually bigoted; it's just that she likes hierarchy. She approves of it, as long as she's high up. She wants there to be layers beneath her so that she can enjoy the elevation of her own position.'

Jessie looked astonished, and I knew how bad that must sound to her. Maybe to anyone.

'It's the way it is here,' I said lamely. 'You and I don't fully understand it. We can't – we didn't grow up here.'

Jessie looked at me and said nothing, and I knew what she was thinking: even if she had grown up here, she would never, ever, think as Bet did. Bet, who called everyone Moroccan who wasn't white, with a lazy ignorance that edged towards racism; who knew the rules too well.

'And Marina?' Jessie asked.

'Not sure. I think she just goes along with it, really . . .' Marina was dancing to the music from Alec's speaker, amiable and indifferent.

'I think you're right.' Jessie smiled. 'She's a bit like a clockwork toy that you wind up and it just keeps going – smiling, laughing, dancing – until finally it winds down again.'

'Look!' I pointed into the tops of a cluster of giant chestnut trees above us, their broad fan-like leaves turning brown and crinkled at the edges. A flash of emerald green had caught my eye.

'What is it?' Jessie asked.

'A parakeet. Probably more than one. There are flocks of them around the city. Apparently someone brought them in for an aviary, as an exotic curiosity, but they escaped and survived so successfully that now they're just pests. They're stronger and more aggressive than the native birds, so they win the battles for food and whatever else birds need. Isn't it funny, to think they went from being something beautiful and strange to vermin? And all because they're too good, surviving instead of dying.'

'Sounds all too likely,' Jessie said. Then, thoughtfully, 'Aggressive and entitled and flashy. I know who they remind me of.' She glanced at Bet, on her way back with her Coke. I wanted to laugh but didn't, because I still hoped the two of them could be friends. Or maybe I knew they never could be, but didn't want to annoy Bet.

'Let's take a photo,' Nico said then, which surprised me because I had never seen him do anything of the sort before. None of us did: we were busy living life, not looking at it, or taking photos of it. It was one of the things we insisted on, made a big deal of. 'Not here. The other fountain, with the water in the background.'

We all grumbled and said we were too hot to move, too tired, that we looked wrecked. Couldn't he wait? Why did it have to be now? But he insisted, so politely and charmingly that, of course, we did exactly as he wanted.

He made us sit on the rim, me, Bet and Jessie – Marina refused, said it was so hot she'd throw herself in and catch swamp fever – so, with Bet's arm around my shoulders and Jessie beside me, I smiled into the camera but really I was smiling through it, at Nico, on the other side, and at my future that lay there, with him, and because the camera was there I didn't have to pretend to be looking somewhere else. I could look straight at him, the way I wanted to look.

Around us, the air was filled with a fine mist from the jet of water behind, sent up fast and hard, to drift gently down on our faces. I turned mine up towards it, to catch the play of feather-light rain, and Nico sighed. 'Stop moving.'

He took several pictures, seemed strangely critical of the first results – 'You all moved,' he said. 'Stay still.' Then, to Jessie, 'You're hidden behind Anna. You need to lean out more. And, Bet, lean back, you're too much in the centre.'

'Who are you? Mario Testino?' I asked, laughing, pretending to be impatient when really I could have stayed on the cool damp edge of that fountain forever, watching him, knowing he was watching me, that together we were trapped in the moment.

'That's enough,' Bet said, standing and stretching. 'I need to get into the shade. I'm melting. Jessie, you're the colour of a beetroot.'

Jessie was certainly pink, and blushed redder again at Bet's remark. She started to say something, then stopped and shrugged. I smiled, to let her know that I appreciated her biting her lip. And then, because I was watching her, I saw Nico watch her too, and he too blushed, just as she was blushing, so that their faces were washed over with the same glow, as if they had been illuminated with an identical light, invisible to the rest of us. Jessie turned towards him, tangled in the intensity of his glance, and suddenly she was blushing even more, her face a furious red.

I saw all this as if underwater, so that it was distanced from me and didn't assemble itself fully, just drifted past me in waves, but waves that were chilly and choppy.

'What will you do with the photos?' I asked Nico, because, suddenly, I needed to know.

'I'll get them printed and give you one,' he said, but he said it to Jessie. Not to all of us. Not to me. To *her*. It's because she's leaving first, I told myself. Because he knows she'll be gone, so she'll need a photo. I won't. I'll be here.

'Thank you,' Jessie said. 'Or you can just give it to Anna and she'll pass it on to me.'

I pretended I hadn't heard. 'I'm going to sit down,' I said, turning away, taking what I had seen with me so that I could examine it better alone and in silence.

'Me too,' Jessie said instantly, but I didn't wait for her. I walked off quickly and sat down beside Bet on a plaid rug too small for another person.

'Any more beer?' I asked.

'They're in the fountain,' Bet said, 'keeping cool.'

'I'll get you one.' That was Pierre, so silent until that moment that I had barely registered him close by. I drank the beer and then another, ignoring the headache that told me I needed to stop, to sleep, to drink water. I was too agitated to doze so I insisted we play silly games instead. Games in which we threw stones to hit certain things, scoring points for accuracy, or balanced stones one on top of another, scoring more points for height. I flirted with Pierre, because he was there, laughed and chatted with Bet and Marina, even Alec, and tried to ignore what was in front of me, beside me, behind me, worst of all inside me: Nico and Jessie on another blanket, talking quietly, heads close together.

'They're getting on well,' Bet said, with a nod to where Jessie lay, propped on one elbow, with Nico beside her. I looked, trying to see what Bet saw, in case it was different from what I saw.

'Yes. Isn't Nico nice to make such an effort?' I said airily.

'Nice,' Bet agreed, with an enquiring look at me.

'And Jessie,' I carried on, insisting now, because perhaps there was some mistake after all, and what I said was right, not what I saw. *Nice*, nothing more. Nothing worse. 'So good of her. She must be exhausted and longing to go by now.'

'Must be,' Bet agreed, the enquiry in her voice now, as well as her face.

'In fact,' I said, 'I think I should go. I really should take her home. Jessie,' I called, getting up, 'we should go, right? You must be wrecked. I know I am.'

'Whatever you want,' Jessie said lazily, 'but I'm fine. If you want to stay.'

'I can drop her back later,' Nico said. 'On the bike.'

And then I knew there was no mistake, no mix-up. This was not a question of politeness or drunkenness or tiredness or niceness, not something innocuous that would dissolve, like dust, in a day. It was real and I had to make it stop.

'No, we have to go,' I said, and my voice was high and sharp so that Jessie looked properly at me, not the slow, sunny-afternoon vague look of a moment ago, but an anxious, searching one.

'Okay,' she said, getting up. 'I'm coming.' I was already walking, so she had to run to catch me up.

'Your jacket,' she said, holding it out. 'You left it.'

'Oh, right. Thanks.' I turned and waved at the others, sitting like islands on their blankets, in a sea of empty beer bottles and crisps packets. How disgusting we are, I thought briefly. How trashy and complacent. *Canaille.* I mimed 'Phone you later' at Bet, then risked a look at Nico. He was lying down, eyes closed, arms behind his head, while Marina trailed a leaf over his nose and forehead.

'Are you okay?' Jessie asked.

'I'm fine. Just tired,' I said.

We went back by Métro, with all the other weary late-afternoon travellers: cross mothers with crying babies; teenagers, sick of trying to make their handful of coins stretch to all the things they wanted; men who had been drinking and had felt the exuberance of the early beers turn into the sullen headache of a hangover. Jessie and I said little, but as the train barrelled forward I felt it was taking us into a different realm, far away from the enchanted grounds I had lived in since I'd arrived.

Back at the flat, I said I was tired and going to bed. 'I'm not hungry. Are you?'

'No.'

'There's probably bread in the cupboard.' We both knew there wasn't. 'You could have toast.'

'I'm fine. I'll go to bed in a bit. I might ring my mum.'

'Fine.' I wanted to be asleep before she came up the stairs to the one bed. Sharing it had been lovely those first nights, because we had chatted and laughed at silly things, then fallen asleep tucked into each other, the muscle memory of all the beds we had shared from childhood onwards – at my house, hers, friends' houses, at parties – settling us so easily together. But tonight I knew the charm would be broken and we would be awkward, without enough space, all sharp knees, elbows and my unspoken anger.

CHAPTER 22

Now

Jessie went to watch TV with Rudi, her face distorting as she saw Anna take a packet of chicken from the fridge for dinner. And even so, even though she knew well the girl just wanted to escape from the kitchen, from her, Anna took it as a victory that she hadn't gone back up to her room, or for a run. Every moment she spent downstairs, with them, now, was a victory.

When Jessie had agreed to go back to school, without fuss, the day after her self-prescribed sick day, Anna had felt triumphant, hopeful, as if Jessie had made a choice that could lead her to more choices, good ones, that would accumulate to take her back to the person she had been.

It didn't work out that way. Jessie went back to school – 'It's something to do, for now', she had said, shrugging – and nothing came of it, just the same wary eyes avoiding Anna's, staring at the ground, her hands curled like claws inside the rough sleeves of her outsize hoodies. And yet it was a small weight in the balance of good versus evil, a step towards light, not dark, and Anna celebrated it as such.

She would go days without ideas or hope or any expectations of better, and then she would think she saw some faint glimmer in the dark ahead because Jessie laughed at something Rudi said or finished the small amount of food on her plate, or offered to wash up instead of bolting out of the kitchen the second she was allowed to leave the table.

Now, as she rustled through dinner preparations, chopping and mixing, with the sound of the television, Rudi and Jessie laughing, she thought how like a normal family they seemed, even though 'normal' was another word Alison had tried to get her to stop using.

'There is no normal,' she intoned, in her deep, monotonous voice. 'No single way for people, or families, to be. It's an unhelpful concept.'

'Okay, but pretending it doesn't mean something is unhelpful too,' Anna had said. 'We all have to benchmark ourselves against something, and that something is what we call "normal".'

'So what does it mean to you?' Alison asked, oh-so-predictably.

'Same as to anyone, I suppose. People getting along together and enjoying one another's company. Just basic pleasantness, some kind of shared interest, even if it's only *Eastenders*.'

'And don't you feel you have that?'

'God, no. Not now. We're like people at a station, waiting for the same train but determined not to make eye contact in case we get stuck talking to that person for the journey. There is so much wariness. Except Rudi.' And then, when Alison didn't answer, or ask another question immediately, Anna rushed in with her own. 'Is it because I was embarrassed about breastfeeding her?' she asked, as she had been planning to ask for a long time. She was getting good at this – revelations that weren't revelations, scraps to throw to Alison to keep her happy. Keep her occupied.

'No. But talk to me about that.' Alison was wearing a crisp white shirt with frilled cuffs, which she smoothed down over the backs of her hands. Anna could see that the cuffs pleased her, their starchy frilliness.

'My mother didn't want me to feed her,' she began. 'She said she couldn't see why I'd bother and a bottle would be much easier. But really she meant she couldn't stand the sight of me feeding. She thought it was disgusting. I know she did, because of the way she'd sit, turned away so she didn't catch sight of a breast or, worse, a nipple. And the way she would pass me a blanket or a coat or her cardigan, anything, to make sure I covered up. Poor little Jessie, all bundled up in layers for my mother's benefit. And if my mother was holding her and Jessie spat up, my mother would press her mouth closed, like she was going to vomit because she saw my milk dribbling out of Jessie's mouth. She'd hand Jessie back to me straight away, saying, "I think she needs cleaning up," as if she was a dirty plate. I wonder if that made Jessie think food was something to be ashamed of.'

Alison, instead of responding, engaging with the decoy, as Anna had hoped, changed the subject. 'We're talking about Jessie again, not you,' she said. 'Instead of guessing at the reasons why she does what she does, talk to me about your response to it.'

'I no longer have a response,' Anna said wearily. 'I don't have any more ideas.' Instead, she threw out more random incidents from their past. She plucked moments from the many years of her and Jessie's lives together, and laid them bare. She described the artlessness with which Jessie used to say, 'I'm going to leave on my gymnastics leotard so everyone will ask me what I've been doing and I can tell them I got a medal,' and admitted how secretly embarrassed she was by the way her daughter's thighs and stomach rose out of the pink crushed velvet, how she wished that her teacher could have favoured something discreet and black, but how she'd smiled all the same and said, 'Good plan!' because she didn't want Jessie to feel, as she had so often felt, lesser or too much.

And the way Harriet's mother had bumped into them in the supermarket one day and said, 'Aren't you a fine girl?' to Jessie, in a voice that said what she really meant was 'Aren't you far too big for that tiny leotard?' so that all Jessie's joy in the day had been spoiled and she had looked at Anna in accusation, because Anna should have saved her from it and hadn't.

There were so many such stories. In fact, once Anna started looking, she couldn't find anything else, only specific moments of failure and humiliation that all seemed, now, to have led to this point. A point where her daughter hated her so much that she chose to reject the entire world because Anna was in it. Because that was how Anna read what was happening, and nothing Alison could say would change that.

'I'm all out of ideas,' Anna said again. Except that was just something to say and was no truer than anything else she said to Alison – only a bit true, never entirely true. What hope had words of capturing anything, really, when they were simply flat discs that escaped, to be piled one on top of another?

'Do you want to consider recommitting her?' Alison had asked then, carefully non-judgemental. 'I believe there would be grounds for suggesting another residential stay, if that's what you, as her mother, want.'

'Definitely not,' Anna said, sharp against her own desire for space and peace, for time off from being an endless unwilling witness to Jessie's battle. 'That place is part of the problem. She went in a confused amateur and came out a hardened professional. She learned things there that have only made her worse. I'm not sending her back, no matter what.'

'There are other places,' Alison said, conditioned to keep doors open, possibilities alive.

'No.'

There was silence then, and Anna considered letting it run on until the end of the session, even though it was excruciating for someone like her, conditioned to fill any void with chat and charm. Or maybe she could veer off again, ask Alison more questions about process – 'What if we tried supplementing with magnesium? Massage therapy?' – keep waving the flags of distraction.

Maybe you do need to talk about yourself more. The words, still in Maurice's cautious tones, ran through her. Because of them, and because Alison wanted Jessie back in the place where she had learned all the wrong lessons, Anna blurted out, 'How is it possible that it's not enough to love someone?'

'What do you mean?' Alison sat forward a little.

'You love them so much, and that isn't enough to change you. Make you better.'

'Tell me what you mean by that.'

And because Anna felt by then as if Alison already knew – because that was how Alison operated, always letting on that she knew before you told her, so that telling her became no big deal – she told.

'There were times . . .' was how she began, knowing that she had no end point in her mind.

'Yes?' Alison encouraged, sitting far back again in her armchair, careful not to betray any eagerness, although Anna thought she could see her nearly twitching with excitement.

'Times I sort of lost it. Lost my temper, and myself. When Jessie was very small mostly.'

'Yes,' Alison said again. *Yes, I thought so,* went the speech bubble. *Yes, of course you did.*

'It didn't happen all that often,' Anna said, in a rush. 'But when it did happen, it was bad. I lost it completely.' She remembered the feeling, the anger that came on her from nowhere, a thing with vast jaws that surged up from the depths and closed around her in one swift snap. Then she would start to shout, and even though she saw the fear in Jessie's eyes at the angry punch of her words, she couldn't stop; her daughter just another impediment to rage against. Because the child's fear was so like her own fear – fear that she couldn't keep her safe, protect her from the world or from themselves. Fear of what she could do. Of what she had done. And the sight of that fear, reflected back, maddened her.

'She was much too young when she learned to forgive me for things no one should be forgiven for. "It doesn't matter, Mama," she would say, patting my arm or my face, wherever she could reach.' The memory choked her and she stopped. 'I let her say it, because I needed her to. I thought I could say I was sorry, that I loved her, and somehow it could be as if nothing happened. And she let me, because she was so loving, so kind, when she should have turned her back on me and refused ever to forgive. And now I guess that's exactly what she has done.'

'Many mothers experience frustration and anxiety when their children are small,' Alison said, the careful blandness of her voice in overdrive now.

'Not like that.' Anna refused to take the absolution that was offered. 'It didn't happen very often, but it was enough to show what I'm capable of.'

'Show who? Yourself?'

'No. Jessie. *I* knew already.'

'Where do you think it came from, the anger?'

'I don't know,' Anna said. 'I don't understand.' Even though she did. Suspected, anyway. 'I mean, I know I was on my own with her all the time, a "single mother".' She deliberately put quotes around the words because that was never how she had seen herself. 'I was tired, really tired sometimes, and worried about what would happen to the two of us, but mostly it was fine. She was such a sweet baby, so good, and I loved being with her so much. But . . . '

'Yes?'

'But sometimes . . . it was like I was possessed. Afterwards,

I would hardly remember what had happened, just the feeling of the shouting in my head, the soreness of my throat, and the exhaustion of having used myself all up. I don't understand. I love her so much. Where do you think it came from?'

'Anger can come from many places,' Alison said, voice low and calm in a way that made Anna want to dig her nails into her palms with irritation. 'It can be many things. Fear, anxiety, guilt.'

'Yes,' Anna said. 'I suppose it can.' *Fear, anxiety, guilt,* she thought. Any of them. All of them. 'Does it really matter, though, where it came from?' she asked. 'Surely the point is that it's there. Was there.'

'I believe it matters,' Alison said. 'Can you tell me a little more about those times?'

'Not now,' Anna said. 'I don't really remember.'

Now, hearing Maurice's key in the lock, the satisfied sound it made, Anna laid food on plates. Rice, chicken and mushrooms in a creamy sauce, steamed broccoli and green beans on three plates, just the vegetables and some plain chicken on the fourth. Automatically, she counted the green beans and spears of broccoli as she put them onto Jessie's plate, knowing she would need to recount later when her daughter handed the plate back, and then called, 'Dinner!'

They sat and ate. She and Maurice chatted about their respective days, about a party that weekend that he thought they 'should' go to, and whether anyone they liked would be there. Anna tried to ignore the noises he made as he ate, the chewing, swallowing sounds that she knew were making Jessie flinch, that spoke loudly, rudely, of his untainted enjoyment of his food. Anna hated him for it. If only he could understand that he was part of this too, that it wasn't happening on the sidelines, but on the pitch.

She thought again about allowing Jessie to take her meals upstairs in her bedroom, the way she wanted to. 'I hate people watching me eat,' Jessie had said.

'I'm not watching you,' Anna had protested. 'I just like us all being together.'

'Well, I don't! I hate it, and I don't see why you should always get what you want,' Jessie had said, too weary to be properly angry.

When she looked over now, Anna saw that Jessie had arranged her beans into a neat box shape, inside which she had imprisoned the broccoli, tidy, regular, almost untouched. The four pieces of plain chicken Anna had placed on the plate were now three and she made a mental note to check the radiator behind Jessie when she cleared the table, both because she needed to know what she had eaten, and because before, when Jessie had first started hiding food there, it had taken Anna days to find where the disgusting smell was coming from.

Beside Jessie, Anna saw suddenly, Rudi had done the same thing with his vegetables, the same stockade made of beans, neat barriers behind which the broccoli rested.

'Rudi, eat up,' she said, her voice loud with alarm.

'I'm not hungry,' he said, interrogative, with a glance towards Jessie.

Jessie looked at him, started to smile, then caught sight

of his plate mirroring her own and stopped. 'Rudi,' she said, 'don't be ridiculous. You have to eat.' She said it with a glance towards Anna that was frightened, almost apologetic, and reached out a fork to disrupt Rudi's box-shaped arrangement. 'Eat,' she said, picking up a bean on her fork and lifting it to his mouth. Then, when he accepted it and began chewing, she got up. 'I need to be excused now,' she said.

CHAPTER 23

Jessie

When Jenna stopped talking to me at school, she still messaged me. She told me she had to not talk, that Harriet would kill her if she didn't do what Harriet was doing. I knew what that was like, so I couldn't blame her, but it was weird. At school she wouldn't even look at me, would walk past, with Harriet, as if I was a wall or a bin, and once I got home, the storm of messages would start, always beginning with how sorry she was, then on to things Harriet had said, lessons we'd had, stuff other girls had done and said. At first I would race home and wait for the messages, when I was at Gran's. I'd go back and say hi to Gran and she would ask if I wanted anything to eat and I'd say no I'd just eaten and run up to my room – Anna's old room – to get away from the kitchen because Gran's idea of a snack would be a crumpet with butter, or toast with butter and jam, or a banana sandwich, and I didn't have nearly as much willpower then as I do now because I was just getting started.

I'd go up and wait for Jenna's texts and text her back, pretending I didn't care and I thought it was all pretty funny, and we'd laugh at Harriet behind her back and say the way she'd done her hair that day made her face look like she'd stuffed nuts into her cheeks. And all the time I was waiting and waiting for Harriet to tell me I was forgiven and to talk to me again.

I thought when she did, it would come through Jenna, like a messenger, but in the end it didn't. Harriet just messaged to say *goin shppn@3. comin?* and I messaged back *k.* and that was it. Then when we met she linked her arm through mine and said, 'God, babes, I've missed you. Jenna is so weird. Guess what she did the other day? Zach was totally grossed out . . .' I laughed at what she told me – something about the way Jenna ate noodles – and made faces of disgust and never said a thing about us texting.

And then, when it was all over and I told Anna what Jenna had been like, because I thought it would make her like Jenna more, she was really angry and said that was even worse because Jenna didn't have the guts to stand up for herself or for me. That she was a coward, *un lâche*, she said, in French, which sounded much worse, and made Anna seem like she meant it much more.

So I don't tell her anything about Harriet and Jenna now, about how they're all over me, wanting me to do stuff with them, meet them, hang out, go to their houses. I say no, and I don't tell Anna. Partly it's because I don't care about them any more. But partly it's to protect her too. She'll only get excited and encouraging. 'You should go; it'll be fun. Or they could come here. You could have them on a sleepover. We can order pizza . . .' I can just hear her, all carried away and giddy.

Pizza. As if.

Habits are hard to break. Even now, I can't just cut Anna loose. I still get the feeling that I want to make her happy and stop her getting that look on her face, not the one that used to scare me, the one that upsets me because it's like a different Anna shines through, an Anna who doesn't know what she's doing. That one is scary too but in a different way.

I'm protecting her from Maurice as well. I know she's up to something. She's weird about her phone, pouncing on texts, saying they're from him when they obviously aren't. Looking at them for ages but not answering, and hiding her phone. It's always in her bag now. It used to be out, on the counter or the sofa, and she never had any idea where it was.

'Where's my phone?' she'd yell. 'Help, I've lost it!' We'd all run around, looking, until one of us found it, in the loo or under her pillow or somewhere. Now, she never loses it.

She's up to something. She thinks I don't see because I pretend I'm not looking, but I am. That habit is hard to break too.

Harriet said something to me once. Harriet, who I always think is so dumb, thinking about guys and how big her boobs are. She said, 'It's like you think you're her,' about Anna. I thought she meant it was like I wanted to be like her, which I did then, but Harriet said, 'No. It's that you think you *are* her. Or she's you. That you're the same person.' She said she thought it was because I had no dad and it was just the two of us so that we were mixed up between who was the mother and who was the daughter; who was supposed to take care of whom.

I hated Harriet talking about me having no dad, because sometimes she did it meanly, but not that time. She was just being matter-of-fact. Then she went back to looking at bras online and asking did I think Zach would like that one. I didn't say anything but I sort of knew what she meant. Me and Anna, all wrapped up too tight together.

CHAPTER 24

Now

That night, when Anna woke alone in the spare room, as she so often did now, into the charcoal world of pre-dawn, she found herself without the energy to pick up the whirling bits of worry that flung themselves at her. She couldn't grasp them, sort them, tidy and subdue them, as she usually would. They were beyond her now.

What had she let loose, talking to Alison? And where was she supposed to go with it now?

There was an alternative. She'd done it before, so she knew she could do it again. She could run. Cut her losses, and run. Run to Andrew, the clean slate, the unknown. She knew he'd take her. She could leave all the bad stuff behind – the failure with Maurice, the greater failure with Jessie. Just like the last time, she could start again. Wipe them out, pretend they'd never happened. Find another man. Another rescue. Another placard for her mother to wave, but this one wouldn't read 'Knight in Shining Armour', it would be 'Home Wrecker'.

Maybe she could take Rudi, she thought. He wasn't one of her failures. But he will be, she knew: if I do this, I'll just push the rot into his future, and then I'll have to face it all again, only bigger and worse.

You can't always run away, she told herself. No matter how much you want to.

She had begun to learn that the hard way. Because talking to Alison, saying aloud what she had never before dared to say, had brought her a different understanding of it. The chapters of her life did not close as neatly as she had thought. The summer of Jessie's conception wasn't, after all, a page turned and sealed off.

She had started Jessie's life weighed down by a millstone of guilt that she had ignored, even denied. But the guilt had succeeded in making her pay anyway, hedging her around with constant small anxieties that erupted into occasional hot rages. They were the legacy of denial. In trying so hard not to be the person she had been during the summer she'd got pregnant, Anna had made up a new version of herself, but so imperfectly, with cracks and leaks everywhere.

Why was her daughter suddenly asking about the First Jessie now? What did she mean when she said she'd been talking to her? Why the questions about what had happened? Anna didn't understand, but she felt uneasy and found herself listening hard to the silent house. For what? For the creakings and light thuddings that would tell her Jessie was disturbed and moving around? The girl slept badly, often wandering around the house in the dark, as if looking for something, disoriented enough to ask 'What? What?' in tones of sharp alarm, when Anna intercepted her on the stairs or in the sitting room. Or was she listening for the mutterings and rumblings that would betray someone who shouldn't be there?

She found herself thinking about First Jessie in a way she hadn't for a long time – not as someone locked in the past, a person finished, caught in the forever fly trap that was death, but as someone with reach and momentum, with changing moods and ways. Who would she be? What would their friendship now be if they had got through that summer together? She realised, with a sudden cold jolt, that she had, for these fifteen years, cast Jessie in the light she needed to see her – warm and loving and understanding – but that there might be another version, an angry, vengeful Jessie. And into her mind came Jessie's face, not with the bright smile and sparkling eyes Anna usually saw when she remembered her, but with a hard black stare and twitching, clutching fingers. A Jessie who had given enough and wanted something in return.

The picture frightened her and she told herself that her agitated imaginings were the understandable product of worry and strain. Jessie was dead, and raking back through that story would help no one.

She turned and lay flat on her stomach, arms stretched out in a V above her head in an effort to get back to sleep. She had a big meeting in just six hours – a junior minister she knew slightly who had been accused of sexual harassment by a woman he had worked with at least ten years earlier. It was the firm's first big piece of political work, and Andrew was incredibly excited. 'This will make our name,' he had said to her, when the call had come in. 'It'll lift us out of the world of commerce, and get us into political strategy, government campaigns, public policy.' The words, as he said them, rolled around in his mouth, like a boiled sweet. 'We need to blow them away tomorrow,' he had said to them all later, at an office meeting. 'I want everyone on their A-game.'

Light, Anna saw, came in differently through the spare-room windows, fuzzy orange gleams from the wrong places, casting shadows she wasn't used to, so that sleep stayed away, mocking at the edge of her grasp, always out of reach. First Jessie's face moved in and out, alternating between love and anger so that Anna was confused and frightened.

She switched rooms, getting in beside Maurice for the warmth of his heavy sleeping bulk that now seemed reassuring rather than infuriating, but even that didn't work. Jessie's face spun inside her mind, a face filled with spite and hate. Only when dawn came and the room was filled with light, instead of sliding shadows, could she see her fears for what they were: silly, inconsequential.

She got up and went to make tea, then woke Maurice with a cup, and laughed off the look of surprise and caution on his face as he asked, 'Why?'

'Because I was up, and I felt like it,' she said, leaning forward to kiss the side of his face, carefully up near his ear in case he misread and thought she wanted his mouth.

'Okay,' he said, still cautious. 'Thanks.'

She went to call Rudi, who rolled farther up inside his duvet, like a little woodlouse disturbed under a rock. 'Come on, bug,' she said, 'time to get up. You've got art today. You like that.'

'Okay,' he said sleepily. As long as she could find something – art, sport, a playdate, pancakes for breakfast – to persuade him that getting up would be worth his while, he was cheerful enough, in his black-and-yellow Batman pyjamas.

'Jessie,' she called up the stairs, 'time to get up.' Silence. 'Jessie,' she called again, 'come on, it's time. I'm going in early, so I can drop you. But you need to get up now.'

But Jessie ignored her so Anna had to walk up the stairs. She was up, sitting in her bed, back against the wall, duvet pulled around her. Her hair was matted and grey-looking in the morning light and she was still wearing the T-shirt she had worn for bed. It said 'Clown Princess' above a picture of a ragdoll. Anna had washed and folded the T-shirt the day before, putting it into Jessie's cupboard. She would, she knew, be washing it again that evening.

'I'm not going,' Jessie said.

'Jessie, not this again,' Anna said, but mechanically. She was already preparing to concede, walk down the stairs and away, because she knew she didn't have time to fight it, could no longer see what she was fighting for, and knew she wouldn't win. 'Why?' she asked, in order to say something, but not too much. 'Is it because of Harriet's mother?'

'God, no,' Jessie said, with disdain.

'Well?'

'I don't feel like it, and it's a waste of time.'

Anna started to say, 'Right, and you're so busy,' in withering tones, then caught sight of Jessie's foot, poking through the end of the duvet she had dragged up to her waist, and stopped. It was bluish, the skin so dry it was scaly, like the foot of a delicate reptile, the nails thick and yellow.

She wondered would Jessie begin to grow hair all over her body, like a little monkey, the way some did, and how she, Anna, would feel then. The same, she supposed: repulsed, furious, infinitely tender.

'It's called lanugo, and it doesn't always happen,' Alison had said, when Anna had broached it. 'It's usually in more advanced cases than Jessie's. It's the body's way of protecting itself from heat loss, or creating a layer of insulation.'

'Like growing its own blanket?' Anna had asked.

'Something like that, yes.'

'How disgusting.'

But Alison had refused to be drawn. Refused to admit that there was, too, a horrible bodily component to this most existential of ailments, the slow abstraction of being to non-being. That alongside the shy demand for less and less space in the world, there was a place of rancid breath, and urine that smelt sickeningly of fruit tea, so that sometimes you recoiled, thrust back by the instinct in all living things to shun death, even when it takes up lodgings in someone you have sworn to protect.

Alison preferred to stay in the realm of 'How does that make you feel?' and 'What would that look like?' than tread outwards into less equivocal territory.

The foot – Jessie's foot, Anna reminded herself – looked lifeless, as if unconnected to a body or blood supply. It seemed heavy and hopeless, as if no effort would be enough to lift it. Staring at it, Anna remembered the wonder of those tiny feet the night Jessie was born, the way the light shone through them, translucent and rosy, lit by the same fire that ran through the small body, so that even though she was fragile, she was also sturdy, wriggling and demanding.

Those feet and the feel of them, cupped in Anna's hand in the first hours of her daughter's life, so completely trusting, had given her back a link she had thought was lost. A reason not just to live but to live with vigour and all the joy she was capable of. How hard it was now to see all that determined babyish thrust come to this, the slow rejection of everything, a slipping out and away.

She wanted her baby back, not this pale, bitter girl, who watched her and judged her and found her so lacking. She wanted her baby, the cheerful child, who looked up at her with love unclouded, like the sun, like water flowing to the sea, merry and certain. Until even that became complicated.

And so, instead of fighting or making demands or issuing conditions, Anna just said, 'I'd better show you how to put on the heat if you're staying at home.'

She did not speak the words that ran through her head, each one as harsh and distinct as a hammer on nail heads: *I will save you. I will save you, whether you want it or not.*

On the way to work, she considered again the previous night – Rudi's mimicry of Jessie's plate; her daughter's reaction. It was, Anna decided, a good sign, something to prove that she wasn't yet, no matter how much she pretended to be, beyond them.

The junior minister arrived looking drawn, with his advisors and a lawyer. He kissed Anna politely on the cheek, and they spent a moment discussing mutual acquaintances before the meeting – the war council, as Anna thought of it – began.

'Right,' she said, as Andrew sat down and nodded to her. 'I think it's pretty clear what we do here.' They looked at her expectantly, and Anna enjoyed, momentarily, the feeling of being in control. The office was the only place where she felt that now, and even there only occasionally.

'This is one woman's word about an incident that may, or may not,' she held up a hand to silence the junior minister who had opened his mouth, presumably to protest his innocence, 'have happened. There is no evidence of what she claims. I think we,' she had noticed how well clients responded to 'we', feeling supported by the firm's reputation, 'issue a statement in which we offer sympathy to a woman so obviously in distress, but also, clearly, state that these things did not happen. And we don't give any interviews.'

She sat back, looked around the table, expecting nods, even smiles, and saw only shock. There was a pause that seemed to go on forever.

'Anna, did you not see the news this morning?' Andrew asked, tight and still.

'I was busy,' Anna said defiantly, heart sinking. 'Why?'

'Two other women have come forward, with similar allegations.' This was one of the advisors, clipped, angry. He all but slammed his mug onto the table.

'This isn't about issuing statements any more,' Andrew said. 'This has moved on. We are in a different space entirely.' He couldn't meet her eyes.

The junior minister sat silently, waiting for his fate to be decided, for those around him to spring to his defence or throw him overboard. He was like a child, Anna thought, in the headmaster's office, with a debate conducted over his head, in language he didn't understand, waiting only to be told that he had survived or lost.

'Right,' she said, dredging furiously, ransacking the furthest reaches of her mind for something that would save the firm, save her. Something that would reinforce her reputation for brilliance, competence, for being a safe pair of hands. The kind of thing she would have found without trouble a year ago. Nothing came. 'Well, we . . .' She petered out humiliatingly, dropped her eyes to the table, to her hands, trembling slightly beside her coffee cup, allowing Andrew to step into the jagged breach and try to cover the damage. He did it, but only after giving her a look.

'The first thing is to get some background on these women,' he said. 'And we need to understand the specifics, dates, times, all that . . .' He was off, proffering not solutions but delaying tactics, things that would buy them another hour, another day, when something else altogether might save them.

It was a tactic she had schooled him in: when there's nothing to be done, buy time. Create small diversions and wait it out, because in this world anything can happen. Tomorrow might bring war, an election, a bigger scandal, a freak storm. If you can buy time, you can win, she had told him, no matter how bad things look. But if you run out of time, allow yourself to be raced through it, you're finished.

It was, she realised, listening to him, good advice. The gamble was that time would also allow your enemies to mobilise, to produce something so dreadful that nothing would make it go away. But it was a gamble worth playing to.

And, she understood, this was the same approach she used with her daughter. Buy another day, another hour, another minute. Buy time in the belief that time would work some magic that Anna couldn't, could present Jessie with proof that life was worth the undoubted effort. That *she* was worth the effort.

Except that time, she began to feel, was running out for Jessie. Maybe for her too. She put away the thought.

She wondered would Andrew remember that these were *her* insights, that it was her teaching he was now offering. She assumed not, and considered how she might remind him.

The junior minister and his crew left, with a farewell to Anna which was far chillier than the greeting. The office stepped lightly around her, giving her space and distance. Except Andrew.

'We need to talk,' he said, walking into his office where she had no choice but to follow him.

'What the fuck was that?' he said, closing the door, but not fast enough for his words not to be heard by those in the open-plan area. Anna saw a girl called Brenda flinch. It reminded her of just how hard she had worked to become the person she was now, how she had dragged herself from fear and uncertainty and a strong desire to begin every sentence with an apology – 'I'm sorry, but can I just ask . . .' How she had taught herself to believe that she was someone, even when her upbringing had told her she wasn't. She pushed back her shoulders and turned to Andrew.

'That was a fuck-up,' she said, almost accusatory. 'A proper fuck-up. And don't say you've never had one yourself.' He mumbled something, and she knew she had him. 'I fucked it up, and I'm sorry.' She made sure she didn't sound it. 'No one is more furious about this than me.' That was probably true but, conveniently, it also stole more ground from under Andrew's feet. 'I had a busy morning, and I didn't catch the updates. I don't know why no one thought we should spend five minutes together before going into that meeting, under the circumstances.' She allowed a faint accusation into her voice. 'I don't know why you didn't mention it in your texts.' That, she knew, would silence him. They never spoke about the texts or, indeed, anything that happened outside the office. She never let him. If she didn't talk about it, it hadn't happened.

'I presumed you knew.' He sounded guilty and sulky now, rather than outraged. She was winning, just as she'd known she would. He was ruthless, yes, but not invulnerable.

'And I should have known,' she continued, more gently, 'but as I say, it was a busy morning.'

'Anna, I know you're under pressure right now, and if you need time—' Andrew began, but she couldn't bear to let him have that. Whatever there was between them, it must have nothing to do with Jessie, her family.

'It's nothing to do with that.' She let silence fall, and the Keep Out sign to flash between them. Then she changed tack: 'Just between you and me, I got a call last night, from someone . . . well, let's just say, if you think our JM' – their code for the junior minister – 'has it bad, you should hear what's rattling in this guy's cupboard, and he has a whole lot more to lose. A whole lot.' She was making it up as she went along, stringing a story that would suit her purpose, buy her time until something real came along to save her.

'Who?' He was caught, reeled right in. 'Who is it?'

'I can't tell you yet, there's too much riding on it. I can't tell you anything about it until I do some more digging. It might come to nothing' – she flipped her hand to convey that it would certainly come to something – 'but I'm going to see him this afternoon. If it ends up with us, it'll be big.'

Andrew gazed at her with admiration and relief. She knew very well that he believed her because he had the habit of believing her, and because he wanted to believe her.

'Don't worry about Simons' – the JM. 'I'll ring him later. I'll tell him enough that he'll understand. And by the way,' she turned back at the door, threw over her shoulder, 'nice use of the buy-time strategy. Always works.' It was the subtle reminder that the strategy was hers. She made sure to be laughing as she left his office, then to wave back and say, 'I'll ring you later. I'll let you know how it goes,' because she knew the entire office was watching.

CHAPTER 25

Jessie

Everyone has a special talent. That's what they used to tell us in school. I decided it was a lie – just more of the nonsense they tell you – because I didn't have one. Now I do.

I'm good at this. I've never been much good at anything before – not school or art or sport, just okay – but this I can do well. Except for the start, I've had hardly any lapses. I don't fuck up. I don't binge and tell myself I'll make up for it later. I don't collapse and pour stuff into myself until it comes back up again, still cramming in as it comes out, the flow of food one way meeting the flow of sick the other. Isolde says she's seen girls do this and they're crying and it's so disgusting that, if it was her, she couldn't live with herself. I don't think she's great at living with herself anyway, but that's not the point.

She says she used to do it, and told me about the burning in your throat as the sick comes up and the burning in your tummy that makes you carry on forcing food down. She says it's like a hand coming up from your stomach, along your throat and reaching out of your mouth to pull the food into you. Ice-cream and pink wafer biscuits and tinned peaches and cream and custard, like some kind of insane trifle: that's what Isolde remembers.

I can see how it might happen but I don't let it happen to me, and when I read what other girls have written about it, I write 'Stay strong' underneath, but I feel a bit smug and want to tell them I never do it.

Sometimes my tummy feels so angry and empty that I think it will suck all of me into itself and swallow me. Like the way a volcano might suck a mountain down into it so that all that would be left would be a hot ember. Like that painter whose pictures Anna showed me once, a guy called Bosch, who drew bladders and stomachs with legs and nothing else, walking around. That's what I feel like some days, but other days, other times, I feel so strong and free. Like I'm free of the stuff that holds everyone else back, that chains them to their disgusting bodies, which order them around, forcing them to eat, to shit, to go here and there, like a monkey on a string.

In my sleep or maybe in the moment that I wake, Other Jessie is there and she's counting the knobs on my spine, brushing her fingers down my back, pausing at each bony hump, swirling the tip of her finger over it, and whispering to me. I think she's saying, 'I'm here, I'm here,' to comfort me but then I realise it's 'She's here.'

Who's here?

She leans over behind me so her mouth is near my ear and her breath smells bad and she's breathing and whispering and

I can't move, until suddenly I can and she's gone. But only over to the other side of the room where she sits in a corner, watching me.

The way she sits, she's doing the broken-leg pose, same as Anna is in that photo, except with Other Jessie you can tell it's real: the legs really are broken, or so bent and crumpled that they don't hold her up properly. She's like a bundled-up bunch of old clothes with different bits of body in them that don't add up to the full thing. She's wearing a red T-shirt with a target printed on it, like a bullseye, except the red has soaked into the white of the target, so it's wonky.

They say that if you die in your dreams, you die in real life too. Is that true? I need to know if it is.

CHAPTER 26

Now

Defiant getaway carried off successfully and safely in her car, Anna wrapped her arms tight around, trying to hug some kind of conviction back into herself. What the hell was she going to do now? The enormity of the lie she had told Andrew shocked her, even though she had quickly decided she had no other choice, and that she had to trust that, somehow, it would all come right.

But why had she tied herself further to Andrew with this complicity, this stupid thing that might blow up in her face? Because if it did, he would have to choose whether to sack her or stand by her, which would force into the open everything they never spoke of. The texts that came late, unasked for, often just a question – *Now? Tonight?* – or a question mark. Sometimes she answered them, sometimes she didn't. Sometimes she diverted from a plan made, to see a friend, a film, and went to him, even though, once there, they didn't speak much, just sat in long silences so that Anna wondered why she'd come.

She rang Jessie, in case there was some way to tell her so that she would see the funny side of Anna's lie, the dreadful hilariousness of it, as she once would have, but she didn't answer. What did she do, Anna wondered, all alone in the house? She tried to imagine Jessie moving around, maybe watching TV or reading, but she could come up with no images, except of Jessie in bed, dozing in the lizard-like state that conserved her energy and heat. What, Anna wondered again, had she meant by saying she was talking to Jessie, to Anna's Jessie?

Because she had time – on her fictitious errand from the office – and because she couldn't bear to go home, or sit in a café, or meet her mother, Anna went to the place where she and her friend used to go together: the tumbledown sea wall where they had sat, legs swinging over the side, dangling down towards the water, and talked about themselves. This was where they had told secrets as children, after the short walk from Jessie's house, from which an even shorter walk would bring them to Anna's house.

Once they were old enough to be allowed to go alone, they would bring enough money for bags of crisps – cheese and onion for her, salt and vinegar for Jessie 'And no sharing!' – then sit, sometimes for hours, chatting and laughing, whispering about people who passed by or who waited for the DART below them.

This was where they talked about boys they fancied, girls they disliked, things they planned to do, the fact that Anna's parents barely spoke to each other, and all the other bits and pieces of their growing up that overlapped and intertwined, like ivy, across their lives.

They came here when they fought – and they did, of course, sometimes even physically, pushing each other when they got cross, until one pushed too hard and hurt the other so that they instantly said sorry, or until they made each other laugh with the pushing, and forgot what had caused the fight. On the days when they were still fighting, they sat silently, apart, until something – a lady struggling up the hill on a bike, in the teeth of the sea wind so that she seemed to stay still; a dog they wanted to befriend; a man who called something to them – made them draw together, close the gap between them and resume the friendship that was the best thing either had.

'I'm not saying sorry but you don't have to either,' Anna would blurt, before Jessie started to forgive her. Jessie was always the one to forgive first, which made Anna feel bad sometimes because she wasn't usually the one to start the quarrel. That was Anna, and she did it for reasons that had nothing to do with Jessie. A fight with her mother, a question from her father that revealed his indifference to her beyond her academic life, a girl at school who had been mean – those were the things she brought with her that made her spiky and resentful so that she threw Jessie's greeting back at her or found fault with a plan she'd suggested. Those were the reasons they fought, or simply because Anna was jealous of the warmth and love Jessie stepped out of to meet her, into which she would return, while Anna went home to something colder and more remote.

How old was she when she realised she was jealous? she thought now, as she bought a bottle of water from the newsagent in the DART station and crossed the footbridge to the wall. Maybe ten, when she began to understand that the delight she felt at being with Jessie in her house, surrounded by her family, also came with pain.

She hoisted herself up on the wall, noting that she hadn't been there in years, although she had spent so much time there when she was pregnant: sitting, staring, listening to the waves that came and went. It had always been a church for her and the First Jessie: a place to pray and think and talk, to tell each other secrets and hopes that were even more secret, pledging their faith to the world and to each other – 'This is what we will be like. This is what we will do, how we will be.' She had broken nearly all those promises, she realised now. One by one she had unknotted them, abandoned them or chucked them away. Nothing was left of the future she and Jessie had painted for themselves and each other, except her daughter. In her, everything they had dimly felt about what mattered had come true. And now her daughter was being taken, dragged out of sight by an undertow that couldn't be seen, that showed only in the ripples and disturbed surfaces of Jessie's skin: the knobbly joints and loosened hinges of hip, elbow, ankle, the ragged surface pitted by tiny bumps and pimples.

'I'm so sorry, Jessie,' she prayed now. 'I'm so sorry. I'm so sorry.' She gabbled the words silently. 'I'm so sorry, but please don't do this. Don't make me do this.' First Jessie had never been vindictive, always in a rush to forgiveness, but who knew what she was like now, after all these years?

It was so long since Anna had dialled that number, but her fingers found it again without hesitation, walking their way through the digits. Would it even work? Did anyone have a landline any more? It worked, ringing for a long time so that Anna saw the telephone in her mind, shrilling from the little table in the crowded hall with its worn carpet, the excess of coats and hats on a battered stand.

'Hello?' The voice was fainter but still crisp.

'Margaret, it's Anna. I'm round the corner. Can I come and see you?'

The house was the same but emptier. The curtains and carpets framed rooms that no longer carried the clutter of a large family in a small space. The coats and hats in the hall were gone, except for two, and the kitchen no longer spilled cups, glasses and plates from the confines of over-full cupboards.

'Will you have tea?' Margaret asked. She had shown neither surprise nor pleasure at Anna's arrival, had treated her with a matter-of-factness that could have admitted her right to disappear from their lives for so many years, or been a reproach. It was hard to tell.

She moved around the kitchen preparing tea and Anna could see, in the way she did so, that there was still a space around her, where Jessie should have been, and that she made room for her, even though she wasn't there. It was the way Anna unconsciously made room for her own daughter, who used to take up space and now didn't.

'How are you?' Margaret asked cautiously. 'How is your mother?'

'Fine, great – she's well. Same as ever.'

'And your father?'

'More or less the same.' She wished she could stop saying that things were 'the same' when for Margaret they weren't and never would be. 'He complains more than he used to, and it's hard for my mother to leave him alone now, even for short periods. He doesn't like to be left with anyone else and he won't stay on his own, even though I'm sure he could. What about Mr McDermott?' Jessie's mother had been 'Margaret' ever since Anna was a child, while her father had always been 'Mr McDermott'.

'He's in a home now – has been for years. It got so he couldn't be left at all. Always looking for Jessie, walking round the house in the middle of the night, calling for her, falling over things because he wouldn't put the lights on in case he disturbed her.'

Anna said nothing because there was nothing she could say. She reached out a hand and squeezed Margaret's arm, then took her hand away again quickly, before it could become an affront.

'He still asks for her,' Margaret continued. 'Still talks about her as if she's here. It's the cruellest thing. Or maybe it isn't,' she corrected herself. 'He gets to live as if she's still with him. There's that. I used to think he could see her – the way he talked to her like she was right there with him, carrying on a conversation as easy as they ever were when she'd come back from school or work and sit on the arm of his chair and chat about her day. He always wanted to know every single thing, and she, bless her, she would tell him. And when his mind started to go, she'd tell him again and again, as many times as he asked, and never be impatient or give a shorter version because it was the third or fourth time she'd said it. "He just needs to feel that he knows what's happening, Mam," she'd say. "I don't mind how many times I tell him, once he feels that.'"

'What kinds of things does he say to her now?' Anna asked, even though the back of her neck was washed over with cold at the thought of Mr McDermott talking, talking, talking to someone who was no longer there.

'Any old stuff – things he said he'd read in the newspaper, although he hasn't read a paper in years, sporting stuff from the telly. But it's the way he talks to her, turning his eyes and his face, like he's keeping track of someone moving around the room, stopping and listening for replies, then answering as if she's asked him a question.'

'It must be very hard for you,' Anna said, because she had no idea what else to say. She hated the hopeless inadequacy of the words. Hard?' Was that really what it was when your beloved daughter went on a holiday to be with her best friend and only the broken shell of her body came home? Was it the word for fifteen years of half-life in which only habit and duty, perhaps, kept you from screaming, until your throat tore itself into silence, for a child you had borne and loved and protected and watched with a self-replenishing joy that filled like a fountain and poured right down over the cupped hands of your life, bathing everything in its miracle? Hard?

She had understood some of Margaret's pain when Jessie died, more still once her own Jessie was born, and now, finally, as her daughter moved beyond her reach, she began to feel the full weight of it.

There in that kitchen, through which she could still have moved with ease if blindfolded, Anna saw the terrible symmetry of what was upon her.

In that house where so little had changed – she knew that if she went upstairs, she would find Jessie's things, her clothes, books and hairbrush, all waiting, in case a mistake had been made; in case the last fifteen years had been a terrible dream; in case Jessie was coming back – she understood that the past was still beside her, and that she owed it.

'A few weeks ago he stopped doing that,' Margaret said. 'He told me Jessie was gone on somewhere, to someone else, and then he didn't say anything more about her. He hardly speaks at all now, except he keeps thanking me for things I haven't done. "Thank you. Thank you," when I've done nothing at all. The doctors said this would probably happen, that there are different phases. I didn't realise how much I would miss the sound of him talking to her,' she said. 'I didn't know it would feel like losing her all over again.' And then, when Anna said nothing, 'Is there anything of hers you wanted to take with you? Her things are all upstairs.'

'I have her name,' Anna said. 'Well, my daughter does.'

'That's right,' Margaret said. 'You do have her name. Your Jessie does. I hope my Jessie will look after her.'

Hearing Jessie's mother speak those words, Anna felt a prickle of horror, because finally she knew that, for all these years, she had been moving Jessie's mouth like a ventriloquist doll to say, 'I forgive you. I forgive you,' and now that she listened and moved nothing, she understood that what Jessie actually said was 'I don't forgive you.'

That evening, Anna went through her emails, dealing with the usual invitations, photocalls, pompous press notices, by sending to each a polite no, then checked Facebook, where her mother had a habit of tagging her in things in which she had no interest, getting annoyed if Anna didn't respond.

There, curled like a claw among the various notices for autumn wreath-making workshops and mind-body-spirit events, was a message, monstrous in its few abrupt lines of French: *Hi, Anna, it has been a long time, I'm sorry. But I would like now to be in touch with you. And with my daughter. Some things have happened to make me understand that I must change my behaviour. Can you telephone me?*

A string of numbers, and that was it. Those few short lines, their meaning ambiguous for all the outward brevity. What could have changed, Anna wondered, to convert a flat No into this Yes, which came at her like a rock flung from on high, gathering speed across fifteen silent years so that it slammed into her with such force that she had to sit down?

She remembered so well their last conversation. The look of embarrassment and what might have been disgust on his face when she'd told him, the immediate leap he had made to 'How do you know . . .' that had floored her with its banal predictability, the squeamishness with which he had listened when she explained how she knew, a question of blood and timing, the polite regret with which he had outlined the many reasons why he couldn't get involved, and his insistence that this would not be a good idea for either of them, followed by the appalled revelation that she was an Irish Catholic and therefore the way out he proposed might not be as easy as he had expected.

'Surely you don't think like that,' he had asked, bending towards getting her to say that, no, of course she didn't, that she was modern, a grown-up, someone sensible and expedient. 'Surely there is a better time, later, for you to have a baby.' A time that didn't have him in it, she knew he was thinking.

'It's too late,' she had said. 'My parents are here. They know. They would never permit it.'

At that, he had accepted defeat, and gone into retreat.

'So you will be leaving soon?' he had said, with no effort to disguise his relief. 'I will call you before you go.' He hadn't. She had known he wouldn't, that he wasn't meant to. He belonged there, on his own, nowhere with her.

Clearest of all, she remembered she had been so shocked still, while telling him that she had shivered uncontrollably at times, her body shuddering through the stages of grief, from denial to terrified acceptance and back again, all within minutes, so that she was permanently exhausted, as though she had run a race only to be disqualified and made to run again on legs that bounced sickeningly beneath her. How the news of Jessie's death had been so very swiftly followed by knowledge of the pregnancy that the two were lodged together in her mind.

She remembered, too, her parents, smug within the walls of their self-righteous disappointment and shock. How they had asked what her plans were, as if they could not be expected to have any real part in those plans. When she had told them 'He doesn't want to know', they had accepted it instantly, with grim pleasure. Of course he didn't want to know. How quickly they had moved to ensure that he had no part to play. They had never been in touch with him, had never suggested communicating with his parents, or even making sure he could get in touch with them, should he ever want to. They had taken Anna, her news and her beaten-up confusion, and brought her home, where she had begun to wonder if she had dreamed the entire summer, even as the living proof that she hadn't grew larger and larger inside her.

And now, when Jessie was so fragile that it felt as though a loud noise might break her, here he was, trying to effect a return.

What must she do?

She had no idea, but she had to do something, because she could feel him approaching, feel him tearing through the space between them.

It's her was the thought that sprang to her. *Jessie is doing this. For revenge.* But how could a dead girl do anything? She stared down the thought for the nonsense it so clearly was, and tried to ignore the way it prickled her.

Because if that was true, anything could be true. For Anna, the important thing was that not everything could be true. Not everything – just the things she told herself, the story she stuck to.

She got up to clean the kitchen, to order and organise

around her, then texted Bet – *It's Anna. Can we talk? Something's happened* – and sent it into the empty distance, through the years in which they hadn't spoken. How long? Four anyway, maybe five. They had tried to stay in touch but it hadn't worked out. The things they didn't, couldn't, talk about dwarfed the things they did and could, like icebergs looking over tiny ships, Anna thought, silent and menacing, until eventually it was easier to stop altogether.

Bet rang promptly, almost as if she had been waiting.

'Anna. How nice.' Her voice, still surprisingly deep, was a jolt, a reminder as no photo could ever be of those long-gone nights and the dust of their peculiar doings. It was also, now, distinctly London. Bet had married an Englishman and moved to London where, despite her lack of a degree, she worked for a production company that made scripted reality shows, featuring oddities – the very posh, the very religious, the very bigoted.

'Bet, I'm sorry. I don't mean to drag you into this but—'

'It's him, isn't it?'

'Yes.'

'Thought so. He messaged me a few days ago, wanted to check how he could get in touch with you. He's married now, just had a kid, a boy. I told him I wouldn't help; he'd have to figure it out for himself.' She sounded proud of herself. 'I guess this means he did?'

'Yes. Facebook.'

'Bloody Facebook. May as well run up a flag visible from all corners of the earth to say, "I'm over here!" So, what did he want?'

'He wants to see Jessie. My daughter.' As if there could be any confusion.

'Jesus. Now? After all these years?'

'Yes.'

There was silence then as they both thought about the years, and what they meant.

'She's, what, thirteen?'

'Nearly fifteen, used to not having him in her life and doing fine without him.' She was defiant.

'And yet he's her father.'

'That's a technicality at this stage.'

'Maybe . . . but there's a brother now too. Half-brother anyway. Why not let him get in touch with her? I'm sure it won't amount to much.'

'That's part of the problem. She doesn't need that kind of disruption, not now. Someone entering her life only to leave it again.' It was true, but it was, as she had said, only part of the problem. The real problem was that if he spoke to her, knew her, he would tell her what Anna had done, and she would know, and then, Anna saw, she would lose her. Really lose her. For good.

'What does he do now, anyway?' Curiosity, and maybe something else, got the better of her.

'He's a financial consultant, would you believe? Weirdly good at it, too. Loaded, I think. I haven't seen him in a while, but we half-stay in touch and whenever I go back to Brussels, which is less and less often now that my parents aren't there any more, we have a drink or something. He married some rich Belgian girl. He's practically native now.' She said it with amused contempt.

'And do you see . . . anyone else when you go back?' She couldn't stop herself, even though she knew perfectly well she needed to leave those doors the way they were: closed, inaccessible.

'No one else there to see,' Bet said. 'They've all moved away, or disappeared. Scattered to the winds. You know about Pierre, of course' – Anna did know, because Bet had told her, some years before. His mother had died, and Pierre, Bet said, had become 'very strange'. She had said it with curiosity, not pity. 'Alec met him, shuffling around the street in pyjamas like a zombie.' Later, Anna had heard, Pierre had died. She had cried then, far more than she had expected.

'I'm sure I could find traces of the others if I tried,' Bet asked now. Her voice and insinuation were sly.

'God, no, just idle curiosity. How's Marina?' She changed tack quickly.

'She's good, I think. I hardly see her any more either. Far too grand for us.'

Marina, to Anna's secret astonishment, had married a man who turned out to be a count – 'An Italian count. Papal,' Bet had said, 'hardly counts.' Then laughed hard at her own joke, repeating it, 'The hardly count,' until Anna had laughed too, or pretended to. She had moved with him to an estate and a beautiful old house in the hills outside Florence, then thrown herself into having children and raising horses.

'So what should I do?'

'I don't know . . . it's tough. Because if you just ignore him, he'll find her himself, just as he found you.'

CHAPTER 27

Then

The days of Jessie's visit wore on. They were like a nightmare in which I swung between loving and hating her: my friend, my enemy, friend, enemy. I wondered where the swinging would stop, because it had to. I knew I couldn't keep it up. That I was breaking up, breaking apart.

I felt sick, a nausea that came in waves, bringing dizziness with it that I blamed on heat so relentless that even the darkest churches were soaked in it, their interiors, which should have been cool, muffled in a stifling blanket. My mind ran itself ragged, like a rat in a trap, always and only on him. My skin craved him, my arms were empty without him. Wherever he was in a room, I turned towards him.

Since that summer I've read about cults and how they operate, limiting food and sleep, repetitive movements and chanting, drugs, the imposition of routine, the threat of outside danger. Unwittingly, I guess, we replicated those

286

exact conditions. No wonder I was dazed. No wonder I'd sleepwalked into an obsession I believed was something holy. No wonder.

It makes me laugh, almost, to think how neatly, all unknowing, I mirrored the conditions, by instinct alone. I couldn't have set myself up better if I'd tried.

Jessie worked so hard at first to step between me and my obsession, but she couldn't because she was now a part of it. She was the obstacle, so I moved to dismantle her.

Mostly I was hostile and suspicious with her, then sometimes I was myself again, but not for very long and never when any of the others were around. And I arranged it so they nearly always were, so that Jessie and I were rarely on our own together for long, because I couldn't bear it.

I got up in the morning and left the flat while she was still asleep. By the time we met up in the afternoons, I would have called in the camouflage of others, but even when I wasn't with her, I couldn't stop the gnawing wondering: what did she do when I was at work? Where was she? Most of all, who was she with?

I wouldn't willingly let her out of my sight. When she suggested she go somewhere, take a trip and visit another city, I protested violently.

'I need to keep you safe,' I said, because of how much I wanted to hurt her, thrust her from me, to lose her in the narrow cobbled streets. I dreamed of taking her to Bruges or Ghent and leaving her, like in a fairytale, unable to find her way back. And I would have done it, except I did not trust her not to reappear, a puzzled smile on her face, after a day, a week, two weeks, saying, 'I'm sorry! I lost you! It took me so long to find my way, but I'm here now.'

I promised her we would go together 'in a few days', days that never came because, as long as Nico was there, I couldn't leave.

I wore myself out. Bet, I soon saw, was as tired of my obsession as I was. 'You should just fuck him and get it over with,' she said, one evening, watching me watch Nico, who was playing pinball with Marina.

'What?' I whirled round to her, shocked.

'Nico. You should just fuck him and get it over with.'

'I already did,' I said.

'Oh. Right. Oh dear.' Bet was clearly delighted. 'So now what are you going to do? Aleah's coming back in a couple of days . . . And Jessie's here now, but she'll be gone soon. Well, this is a mess.' She sounded delighted.

'It's not,' I said, through gritted teeth. 'It's fine. It's not a car crash, Bet, to gawp at. There's nothing to see. And anything you think you do see, you've made it up.'

'Okay,' she said. 'Whatever you say.'

'I'm worried about you,' Jessie said, a few days after that. We were alone together, as I tried so hard for us not to be. 'You don't eat, you don't sleep, you drink way too much, and you take drugs like you need them, not just for fun any more.'

'I don't need them. I just take them.'

'Well, they can't be doing you any good.'

'"Leave nothing on the pitch,"' I quoted wryly. It was what our hockey coach used to say when we were kids – 'Leave nothing on the pitch': do your best, give it your all, walk away knowing you couldn't have done better. As teenagers, Jessie and I had adopted it as a motto, our own shorthand for trying everything. 'Because we don't want to be bitter middle-aged women, looking resentfully at girls and saying things like "Isn't it well for ye?" in that miserable way they have,' Jessie had said.

'Too right,' I had agreed. 'By the time we get to that age and have to give up the fun stuff, let's at least feel like we did it all while we had a chance.'

I said it now, but mocking, because we were no longer the friends we had been back when we used to say it to each other, but also because I knew neither of us had ever meant that we should go this far.

Jessie was right: I was lost somewhere inside the long, long nights and short, increasingly confused days. Sometimes I would have aural hallucinations, in which I thought people were speaking to me. 'What did you say?' I would whip around to the nearest person in work, only to find them staring at me, bemused.

'Nothing. I said nothing.'

Even the few nights I didn't go out, I couldn't sleep. It was too hot, the flat too airless, the sheet on the bed too heavy and wrinkled, Jessie, beside me, too deeply asleep.

I would get up and lie on the battered sofa, bathed in the tight orange light from the street outside, my head hanging backwards over the armrest, and stare up at the sky – a darker, fuzzier orange – outside the window for hours. Sometimes I was still there in the morning when it was time to get up.

I would think about Nico, replay our night together, looking at it from different angles, although I wasn't sure any more which bits of it were real and which I had added. I would think about what I needed to do – be thinner, more popular, more indifferent – to get him. I still knew I could, that he was mine but had lost his way towards me. I had to burn brighter, harder, so that he could find me. When Jessie was gone, he would find his way back. He was distracted by her, confused. That would end once she had gone.

We didn't talk about him any more, she and I. Ever. We had come close, the day after that time in the park. I had been so cold, so offhand, ignoring or sneering faintly at anything she said.

'I don't know why I'm here,' she had said at last.

'You can just go if you're not having fun,' I snapped.

'It's not about having fun. And I'm not going. I'm worried about you.'

'So you say.'

'Well, aren't you going to tell me what's wrong with you?'

'Nothing. You know bloody well.' It was as close as I could come to admitting.

'I don't know, Anna, because you won't say. I only know what I think.'

'Well, and what do you think?'

'That this is about Nico. That you think . . . I don't know . . . that I'm flirting with him or something, or . . .'

'Or what?'

'Well, that he likes me.'

There, she had said it, and had made it sound just as pathetic as I had known it would, spoken in the open like that. Which was why I kept my silence, because words were only ever going to do that – cheapen it, make it small, silly and childish: *He likes you more than me*. The stuff of schoolyard crushes, when this was not that. I could tell she didn't understand. Hadn't a clue what this was. Didn't know anything about what it was like to love someone the way I loved Nico, with the certainty that we were for each other, until she came along and stepped into the middle of us.

'It doesn't matter what you think or what you do,' I said, 'because whatever it is you do, I will outdo it and undo it, so it will be like you were never here.'

'Anna, you know this doesn't sound like a good thing? Don't you want a relationship where he wants you?'

'He can put a dog collar and a lead on me for all I care, as long as I'm his.'

'You shouldn't feel like that about anyone!' Jessie said. 'That's crazy!' She was shocked, as I knew – had hoped – she would be. I wanted her to realise that she couldn't begin to understand the way I felt, that I had moved beyond her into a place she could not follow or imagine.

'Well, I do and it's not.' It was, I thought, magnificent.

And so we stopped mentioning Nico. Instead, we talked – in as much as we talked at all – around the idea of him, around the idea of ourselves, with all the careful neutrality of hostage negotiators.

And meanwhile I knew Jessie was living for the day of her

departure. That she was too proud to leave early, too loving to let me stay behind in the state I was, but desperate to go.

'I'm going to cook something.' It was a few miserable days later, and Jessie, trying so hard as always, sounded resolute. 'Something proper.' It was late afternoon, the evening starting to suck light from the sky.

'You can't,' I said. 'There aren't any pots.'

'There's one pot, and an ancient frying pan. They'll do.'

'Well, I don't want anything.'

'Anna, you need to eat. Seriously, you live off crisps and yoghurt. Your bones are sticking out, and not in a good way any more. You've gone from "too thin" to "creepy thin".'

But I couldn't bear her to care for me, cook for me. I couldn't bear to eat, the two of us together. I couldn't bear to eat at all. If I eat, I will get fat, and he will never love me, I thought. And I meant it. But I also knew that the signalling of my distress was effective. The slightness of my form told a story I wasn't willing to tell in any other way.

'I'm going out,' I said. 'I'll be back later or I'll call and let you know where I am.'

But I didn't: I went to Bet's house and stayed out till there was no chance that dinner would be edible, and still I didn't call. When I did go back, at last, Jessie wasn't there, the emptiness of the flat shocking. I felt frightened when I called for her in the dark and found no response. The place, I noticed absently, was filthy. Neither of us bothered any more to clean up or go to the launderette. Dirty clothes lay in piles; towels were draped across the back of the sofa and chairs. In the heat, they smelt sour.

I looked up, at the shape of a body in the bed, hunched and disordered. 'Jessie,' I called, panicked suddenly. 'Jessie, I'm sorry I'm so late.' Only silence. 'Jessie!' I called again, feeling sick. Nothing. I scrambled up the wretched stairs and tore at the sheet in the frenzy of fear. Nothing, except more sheets and a hot, damp smell.

I couldn't stay there, so I raced downstairs and into Chez Léon and there she was, sitting up at the bar with Cécile.

'Anna!' She jumped down. 'Where were you? I was worried.'

'I was out,' I said, offhand again, dismissive now that I had found her safe. Jessie, climbing back up onto her stool, was upset, and Cécile gave me a filthy look. *'Qu'est-ce que tu fais, copine?'* What are you doing, girl?

Cécile was crazy, but she was loyal too, and she was her own kind of crazy. By then, I was every kind, and everyone's kind, of crazy.

'Let's go,' I snapped at Jessie, because I wanted Cécile to see that it didn't matter what I did, that the friendship between us was bigger than that, more fundamental, immune even to my day-to-day meanness scratching at the surface. I wanted Cécile to see it, and I wanted to feel it, to have it proven to me, again.

Jessie gave me a long, steady look, without moving from her stool and then, just when I thought she would turn her back on me and talk to Cécile, she sighed and said, 'Fine. I made chilli. It's probably dried up, but I'll try to revive it.'

And that night we were almost merry together. I knew I had gone too far, been too cruel. I was filled with shame and remorse, and I swore to myself that I would stop being horrible, would be myself again, my usual self, not the self I had discovered there, with them. I hugged Jessie and told her I was sorry. And Jessie? She hugged me too. Even though she was confused and hurt, she refused to let me be as bad as my behaviour made me. She stuck with me, accepted my pathetic apologies and allowed me to come back to her when I tried.

'You just need to get away from here,' she said. 'To come home. Sleep a bit, eat a bit, get your head straight.'

'I will,' I promised, even though I knew I wouldn't. 'It's like there are two switches inside me,' I said, 'and when the awful me is switched on, I can't seem to be anything else. Only when it's off, at last, am I back to myself.'

'It's okay,' she said. We were arranged at either end of the sofa, bare feet in each other's laps. She squeezed my foot. 'You'll be okay.'

CHAPTER 28

Now

The first thing Anna saw when she checked Facebook that morning – and the first thing she did when she got to the office was check – was another message from Jessie's father. This one was curt. '*Anna. I need you to answer me. I have the right.*'

Just ignoring him wasn't going to make this go away.

As she avoided Andrew's eye – she knew he was eager for an update on what she'd told him – by keeping her head low and clicking through emails, Maurice rang. She hadn't seen him that morning – had left early, before anyone was up.

'Hi.' She put as much can't-talk-now-I'm-busy into her voice as she could muster, in case he wanted her to do something for him. In case Andrew heard.

'I was thinking I might take Rudi to stay with my mother for a while,' Maurice said. No hello.

'Why?'

'Give you some space.'

'I don't need space.'

'You and Jessie, I mean.'

Save your child, you mean, she wanted to shout. *Save your child, not my child. Save your child from my child.* She remembered again the prison box of beans, the incarcerated broccoli, and fought back her first, snappy response. 'I don't think that's necessary.' She kept her voice modulated.

'I do.' There was silence between them. She could hear him breathing heavily, so she knew he was hating this, just as she was. 'My mother would love to have him.' As if that was the point, Anna thought. 'Only for a few days,' he said then. 'Just until we all work out what to do next. This can't go on, Anna. You know that.'

Which bits of it? Jessie's bits? His? Hers had been going on for so long that they seemed to have taken on a life of their own.

'Okay,' she said, because there didn't seem to be a single other thing to say. 'But only a few days.'

She went to Alison, because there wasn't anywhere else to go, even though it wasn't her day.

'Thank you for fitting me in,' she said. Alison was wearing a cashmere roll-neck of palest green, like a misty shoot of spring, Anna thought. Her own charcoal grey dress, in contrast, was severe enough as to be almost institutional. How she envied this woman the luxury of being the one to listen, not the one obliged to talk.

'How are you today?' Alison asked. The room positively hummed with the subduing blanket she cast over everything. A bluebottle droned as it bumped against the closed window. Even that had a sleepy, hypnotic quality so that Anna wondered if it was there on purpose. A prop, an aid, like the discreet box of tissues, angled at her elbow, one white sheet poking temptingly up towards her. *I'm here*, it seemed to say. *Let me help*.

'Not great.' For once, Anna cut short the usual opening of 'Fine. Great. How are you?'

'In what way?' Alison asked, ignoring the 'How are you?'

'All the ways I can think of,' Anna said. Where to begin? 'Maurice wants to take Rudi to his mother for a few days. To get away from us. To get Rudi away from Jessie. And me.'

'How do you feel about that?' God, it was like talking to a mirror, Anna thought. Presumably that was the point.

'I don't want him to. It feels like such an admission. Of failure. That we're not coping. That I'm not coping . . .'

'And?' Yes, Alison was right, there was an And.

'I hate that he wants to save his son and doesn't try to save my daughter.'

'Why do you think he doesn't try with Jessie?'

'He just doesn't. He hasn't, not since Rudi was born. He did, when Jessie was small and we first met. He was so sweet to her, but it got complicated . . .'

'How?'

'She got bigger, and stroppier. Then Rudi came along and she got stroppier still. It's like she expected him to reject her, so she started pushing him. And I suppose I didn't help . . .'

'In what way?'

'When Jessie was small, if Maurice tried to intervene between me and her, ever, I wouldn't let him. I see now that I should have. I should have allowed him some of the responsibility, not just the fun-uncle role I pushed him into, because then he might have formed a deeper relationship with her. You know, if he'd had to go through the hard stuff as well as the easy days-out stuff.'

'When you say "intervene", what do you mean?' The voice was like icing now, pouring smoothly over everything Anna said.

'He used to try to stop me if I got angry with her. He said I went too far. It made me furious, because I knew he was right but I didn't want to hear it. So I refused to allow him to be involved like that, and after a while – quite a short while, really – he just backed off. He stopped trying. I thought that was better, that I was the best person to decide anything to do with Jessie, but I see now that I wasn't.'

'You talk about him not trying to "save" your daughter. Does she need saving?'

'You know she does. Why else would I be here? She won't eat. She's starving herself. That's what this is all about.' It was horrible, Anna decided, this game of Stratego she played with Alison, where the therapist tried to uncover the flag while Anna moved it, trying to stay one step ahead.

'Is that what you meant when you talked about Maurice not trying to "save" her?' Obviously it wasn't, not really, they both knew that, but Anna didn't answer. She moved the flag again.

'I'm drinking too much.'

Alison let her. 'How much is too much?' she asked.

'Every night, a lot. Sometimes I don't remember going to bed. Other times, well, I go places I shouldn't. Meet people I shouldn't.' She thought Alison would chase that hare, but she didn't. She was better at this than Anna had thought.

'Tell me why you say Maurice didn't "save" Jessie.'

'He didn't do enough for Jessie when she was small, because I wouldn't let him, and he should have been stronger and bloody well insisted, but he was weak. And then, when Rudi came along, he was so damn vigilant, barely leaving me on my own with him. He had his mother in and out of the house the whole time. Helping, he said, but keeping an eye was what it seemed to me. And I hated that.'

'Why?'

'Because it was so unnecessary. And because he didn't do it for Jessie.'

'Was it necessary for Jessie?' She asked gently enough, but in a way that meant Anna had to answer. She understood the way Alison's mind was turning now, why her questions weren't about Jessie, either of the Jessies, but always about Anna and, now, far less about how things made Anna feel and instead about what Anna had done.

'Maybe,' she said miserably. 'I mean, you know, I can see now – I could have done with a lot more help, but I was scared to ask for it in case it looked as if I wasn't coping. In case my parents took her away from me. It was always going to be all or nothing with them – they would have raised her because they like being martyrs to life, but they wouldn't help me. So

I said nothing, just struggled on. And it was wonderful, but sometimes it was hard, and I wasn't always equal to that. I wasn't enough for her.' She reached for a tissue, cursing the fact that Alison had been right to position them so discreetly.

'You must have been under a lot of pressure.'

'Yes. There was so much guilt. I know you say guilt is unhelpful, but ignoring it is so much worse.'

'That isn't what I meant . . .' Alison began.

'I know, I know. You also said that it matters, working out what happened. But what if that's not enough? Because you can't change what happened.'

'Do you mean with Jessie?'

'Yes, and other things. We started out badly, me and Jessie. The other mothers knew it, but I didn't. I could see on their faces that they knew the whole thing was a no-go from the beginning, even though they were wrong about the reasons. But I was so excited, I ignored all that.' She wiped, and blew, and reached for another tissue, wondering what to do with the snotty wet one. She couldn't just leave it on the table, sitting there. That would be gross, unhygienic. But she didn't want to hold it either. She tucked it up her sleeve, shrinking a little from the clammy touch.

'Many women raise their children alone,' Alison said.

'That's not what I mean. I was fine with that – happy even. I didn't want him involved. No, I mean the beginning of it all was bad. We started under a cloud, me and Jessie, and I thought I'd get through that; I wouldn't let it hold us back or matter, but it did. Even though I squashed it down, it came up and out in other ways.'

'Anna, what exactly are we talking about here?' Alison, it seemed, was sick of Stratego. She was going in direct. 'Have you ever hurt Jessie?' she asked, in the flattest voice she had ever mustered.

'You mean have I hit her?' Anna was appalled, although she knew she had no real right to be. 'How can you ask that?'

'Is that a no?' Alison pushed.

'Of course it's a no. I never would have.'

'If there's anything you want to talk about, this is a safe place to do that.'

'There isn't.'

'You said yourself you don't always remember.'

CHAPTER 29

Jessie

It's getting harder. Isolde said it would get easier, that you go through a barrier and then it's so simple, but she was wrong, or I'm just not like her because I thought I was through the barrier but I can't be. Not yet.

Isolde pulled out the tube and said it was really easy. Now she knows how easy it is, she doesn't care if they put it in again because she'll just take it out. She's so much tougher than I am. I'm scared of the tube, of what it must feel like when they put it up your nose and down your throat, like when you get water up your nose at the swimming pool and it makes you panic and your eyes water, only worse, much worse, I'm sure, and of how, if they can do that, they must be able to do anything they want to you. Anything at all.

They sent Isolde back to The Laurels, and I haven't heard from her, so that means they're allowing her no contact with anyone outside. They do that because they want us to belong only to them, hear only what they say to us, keep us isolated so they can break us.

If I went in now, they'd break me so easily. I'm scared of that too – that they'll send me back.

I don't bother looking at myself like I used to, mapping out the good bits – knees, ankles, shins, upper arms, hip bones – and the bad bits – thighs, stomach, back of calves where, no matter what I do, there is always a bulge, because I'm not proud of any of it now. None of it feels or looks like it belongs to me. Everything is odd, as if it arrived in the night and no one has sorted it out yet so it's just bundles.

Nights are the worst: they wash in and out like waves, pushing and pulling me. My ears roar and the empty feeling inside me is like a stone, cold and hard. I don't like it. It frightens me. It's too cold and old, and I think I swallowed something by mistake that is growing and living inside me. It's living in the roots of me, gnawing and scrabbling.

There is nowhere for me to settle in the nights. It's like I'm walking the rooms of my mind, looking for somewhere I can be still, but there's nowhere. I'm driven on, driven out of each place by things that shriek at me, 'Not here! Not here!' There are frantic flapping hands to shoo me on: 'Go! Not here. Go!' And the walls shift between sleep and waking, like someone is changing scenery in a play, smoothly and silently moving the boundaries of my existence so that I fall through them without warning, into the past that is more alive than I believed it could be. Other Jessie can move through them just as I can and now she is behind me, breathing into the back of me.

She's pushing me further than I want to go. I don't know

how to stop her. Sometimes she looks like Isolde. Like me. Like Anna. And it's easy for her. She doesn't need food where she is. And you can see it. She burns light, nothing else. Or maybe it's the dark she burns. She must have forgotten it doesn't work that way for us, because she's whispering to me to do more, always more, telling me I can, I deserve this and it's right. But it's been so long since she was here that she doesn't remember I can't do as much as she wants me to. That it's dangerous, and I don't really want to go all the way. Not the whole way.

She tells me I need to be with her, but I don't know where she is when she's not here with me, and I don't want to go there.

Anna always says how funny and kind Other Jessie was. But I don't see that. She's concentrated, not kind. Like an implosion. It's like she's sucking everything towards her, me included. And I'm trying to resist, as if I'm hanging on to bits of furniture and bed legs, but she's pulling too hard, not by touching me, just by the force of her.

I used to see her only in my bedroom. Now she's in the kitchen sometimes as well, always watching me.

She wants Rudi to come too. She says he will if I bring him, that I can do that. That he's just waiting for me to show him. I know she's right because I can see that he watches what I do and wants to copy me.

I can't do this. I'm frightened. She wants too much.

She talks about a place alone together, Rudi and me, so perfect on our own, and her there, too, but not Anna. She says I need to save him from Anna, who will ruin him. Who will ruin me, too, if I let her.

But I don't want that. Not with Rudi. I don't want him here. He's perfect already: he doesn't need to change. He is warm and round and firm and right. She's wrong about him.

Anna wouldn't hurt him. He doesn't need to escape her.

When I see Anna now, I don't feel happy. She looks so alone and lonely, like I used to feel, so I know what it's like. If I take Rudi too, what will she have? Nothing. I can't let her have nothing.

Other Jessie gets angry when I say no. Or, at least, I don't say no, because I'm not strong enough, but I don't say yes either and that's what makes her angry. She blows into my face with her cold, grey breath. Blows until there's a wind whistling through me that comes from far away, the place where she is that's all in shadow and I can catch only a little bit of at a time. I hate that place. It looks terrible. Like it was forgotten so long ago that now it's only scraps of itself, held together by the shreds of memory the people there have, but all distorted and wrong. Jessie tells me it's Anna's fault. That Anna did something and never said she was sorry for it but that can't be true. She must be wrong.

Anna does bad things, sometimes, but she always says she's sorry.

CHAPTER 30

Then

That night, we were like flies before a thunderstorm. Sluggish, confused, looking for a calm surface to flatten ourselves against. For the first time that summer, no one seemed to want to go out. Marina muttered something about 'just a few drinks', and even Bet said she needed to be up in the morning because a man was coming to the house to do something with an armchair – restore it, I think – and she needed to let him in. Her parents were due back in a week and she was starting to fuss about a house that had been used as a hitching post for months.

We were all short with one another, cross and sulky.

'Stop it,' Marina spat at Alec, who was rubbing the underside of her arm with his thumb. She jerked away. 'It's making me twitch. Stop.'

No one said anything, but there was a sudden sense of summer's end, of normal life waiting to resume, checking its watch and tsking at our refusal to understand that the golden days were nearly finished, a well drained dry by repeated visits.

'We could go and check out the prostitutes. That can be fun,' Bet said.

'What?' I thought I must have misheard.

'It's legal here. They sit in windows against velvet backgrounds, loads of them in a row on the same streets, for men to walk past and choose. Like a display of chocolates in assorted flavours.' To my relief, no one responded, except Jessie, who made a face and turned away.

She was due to leave in three days, and earlier that day had said she wanted to visit a bit more of the country 'than just its bars and nightclubs' before she went. I don't know if she said it with judgement, but that was how I took it.

'Go and be a tourist if you want,' I said meanly.

'I thought you might come with me,' she said, without any of the bite she was entitled to.

'I might,' I answered ungraciously. 'But I won't.'

Worst of all, Aleah was due back. Nico would be picking her up at the airport the very next day.

Bet had told me, unable to hide a small smile. I had failed, and she was sorry for it, but she wanted me to know that she knew.

And of course I knew.

After Jessie left, I would no longer be able to put off the question of 'What next?' My job at the law firm was soon to finish. Already there was nothing like the same volume of dusty files arriving to be catalogued. The sleazy security guard came less often, and paid me less attention. He knew I was nearly done. I had originally planned to return home once the job ended, but now how could I? I could barely remember what I used to do at home, what I had wanted for my life. Without the daily, nightly, constant thinking about Nico and preparing to see him, I had no idea who I might be.

We went clubbing, because there didn't seem to be anything else to do, and Jessie came with us because I wouldn't let her go elsewhere. I was afraid he would go with her. That night she wore a red T-shirt I knew well. She'd been wearing it for years, so that it was soft and faded, with a picture of a round bullseye target in red, white and blue. She looked tired and unhappy, and I knew she was longing to leave, to get away from us and from the sulky city that rejected as much as it beckoned. Maybe to get away from me most of all.

How I longed for her to be gone. To wake up and not have her beside me or, finding an empty flat, know it was because she had woken early, on purpose, to slip away before she had to see me. Before I could throw my rudeness and lack of care in her face again.

I wondered would we ever be back to what we once were, and knew that I didn't care. That I had been forced to pick, and I had chosen Nico. I would never look back.

That night I asked him finally, 'Why?' We were sitting on the steps behind the bar and the music throbbed around us, like distant thunder. I was swigging from a bottle of Coke, unable to quench the thirst that seemed to consume me, or quell the nausea that followed me around like a toad. I couldn't drink alcohol or stomach drugs. My body was revolting against the weeks and weeks of excess, drying, fading, my stomach swelling. My hair was lank, my hands so dry and chapped that they bled from tiny cracks between the bony fingers. I looked at them, feeling like some kind of mud-bound creature left too long in the sun, away from the cool wetness, shrivelling and shrinking.

I need to go home, I thought. But I pushed it away. Not yet. I wasn't ready to give up.

'I don't understand,' I said, my French unequal to the task of retaining any shred of dignity while seeking the explanation. 'I thought you liked me.'

'I'm sorry.' He looked it. Looked miserable, in fact, worried and drawn. We're all falling apart, I thought, peeling off, layer by layer. 'I didn't think this would happen,' he continued.

And even though he must have known I was the last person on earth to whom he should have said these things, he began to tell me how he had felt when he first saw Jessie, in the doorway of Chez Léon, and how he had understood then that she was the person he wanted his life to be with. How she was the purpose he had never thought to find, and then suddenly, there it was, in front of him, beside him. 'Never two without three,' he kept saying, so that eventually I asked what he meant. 'First I thought it was Aleah. Then you came along and I knew it wasn't her, that it might be you. But it wasn't. And then Jessie came. The third. The only one.'

Everything he said was an affront. I marvelled that he could put those words together, in that order, and say them to me. Had he really no idea?

I took his hand in mine and held it for a moment, then lifted it to my cheek where I pressed it, and then to my mouth.

I think I meant to kiss it. But instead I bit his finger, so hard that I tasted blood. Too much blood, washing into my mouth in a warm wave, like water heated in a rusty iron pot but so thick that I choked, unable to swallow. I dropped his hand in shock and spat, a mouthful of crimson saliva. His finger was still bleeding and he wiped it on his jeans, as I stammered, 'I'm sorry. I'm so sorry.' I stood up, backing away even while he said, 'It's okay, Anna. It's okay.'

I bolted back onto the dancefloor – to lose myself, but Pierre found me there, caught hold of my arm and said something into my ear that I couldn't hear. When I shrugged, he leaned even closer and said, 'I think I'm falling in love with you.'

I tried to laugh, to show I knew he was joking, and when he just looked at me, so that I knew he wasn't, I found I had nothing – not one word – to say to him. There was nothing left in me that I could draw on to say I was touched, and flattered, and 'I'm so sorry but . . .', any of the things I normally said in such situations. I shook my head, mute, and walked off to a dark corner where I hid for hours in the shadows from where I saw but could not be seen. I saw them all come and go, Bet, Pierre, Marina, Alec, Jessie, Nico. They came and went and sometimes I think they looked for me, but not hard, and I did nothing, just watched. I think I barely blinked.

When it was all over, I went outside, thrusting a crumpled note into Alain's eager hand, and found them, grouped together, waiting.

Bet saw me first. 'There you are! Where have you been?'

'Anna, we were worried.' That was Jessie.

'You were,' Bet said to her. 'I wasn't. I figured Anna was off having a good time.' She smirked at me, an interrogation.

'Pretty much,' I said. 'A fun night.' And I forced myself to smile back at her, to ignore Pierre, whose face that morning was more tragic than ever, to ignore Nico, and Jessie, not to give myself away, not to allow kindness or concern or love or regret to interfere with the wall of rage going up inside me. I could only get through this by being angry, because if I didn't fix the sneering cold within me, I would break up entirely.

'What will we do now?' Bet asked. It was the question that had scratched at me all night: *What will I do now?* I had no answer, so I waited. No one spoke. I think we would all have liked to go home, get away from one another, be alone and begin a trek back into our own selves. But no one said this. We were, I suppose, too young, too silly, too in love, too hopeful, too convinced still that, despite everything, anything could happen. That we were not, even though we so obviously were, at the end of the road.

'I know,' Marina said. 'Let's go to the flea market. It's still early, they'll just be setting up, and that's when you get the good stuff. My mother found a Lalique lamp there once. It's worth a fortune and she bought it for nothing.'

'Okay.' Probably we would have said yes to anything, any plan presented with conviction.

'We can get the Métro,' Bet said. 'There won't be anyone on it at this hour.'

'Nico, I'll come with you,' Alec said firmly. 'We'll see you there.'

'Great,' Marina said. 'There's a place that does really yummy hot chocolate near there too.'

'I might go home,' Jessie said quietly to me.

Instead of letting her go, I insisted, roughly, that she come. 'Nonsense. We won't be there for long. Just come.' As if she was being demanding, childish.

We went down into the Métro, where the air was thick and stale as if some large creature had breathed it in and out too often. The same legless man I had seen on my first day was there with his accordion, playing the same tune, leering up at us with his wet lips. Jessie gave him money, for which he blessed her ostentatiously, drawing the sign of the cross in the foul air around him with a hand so dirty from propelling himself along the ground, it was like a paw. I wanted to kick him. To kick his skateboard, with him on it, so that he disappeared into the dark tunnel.

Marina was singing the chorus of one of the club anthems of that summer, something about 'We are forever people', as we clustered on the empty platform.

'Come and see this,' Bet said. We walked with her to the opening of the tunnel mouth, where a round fish-eye mirror was positioned at an angle. She began pulling faces into it, grotesque and comedic, that looked even more absurd when warped and reflected back. I pushed in beside her to make my own faces, then felt Jessie beside me. She was laughing as I hadn't heard her laugh almost since she'd arrived, and I hated her for it. Hated the sight of her face, eyes crossed and mouth stretched wide, in the mirror staring back at me, mocking me. She was too close. I could smell the sweat and dry ice in her hair, the perfume she had put on at the start of the night, now stale. I hated the sight of her T-shirt with its jaunty bull's-eye pattern, the feel of her beside me, the familiar body so much a part of me. That had breathed beside me in the dark through so many nights, or sat close beside me, so that we were within one circle. I wanted her away from me.

The accordion music had picked up now and was chasing me, teasing me, cursing me, a spiralling whirl of mad music leaping through the grimy air after me, and Jessie was still too close, too warm, too familiar. Taking up my space, breathing my air, taking the love of the man I loved. I needed her gone from me.

And so I pushed her.

I shoved her with my shoulder, hard, with intent, just the way I had shoved her so many times when we were kids and cross with each other. Those were shoves that ended a game, or a fight, or led to another shove. Not that one. I shoved her and she fell and the train came, like a monster, out of its tunnel, surged forward and took her and she was gone.

Except she wasn't gone. She was there, but she was broken and I saw her below me, forced into the too-small space between the tracks and the platform, her bull's-eye T-shirt soaked in blood that was her blood and her legs like sticks chopped up and thrown in a bundle. All of her was just a sack chucked down by a giant, who had been stealing children, had filled the sack with body parts and blood, then thrown it away. I screamed and I screamed and then I let myself go because I couldn't be there and look any more so I fell forward onto the platform in a faint that wasn't real but wasn't entirely fake. I dived below the surface of myself and hid there until the ambulances came, and above me I heard more and more screaming, a thin sound, like wind through bare branches, and I don't know if it was from me or from someone else.

I knew that if I could stay there, in that moment, I could stop this from being true. If I stayed still, everything would stay still with me, and there would be no unspooling of terrible things. No logical progression of inevitable reality. But I couldn't stay. Time wouldn't stay still with me.

There were lights, blue and flashing, and people running, urgent with movement and still I lay there. Someone opened one of my eyes and shone a torch into it and I stared through the light, like I had stared through the camera when Nico held it, and the person said, 'Can you stand?' and I did nothing, said nothing, fell limply back towards the platform when the arm supporting me was removed.

They put me on a stretcher and brought me to hospital where they took blood and shone lights at me while I shook my head over and over and over and said only 'No and no and no and no and no and no.' And they put me to bed in a ward with a drip and said I was badly dehydrated and my blood glucose was too low and I needed to rest. They gave me something, pills that made me choke, but I swallowed them because I knew what they would bring – a whiting out of everything I couldn't look at or cope with.

CHAPTER 31

Now

The house sighed and creaked through the night, mumbling to itself. Whatever was in it was getting stronger, moving deeper in and taking up more space, winding itself into the walls and under the floors, burrowing, stretching. Rudi's door opened once, then closed with a tight click. Anna got up, opened it again and checked on her sleeping son. He was breathing gently, easily, so she left him, wedging the door open with his shoes.

Back in bed she listened again. Silence, but a waiting silence.

She moved closer to Maurice, for heat and comfort, and when he reached for her in the dark of the night, she went willingly, because he was alive and strong and reliable, and she missed him and was frightened of the silence.

Half-asleep, he put his arms right around her, in a way she usually hated because the proximity was too much, but this time she stayed deep in his embrace.

He was heading off that evening, with Rudi, had already packed a neat bag with enough clothes for them both, while Anna had watched, miserable. 'You promise it won't be for long?' she'd asked.

'I promise. A few days.' She wondered did he mean it or would he go and, once away from her, realise how easy it would be to stay gone.

'Please don't tell your mother why you're there.'

'Okay,' he said, not looking at her, busy with the zip of his bag. 'I won't.' But she knew he would. He told his mother everything. It annoyed Anna, but also rather charmed her: his earnest transparency. Rudi had it – the same need to lay out his store of happiness, unhappiness too, for all to see. Jessie, conspicuously, did not.

Going up to Jessie's room the next morning, Anna braced herself for the smell of rot and rage that hung in the air. Her daughter was bundled in her duvet, eyes open, staring into the morning dark. The sheets were wrinkled and bunched so Anna knew she had been turning through the night, one way then another, never finding enough comfort to sleep much beyond the fitful starts of a dog that twitches at something or nothing. The pillow she kept to place between her poor, dreadful knees, to protect them from resting too heavily on each other, had been thrown on the floor.

Anna thought how much those stiff, spindly limbs must hurt, how hard they must be to dispose comfortably, and she wanted to wrap her daughter in something infinitely light and warm that would cushion her and hold her up.

'Are you going in today?' she asked quietly.

'No,' Jessie said, as Anna knew she would.

'Okay.' Then: 'I have to go out, but only for a bit, and then I'll be back. I'll take the day off too.'

'You don't have to,' Jessie said wearily.

'I know, but I want to. I just need to do something first.'

She rang Margaret. 'It's Anna.'

'Anna, how are you?'

'May I visit Mr McDermott?'

'It's kind of you, you're good to offer, but there isn't any real point, the way he is.'

'I know, but I would like to. Just to see him. I won't stay long.'

The nursing home was long and low and brown, with big windows and, outside them, raised concrete beds planted with waving grasses. It might have been a library, Anna thought, or an archive.

Inside there was more brown, layered with cream. Anna had prepared herself for the smell – boiling vegetables undercut with the tang of ammonia, of wee – but the atmosphere of the place caught her by surprise. The sense of waiting – staff waiting for their shifts to end, inhabitants waiting for lunch, for a visit, for the hour to move forward, for it to rain, for the sun to come out, for someone to tell them why they were there, and how a life of bustle had come at last to this place where there was nothing to hurry for.

That won't be me, Anna thought reflexively, catching sight of a woman alone in a sitting room, a newspaper on her lap, hands on the arms of her chair, straining forward eagerly and staring at the door with a look partly bright, partly terrified, as if she knew someone would come through it, and she would have only that instant in which to understand who they were. That won't be me, she thought again, even as another part of her told her, gleefully, that it very well might.

She had wondered if anyone would ask for her credentials in visiting this man she hadn't seen in years, but they didn't. Those she spoke to seemed delighted to see her, help her, have her vary their routine for them.

'In here,' a nurse said jovially. 'He's had his breakfast and he's all ready to receive.'

Did they know how patronising they were? Anna wondered. Did they understand the insult in that register of voice – the high brightness of it – or were they, after years of service, now simply immune?

The years had taken far more from Mr McDermott than they had from his wife. It wasn't just his height and girth, both now diminished: the boom of his presence was gone too, muffled entirely, perhaps even extinguished.

When they were young, she and Jessie had giggled that being in a room with him was like a never-ending game of Granny's Footsteps. Absorbed in a newspaper, he would show no sign of noticing the noise and chaos around him, for so long that you forgot he was there, and then, out of nowhere, he would roar, 'Can a man not get a bit of peace in his own house?' and send his family scuttling to quietness, for a little while anyway, not because they were frightened of him but because they loved him.

He sat in a high-backed chair angled so that he could look out the window at the waving grasses, even though he had never, as far as Anna knew, taken much interest in gardens. His hands, placed carefully on his knees, by someone else she suspected, were like the fringes of a shawl, lengths of uselessness, knotted into bunches at the knuckles. Opposite him a second chair had been placed, with optimism, for any visitors.

'Mr McDermott, it's Anna. How are you?' She pulled the second chair close to him and sat down. He smelt of Dettol and baby powder and, underneath those, the papery odour of age and the failure of hope.

He said nothing. Neither did he turn his head towards her. There was, she saw, a stain on his cardigan, and suddenly she hated the whole world for the way it disposed of the people it didn't want. Dressing them up in easy-to-button clothes, feeding them, but carelessly so they were sent out with stains and spills that said, 'This is the best we can be bothered to do.'

She took one of his hands in hers and he didn't resist, or return her squeeze. His palms were cool, and surprisingly smooth.

'It's Anna,' she tried again. 'Jessie's friend.' She had wondered if his daughter's name would stir him, but it didn't.

'I wanted to talk to you,' she said, 'about something that happened a long time ago.'

The words took a long time coming out because she had no precedent for arranging them in the order she now needed. She had told lies, edged away from the truth, to herself as much as to others, for so long that it was hard to make the words behave as she needed them to. But time, she told herself, was what they had. And so she spoke, slowly at first, then in a rush, about a day and a night and the days that went before and came afterwards.

She told him everything she could remember, as plainly as she could. She told it as it came to her and didn't bother filling in the blanks – Who was Nico? Who was Bet? – just spoke on and on until it was all there in front of them both: *I pushed her; she fell. She fell; I pushed her.*

Everything depended on where she stopped that see-saw.

Partly she hated herself for doing this, for needing to do it, for burdening an old man who was without memories to define him, giving him the weight of her wrongdoing to carry in the dark of his own disturbance. But she didn't know any other way. She needed to apologise to him for what she had done, even though to do so was cruel. And because, even though his dementia had not been caused by Jessie's death, she knew that his hope of comfort had been stripped by it. That, without his daughter, the confusion and exposed terror of so many unknowns piling up around him had been – had to have been – so much worse. The years of his loss were her responsibility. Every time he had learned again, as if for the first time, of his daughter's death, there was pain of her, Anna's, making.

And, too, this was the only place she could think of to look for Jessie. She had tried at the sea wall, and there was nothing. If Jessie was anywhere, still, it was here, in this room. If she was reachable, it was through him. If she was to be stopped from taking Anna's daughter, a life for a life, this was the only way to do it.

He sat silently through everything Anna said, hand resting loosely in hers as if he had forgotten it, or it didn't belong to him, had just been something he was minding. And when she was finished, he said nothing, so Anna returned his hand to him, placing it gently in his lap, and stood up.

'I'm going now,' she said. 'But I'll come back. I want to bring my daughter to see you. She's called Jessie too. She's a sweet girl, just like your Jessie.'

At the door, she turned. He had not moved but now, as she watched, he raised a hand, the one she had been holding, and scratched at the air.

'Thank you,' he said, still staring out at the garden. 'Thank you.'

She knew it was nothing – his wife had complained of this very thing, the strange, unnecessary thanking, but Anna chose to take it as meant.

Back home, Jessie was in the kitchen, sitting in front of a plate on which Anna spotted a few crumbs. Toast, she decided. Toast that Jessie had eaten with cutlery, from the knife and fork lying in meek conjunction. She could imagine it – small, precise squares lifted from plate to mouth, chewed, counted, swallowed. Hands returned to lap to wait until ordered forth again.

'You're back,' Jessie said – almost an accusation.

'I had something I needed to do, but it's done now.'

'Of course it is. The Queen of Competence.' She said it like it was the start of a ditty or rhyme, and Anna waited for her to continue, but she didn't.

'What do you mean?' Anna asked.

'That's what me and Harriet used to call you. The Queen of Competence. It suits you. Always sorting everything out, making things go your way.'

'Or your way.'

'True. You sorted lots of things out for me, at school and hockey and stuff, when I was younger. That's true.' She didn't say it as though she was grateful.

'Perhaps that was annoying of me, all the sorting out.'

'Perhaps.' Jessie shrugged. 'Maybe a bit.' And then, with the bewildering about-faces of her age – love to contempt, indifference to kindness – she added, 'I'm sure I needed it. It can't have been much fun, having to manage such a mess as me.'

'You're not a mess, Jessie. You never were. I think I just have the habit of managing things and I find it difficult to let go of. It's a habit I learned the hard way.'

The girl said nothing, and after a moment Anna tried again. 'Do you think that if I talked to you for a bit, you might be able to listen?'

'Maybe.' But she said it in a voice that was tentative, not surly.

Anna knew what she had to do. She had to talk to her daughter in a way she wasn't used to. Not telling or instructing or lecturing, not showing her or protecting her, not shouting or arguing or insisting. Instead, with all the humility she could find. 'Can I sit down?' she asked.

'Of course.'

Anna sat at an angle, carefully not quite facing Jessie.

'I wasn't any good at managing anything when I was younger,' she said. 'Not at all. In fact, I was utterly hopeless. But I had to learn fast, for your sake. Otherwise, the way I was back then, we would both have been sunk. There was no one else. Gran and Grandad weren't coming to our rescue. There was only me for you. Do you understand that? Because that's the important bit.'

'Gran isn't much use, is she?' Jessie agreed, but kindly.

'She is not.'

'But she's nice in her way,' Jessie said loyally. 'I know she wants me to be better' – it was as close as she had yet come to admitting she was sick – 'she just doesn't know how to say it, or what to do about it.'

'I think you may be right.'

'I can't imagine you any other way.'

'Well, trust me. You think *you're* a mess – I was a total mess. Hopeless, distracted, selfish – so selfish – full of myself. Mean.'

'Mean?'

'Yes, mean. You know I was. I was mean to you.'

'You weren't mean . . .'

'Well, maybe mean is the wrong word. Maybe cruel is better.'

'Anna, no.'

'I'm so sorry, Jessie,' Anna said, in a rush. 'I was so horrible sometimes, and I'm sorry. I'm tortured by it. I was your mother and I didn't behave like one. I was so afraid someone would say I couldn't cope and try to take you away from me, that they would give you to Gran and Grandad to mind, so

I never, ever asked for help. Never admitted I needed it. But I should have done, because it wasn't just about me, it was about you, and I didn't really understand that. I thought if I could get it right, we'd both be fine.' The shame she felt meant she couldn't look at Jessie so she stared at the counter-top. It was made of caramel-coloured stone with flecks of dark grey, aggressively smoothed and polished. She'd always disliked that surface. It looked so hard, as if anything that touched it would shatter into a thousand pieces.

'You think I hold those things against you, but I don't,' Jessie said, in a way that was almost cheerful.

'How could you not?'

'I really, really don't. I'm sure I was annoying.'

'You never were, Jessie. You never ever were. Everything wrong was mine. I couldn't cope, and I exploded, and it was never anything to do with you. And I know you say you never held it against me, but I think you do.'

'You think I'm holding it against you now, don't you?'

'Yes, and I don't blame you at all.'

'I swear I'm not. It's okay. Really it is. You think you were a lot worse than you were. You yelled sometimes, and I hated that because it scared me, and then you did that awful deep-breathing thing, which used to freak me out because you wouldn't look at me, just breathe loudly for ages – weird!' She was almost laughing, so Anna risked looking at her. 'But it's okay. I promise you. I don't hate you for it. I never did.' Anna wanted to take her hand, but she was scared in case that was too much, too grabbing. Instead, she reached out and gently bumped the back of Jessie's hand with the back of hers.

'So who else were you mean to?' Jessie asked.

'Lots of people. To Jessie.'

'Surely not.'

'To her most of all.' Anna remembered the jeering, the eye-rolling, the way she had encouraged Marina, and Bet, who needed so little encouragement, to mock and isolate Jessie, pulling away from her, closing in together, leaving her out. They had ganged up as surely as if they had been twelve years old, giggling in corners without her, and saying, 'Oh nothing,' when she'd asked what they were laughing about.

'Why?' Jessie's question broke in on her bitter recollections.

'That's the worst of it. It was over a guy.' She would never say which guy. 'That's the really shaming part of it.'

'Like me and Harriet?'

'Yes, I guess so.'

'So was that my dad?'

'Yes.' It was a lie, but Anna had already known she would tell it.

'Did you love him?'

And because Anna couldn't say, 'I barely knew him. He annoyed me. I'm not sure he was much of a person . . .' she said something else. Something that was almost true. Or, rather, was completely true, of itself.

'I fell in love that summer in a way I never knew was possible,' she said. 'A way that seems now like a dream. I loved him so much, I was mad, but he didn't love me. Not in the same way. Not at all, really. And I never said I loved him, only to myself. But once you came along, it didn't matter. I was almost glad – loving him would have been a distraction from loving you, and I didn't want there to be any distractions. I know Gran, probably Maurice too, think what happened that summer was "a mistake", that I got into "trouble". But it wasn't. It – you – were everything I needed.' Maybe one day she would tell her more of the truth, so complicated but so simple, but that was enough for now. She remembered Alison saying, 'Everything is relevant,' in one of their early sessions, and now, as then, she silently refused it: *Not everything.*

'And what about Maurice?' Jessie sounded defensive over the man who was all the father she had ever known.

'Maurice was kind, and lovely, to both of us. You remember? He once told me that what attracted him to me when we met the first time was the way every bit of me screamed silently not to be noticed. The way I said no. And I think he was right about that because by then I didn't dare ask anyone to love me – but who else would have thought I was worth bothering with?'

'Right, so why are you messing him around now?'

The sharpness of Jessie's tone startled Anna. And that she had noticed, when she had seemed so utterly self-absorbed.

'I'm not.' The sceptical look on Jessie's face forced her to elaborate. 'I'm not, really. I've been spending too much time with Andrew, from work, but only because he seemed to want me to, and it was nice to feel someone wanted me for a change.'

'Rubbish excuse,' Jessie said.

'I know it is, and I'm going to stop.' That bit, anyway, was true. She never wanted to see Andrew again. There hadn't been an affair, or not if you considered an affair to be something that meant sex, but it had been a betrayal all the same; of

Maurice, but of Jessie and Rudi too. A stranger brought to the gates, nearly let in. 'I may look for a new job,' she said. 'A job with shorter hours.' She couldn't wait to tell Maurice. Perhaps she would even take time off, before any new job, and stay at home for a while. She would ring him later and tell him, and beg him to come home. To bring Rudi. To try with her as she tried.

And he would say yes, she knew, because that's what he was to her – the cheerful Yes that coaxed her from her place of No.

Maurice would help her, she suddenly realised, with Jessie's father. Why hadn't she thought of that before? Of course he would help. He didn't want to lose Jessie any more than she did. Didn't want a man to whom Jessie owed nothing to take the place he had earned for himself, rocky though that place now was. And maybe later, when Jessie was stronger, they could decide together what, how much, to tell her about this technical father, this piece of genetic jigsaw. In the meantime, he could be told to wait, that a sudden appearance after so long bought him nothing but the opportunity to try and prove himself.

'What about Other Jessie?' Jessie asked then. 'Why is she so angry with me?'

'Sometimes,' Anna said, 'if the truth is too much, we tell ourselves stories instead.'

'Meaning?'

'You think Other Jessie is tormenting you, but I think, maybe . . .' really, she had no idea what she thought, was just putting words on an idea that frightened her, to make it go away '. . . I think you're still trying to protect me, just like you always have done.'

'From who?'

'From myself, from yourself, protect me from being as bad as I am. Or was. I mean, if Jessie is the bad one, in your mind, then I'm not . . . something like that?'

'Perhaps.' She didn't look convinced. 'But what happened with you and Other Jessie? Something did, I know that much.'

'I let her down. I was mean first, then weak. That was why she died. It was my fault. I let her go.' And she told a version of the story to her daughter that was near the truth, had some of the truth in it, not a lot.

'But it wasn't your fault.' That Jessie could still, after everything, rush to defend her made Anna sad enough, hopeful enough, to cry.

'It was my fault,' Anna said. 'I let her go. I'm not letting you go, Jessie. I won't let you go.'

CHAPTER 32

Then

I don't know where they took Jessie. Did she come to the hospital, with me, for one last time? Or did she go straight to the morgue? I never found out. Who could I have asked? My parents thought it better not to talk to me about any of it, and I couldn't ask Jessie's parents.

They did their job, those pills. Maybe the weeks and weeks of exhaustion did a job too, because when I came out of the hard white glare, it was a whole day later. My parents were on their way, I was told, and the police were waiting, in a room next door. And I was pregnant.

All this I was told almost with indifference, by a doctor with blonde hair bound neatly to her head in thick plaits. Around her, nurses and orderlies were silent, heads bowed over my predicament, but as though it existed beyond their reach. There had been drama, tragedy, horror, yes, but in this city where Bruegel's *Fall of Icarus* lit the centre, a certain type of indifference seemed to come naturally. The drama and horror were not theirs. They had jobs to do – floors to clean, drips to administer, wounds to bathe – even while I struggled and sank within myself at what I knew.

The police came in and spoke to me at length, but also without any great curiosity. They had a version of events – given to them by Bet, I later learned – and they were happy with it, keen that I stick closely to it. They led me forward very gently, with many pauses, while they allowed their version to reach me and take up residence within me because it was better than mine.

'You were tired, and drunk. It had been a long night.' He sounded almost approving, that policeman. He was so fat that his legs stayed planted firmly apart to accommodate the gut that hung aggressively between them. His gun glinted in its holster, just inches from me, and I wondered what he would do if I lunged for it, tried to shoot myself, shoot him, shots fired in recognition of a warning I hadn't heard.

'The friend, she was clumsy,' he continued lugubriously. 'She tried to look in the mirror, there was not a lot of space. Such a tragic accident.' When I said nothing, just nodded, duplicitous, wary, my eyes still fixed on that gun, on the navy cloth of his trousers stretched tight across his large thigh, he reached out a pale hand and rested it for a moment on my shoulder. His hand was heavy and deliberate. Through it, I felt him press this agreed version of events deep into me, squashing it down so that it mingled with the rest of me, becoming native there.

He got up to leave, telling me to 'take it gently'. Part of me wanted to thank him, wanted to let loose the tears that pricked my eyes at what felt like his kindness, even though there was another part that knew he wasn't being kind at all. I thought of Bet, gloating, *I could carry a Santa bag full of drugs and they wouldn't bother me. I could probably kill someone and they wouldn't do much either*, and wanted to call him back, but I didn't. My parents were on their way. I was pregnant.

The child was Alec's. That much I knew. I remembered the surprising arrival of blood a few days after my only night with Nico. Surprising because I had forgotten my body could do things I hadn't willed it to do. Surprising to find that it still ran a secret autonomous course, like a kind of silent resistance movement.

I remembered Alec calling quietly from the street below a few days after that, late at night when the square was quiet. I let him in because I thought, of course I thought, that Nico might be with him. He wasn't.

There was just one night, because he wanted to, and I thought it would make Nico see what he was losing, might even distract me from him. But it didn't. Couldn't. Because, really, Alec wanted Nico just as much as I did. It wasn't me he wanted, and because of that, he understood me. There we both were, without him, with each other.

I was surprised at how little I minded that the baby was

Alec's. Almost, I was glad. If the baby had been Nico's, it would always remain his. Because it was Alec's, it would be mine.

He wouldn't step in, would wriggle as far away from me as he could. I was glad. I didn't want him.

My parents, I knew, would not help me. But I didn't need them. I would do it alone. I knew I could. I knew Jessie would help me.

Bet came to see me after I left the hospital. My parents were staying at a cheap hotel in the centre, and my mother said she would help me pack up the flat, but when she came and saw it, she couldn't bring herself to touch anything, so I sent her away, to walk around. I said I would pack my own things, and Jessie's things, for her parents to take.

I moved slowly, still in the haze where I had stayed since the morning, and the buzzer, when it went, sounded a long way off.

'It's Bet. Can I come up?' I didn't answer, just pressed the button and opened the door so that she was facing me before I knew what I could say to her.

'Are you okay?' she asked.

'I'm fine. I'm pregnant.' She nodded, unsurprised by the abrupt blurting out of my news. She said nothing. 'It's Alec's,' I said, although I had no idea why I needed her to know that. She just nodded again. 'How did it go with the police?' she asked.

'What did you tell them?'

'I told them what I saw,' she said, her large flat eyes swivelled towards me. 'No one except me saw anything. Marina didn't – she couldn't from where she was.'

'So what did you see?'

'We were in a knot, too many of us. Jessie pushed in and lost her footing. The floor was slippery.'

'Sticky.'

'What?'

'The floor was sticky, not slippery. That much I remember.'

'So you don't remember much else?'

'Not really . . .' I allowed myself to say it, to bring it in, as a possibility, a definite. 'You tell me.'

'Like I said, there were too many of us in too little space.' She was picking up speed and fluency now. 'Jessie pushed in. She slipped and fell. She was drunk. We all were.'

'I wasn't. I didn't drink that night. I felt sick. Now I know why.' I gestured towards my stomach, so surreally flat.

'What do you want, Anna?' Bet said then, so that I knew she knew what I had done; what I might have done. 'What do you want me to say?'

'I don't know.'

She left then, saying her parents were due home that afternoon. The city, the life that had been ours, was now our parents' again, a place for grown-up lives and things. We had made a mess of it, and now they had come to take it back.

I saw Nico one last time. He must have been watching the flat because, soon after Bet had left, the buzzer went again. When I looked out, it was him. I had finished; the place was tidy. We sat, like two strangers in a strange place, and tried to converse. He asked was I okay and I said yes. Was he okay? He said yes, and I chose to believe him because what else could I do? He was no good to me, I knew that. There wasn't any substance. He wasn't a wall you could lean against that would hold your weight. The arrangement of his molecules was too porous. If you leaned, you would fall through, into nothing.

So I was cold and distant, no longer the girl who burned for him but a stranger who held herself politely apart. If he was confused, he was also accepting. I said I was fine and hoped he was too. I didn't tell him about the baby. What was the point? My child would have no part of this life: I wanted there to be not the faintest shadow left between us. Let Alec tell him, I decided, knowing he wouldn't.

'I must go,' I said. 'My mother will be waiting.'

'Okay. I wanted to give you this.' It was the photo he had taken, the morning in the park: Jessie, Bet and me on the rim of the fountain. The spray of water behind our heads made a giant halo. 'I have a copy too.' I refused to see his sadness, to allow that he felt it.

'Thank you.' As if he had given me a postcard or souvenir. I put the photo between the pages of a book and put the book into my bag.

We went to hug goodbye then but held back, both of us, so we sort of bumped against each other, and he was gone. Through the open window I heard his Vespa starting up, then trailing off across the square and into the streets beyond. The sound bounced between tall houses for a while, funnelled into the air above them, then was gone. I looked out, one final time. Below, Jacques was unlocking the door to Chez Léon.

He looked up and shrugged slightly, mouth turning down at the corners. For once, there was no hint of that infinitely patient, understanding smile.

I closed the window.

And then, Jessie, when there was nothing left, there was you. Birth was terrible and tearing, and I was glad, because I wanted to rip apart the two bits of my life so they would not touch, so that the place with you in it would be ours alone.

And it was. Until now. I wrote this for you, but said I would never show it to you. I wrote it for me too, but because of you.

I need to remember what happened, what I did. And what became of the girl I was.

She's gone now. She went with Jessie, and she's gone. I pushed them both, and they're gone.

There's only you.

ACKNOWLEDGEMENTS

Of the three novels I have written, this one is probably the most autobiographical. Not that the events or characters in it are real, but the landscape of half the book is one I remember from my childhood and teenage years.

Brussels, the city I grew up in; still one of my favourite places in the world. Ex-pat life is strange in many ways, and those of us who live it miss out on feeling the kinds of deep roots that can be so reassuring, but there are good things too. In my case, I look back and marvel at the incredible permission of living in a city that seemed almost empty, and where no one knew me.

When I recall those years as a teenager and young adult, I feel again the freedom, the excitement, the whiff of danger. A kind of dream landscape, exhilarating and slightly sinister. And I miss it. I miss the beautiful tall houses, the elegant or shabby streets, the grubby little bars that never closed and were never full, the Métro stopping late at night and starting up again at dawn, the bakeries that opened as we spilled out of nightclubs, and closed, empty, just a few hours later. The long hot humid summers where everything seemed to wither and tempers were so frayed by lack of sleep that anything could happen. I miss the grand boulevards, the sleazy back streets and all the forgotten corners that seemed to have been left to crumble and mould.

I miss the strange encounters with people from different backgrounds, the intimate conversations and confidences that dissolved instantly in the light of day. I even miss the feeling of gunpowder at the edges.

I've tried to capture some of that in this book. And, for the many who won't recognise their city in my descriptions, all I can say is, that's what it was to me.

This book is, in part, about a love affair, with a person, but with a city too. Because I think that can happen – you fall in love with *somewhere*, just as much as *someone*. And when the two kick off together, it is oh-so potent.

Threaded through my recollections of Brussels are memories of my friends from those days. This book is for them; the ones who are still in my life, the ones who aren't, and especially the ones who didn't make it.

As always, I have people to thank: My fantastic agent, Jonathan Williams; Ciara Doorley, an editor so clever and intuitive that it is a joy to work with her; Joanna Smyth and Breda Purdue at Hachette Ireland; Hazel Orme, who did a wonderful edit; Ruth Shern and Susie Cronin for getting the word out so graciously; Brendan O'Connor, who is brilliant at jump-starting waning motivation, as well as being a stalwart friend, and a launcher-of-books like no other. My adored children and husband. My brother Michael, for always being a rock in any hard place, and all my wonderful family and friends. It's not just that I couldn't do it without you guys, it's that I really, truly, wouldn't bother.

My thanks to the Tyrone Guthrie Centre in Annaghmakerrig (with most honourable mention going to Lavinia's scones). For years and years people have been telling me how special it is and how I really should go there. It was only when I finally did, last year, that I realised they weren't in fact exaggerating!

I also want to remember my friend and fellow Hachette author, Emma Hannigan, a joyous spirit who has left a deep and abiding imprint on the world. If ever someone showed grace, and charm, under fire, it was she. I once walked a little way along a very hard road with her, and will never forget how kind she was to me.

Just after finishing *The Blamed*, I decided it was time to do something completely different. So I went to Uganda, with my sister Martha, to visit projects funded by a remarkable organisation called Self Help Africa (www.selfhelpafrica.org – do have a look!). The work they do, in Uganda and across much of the rest of Africa, is an example of just how much can be achieved with understanding that is deep and true. It's not just that they change lives – which they do – they change generations of lives, with education, training, support, and hope.

This book is also for my amazing companions on that trip. People Are Love!

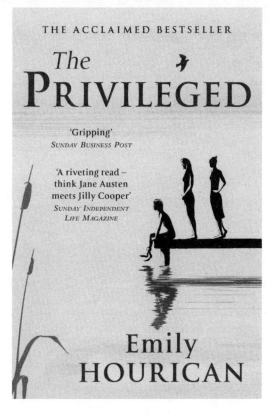

THE ACCLAIMED BESTSELLER

The

PRIVILEGED

'Gripping'
SUNDAY BUSINESS POST

'A riveting read –
think Jane Austen
meets Jilly Cooper'
SUNDAY INDEPENDENT
LIFE MAGAZINE

Emily HOURICAN

n an exclusive all-girls' secondary school, they become friends. They choose the same university, and through smoke-filled nights, lectures, sexual encounters and first loves, their bond deepens: a friendship that seems like it will last for evermore.

But then, at an end-of-year party, something happens which changes everything . . .

Afterwards, they drift apart. Now Stella, a lawyer in New York, lives for her work; Laura, a struggling journalist in Dublin, is still waiting for the scoop to kick-start her career; while Amanda, broken and beautiful, lives a life of slow decay in London.

Then the phone call comes which brings them back together, to the friendship they swore would last, and the night when it all went wrong. *The Privileged* is a haunting tale of friendship, loyalty and how one decision, one night, can decide the future.

Also available as an ebook

From the bestselling author of *The Privileged*

EMILY HOURICAN

WHITE VILLA

What happens when you invite an outsider in?

What happens when you invite an outsider in?

It was supposed to be the holiday of a lifetime – a luxury villa in Ibiza, a group of university friends, and their last chance to cut loose before embarking on their serious adult lives.

But when one of the group invites an outsider, the aloof and beautiful Natasha, tensions begin to simmer.

The days pass amid the sweltering rays, and dissolve into wild, humid nights. And Natasha seems bent upon a path of destruction, leading her to Jennifer's boyfriend, Todd – while Jennifer and the rest of the group look on . . .

Then, one hazy afternoon, paradise is shattered.
Ten years later, the friends reunite. Will what happened that afternoon at White Villa now destroy the lives and façades they have so carefully built?

Also available as an ebook